DEADLY DECOR

When Caprice ran outside, she stopped short at what she saw. Green paint spilled across the asphalt from an overturned can. In the midst of that paint, a man lay, his head bashed in and bloodied.

Caprice's sister, Bella, knelt beside him, crying, saying over and over, "He doesn't have a pulse. I can't find a pulse." She was struggling with the body, trying to turn it over, apparently intending to attempt CPR.

As soon as Bella pushed the man to his back, Caprice recognized him. Bob Preston lay there in the puddle of green paint, and he looked . . . dead.

Books by Karen Rose Smith

STAGED TO DEATH

DEADLY DECOR

Published by Kensington Publishing Corporation

Deadly Decor

KAREN ROSE SMITH

KENSINGTON PUBLISHING CORP.

http://www.kensingtonbooks.com

KENSINGTON BOOKS are published by

Kensington Publishing Corp.
119 West 40th Street
New York, NY 10018

All Kensington Titles, Imprints, and Distributed Lines are available at special quantity discounts for bulk purchases for sales promotions, premiums, fund-raising, and educational or institutional use. Special book excerpts or customized printings can also be created to fit specific needs. For details, write or phone the office of the Kensington Special Sales Manager. Kensington Publishing Corp., 119 West 40th Street, New York, NY 10018. Attn: Special Sales Department. Phone: 1-800-221-2647.

Kensington and the K logo Reg. U.S. Pat & TM Off.

ISBN-13: 978-0-7582-8486-0
ISBN-10: 0-7582-8486-1
First Kensington Mass Market Edition: June 2014

eISBN-13: 978-0-7582-8487-7
eISBN-10: 0-7582-8487-X
First Kensington Electronic Edition: June 2014

10 9 8 7 6 5 4 3 2 1

Printed in the United States of America

Chapter One

"It's a crime to cover that up!"

Caprice De Luca watched Eliza, with her symmetrically styled, sleek, ash-blond hair, anchor her hands on her slim hips and pout.

As a home-stager, Caprice often fought battles with her clients about de-cluttering their homes to present them in the best form to the buying public. In this case, however, de-cluttering wasn't the issue . . . color was. Eliza Cornwall had decorated her mansion in countless shades of purple. The deep purples especially had made Caprice's eyes roll more than once.

Before she could respond with just the right amount of tact, Bob Preston ordered, "Stop complaining, Eliza."

The painter was balanced on an eight-foot ladder, but that didn't stop his flow of words. "Caprice told me Baroque Bedazzle is your theme. Everything will show up better with this cream and pale green as its backdrop."

"It really will, Eliza," Caprice reassured her client.

"You know we've discussed this color scheme backward and forward." Caprice thought about the hours she'd invested in this particular home-staging process.

"And upside down too, I imagine," Bob wise-cracked, with a wink for Caprice.

Caprice often used Bob and his painting crews. Bob himself wasn't averse to personally picking up a paintbrush and working hard when he was short-handed. He had light brown hair and myriad muscles, and was six feet tall. He could also charm the paint off the wall. Caprice knew about his lady-killer tendencies because her sister, Bella, had dated him seriously years ago. Today he wore a red, chest-hugging T-shirt and jeans that weren't any too loose.

The way Eliza was looking at him . . . the way Bob spoke to her with familiarity . . . Caprice suddenly wondered if Eliza and Bob had hooked up. Eliza was in her late thirties, so she might be six to eight years older than Bob, but in this day and age, that difference didn't much matter.

"What if the house doesn't sell?" Eliza asked, with panic in her voice. "What if I have to stay in Kismet instead of moving to L.A.?"

"I can't imagine Christmas in L.A.," Bob remarked laconically, as he expertly wielded the paint roller toward the ceiling. "Are you sure you want to trade Pennsylvania's seasons for sunny weather all year, not to mention mudslides, earthquakes, and wildfires?"

When Caprice saw the corners of Bob's mouth twitch up, she knew he was teasing. Another reason to believe he and Eliza could have once been involved . . . or were maybe involved *now*.

"I won't miss the ice and snow, or Kismet's small-town gossip mill. Not one little bit," Eliza muttered.

Caprice thought about Eliza's comment. Kismet, located outside of York, and a bit farther from Harrisburg, did have a grapevine that tangled through its neighborhoods with more accuracy than most residents gave it credit for. But the town also had community spirit. Neighbors helped neighbors. Eliza had moved here about five years ago and started Connect Xpress, a video and online dating service. If the worth of this mansion was an accurate indicator, she was a multimillionaire.

Caprice had dealt with quite a few of those in her high-end staging business. Before she signed on with a client, they decided on a unique theme that would help the house stand out and sell more quickly than others in the same price range.

Bob, who had been born and bred in Kismet, must have agreed with Caprice's assessment of the town rather than Eliza's because again he quickly said, "Give it a rest, Lize. Kismet's been good to you."

Lize? Caprice had never heard the entrepreneur called by that nickname . . . or any other.

Eliza moved closer to Bob, ready to give as good as she got, when a reverberating *gong* traveled through the house. In the empty living room, the hollow sound echoed off the walls.

"No housekeeper," Eliza said, as if reminding herself. "I gave her the week off because of all the rearranging and painting." She started toward the front of the mansion.

Bob peered down at Caprice and lowered his voice. "She must be low on estrogen today."

Bob's attitude was friendly and conspiratorial, but Caprice wouldn't be drawn into a discussion of her client. Uncomfortable with Bob's comment, thinking about the best way to be diplomatic, Caprice brushed her straight, long, dark-brown hair over her shoulder. The seventies hairdo with bangs was a nod to the retro fashion sense she appreciated the most.

As Bob eyed her fifties-style summer dress and white sandals, he considered her silence and shook his head. "You women know how to stick together. But that's a good thing, I guess." He grinned as he stretched to reach an unpainted area close to the ceiling.

Changing the topic of conversation, he asked, "Taken in any strays lately? That article the reporter did on you a few months back was pretty good. Of course the tie-up of the murder you solved at the end of May was even better. You sure do know how to get press for your business."

"What an awful thing to say!" Caprice erupted, tired of trying to be diplomatic. "I take in strays because they need a home, not to get publicity for my business. And as far as the murder, Roz was a good friend and I had to help her."

"Whoa," Bob said, holding up his roller to stop her. "I was just yanking your chain. Maybe Eliza's mood is rubbing off on you. Or maybe we're behind schedule and you're freaking out."

Yes, they were behind schedule, but she was *not* freaking out.

He went on, "Think about that doctor you're dating for a better state of mind. I spotted the two of you at the Koffee Klatch the other morning. You didn't need caffeine to get revved up over each other. That was obvious."

Caprice felt a flush creeping into her cheeks. She'd been "dating" Seth Randolph for almost two months, but they hadn't enjoyed many full-fledged dates. With his schedule at Kismet's urgent care center, a morning coffee or an evening ice cream was about all they'd managed after their initial miniature golfing date. She'd fallen for Seth quickly, and most of the time, the depth of their attraction and their rapport scared her. Especially considering her track record with relationships.

Bob laughed. "When a girl blushes about a guy, she's hooked."

Caprice was about to tell Bob he was out of line today in several respects, but the voices approaching the living room kept her from doing so. Eliza's voice was the loudest, but she thought she recognized the other one—

Eliza and Caprice's sister, Bella, entered the living room, chattering. Caprice didn't think they were acquainted. After all, Eliza Cornwall and Bella Santini didn't move in the same circles.

Bella was saying, "I've heard about your match-making service and your move to L.A. I've always wondered how matchmakers pair people up."

Caprice took a deep breath. Was Bella wondering about matchmaking because her marriage was in trouble?

"I have a sophisticated computer program that does the initial pair-ups," Eliza explained. "But I also use my instincts with the video footage we shoot during the first interview."

"They must be great instincts if you're going to open a Connect Xpress in L.A. too. How exciting that must be. And moving to California . . . I've always wanted to take a vacation there."

"You should," Eliza encouraged her.

"With children and a budget, that's not in the cards right now." Bella's hand went to her stomach, and Caprice knew her sister was thinking about the child she carried. She wasn't showing yet at three and a half months. But she was looking tired and a bit frazzled. In jeans and a wrinkled blouse and with her black curly hair tied back, Bella wasn't her usual well-put-together self.

"Hey, Bella," Bob called from his ladder. He laid his roller on the tray, then quickly hopped down. "Long time, no see. You're even prettier than you were in high school. How have you been?"

Eliza glanced from Bob to Bella, looking perplexed and maybe a bit . . . annoyed? Caprice was perplexed herself. Why was Bella here? And why was she blushing as if she was back in high school and she and Bob were dating again?

Although Bella and Bob had split up because he'd been unfaithful, any animosity had been laid to rest years ago. The reason was simple—Bella had found Joe Santini, and they'd made a life. When Bella bumped into Bob at Grocery Fresh or at the mall, ignoring him had seemed foolish.

Bella gave Bob a first-class smile. "Busy with two kids."

He gave her another once-over. "You and I will have to talk. Maybe we can have coffee sometime. What do you think?"

She only hesitated a few seconds. "I'd like that . . . a lot."

Bob's smile was rakish as he asked, "Did you come to get decorating tips from your sister?"

"No, just a sister-to-sister consultation. Can you give me a few minutes, Caprice? I just need to talk to you. When I phoned Mom, she said you'd be here this afternoon."

Although Bella had gained color in her cheeks when Bob had complimented her, she'd looked pale when she'd walked in, and there were smudgy blue circles under her eyes.

Not sleeping? Caprice knew there was lots of tension between her sister and her husband, Joe, because of her pregnancy.

Eliza picked up the clipboard she'd left on one of the tarp-covered tables. "I have to go upstairs and work on the list for the auction people. Caprice is ruthless when she de-clutters, but I probably can't use any of it when I move to the West Coast anyway." With a fluttering wave, she headed for the foyer and the stairs.

Crossing to his ladder, Bob said to Bella, "I'll give you a call soon, and we'll go for that coffee."

Bella showing up like this was odd, and Caprice really was worried. She said to Bob, "Excuse us," took Bella's arm, and pulled her out of the painter's earshot.

She and Bella didn't always have the most harmonious relationship. Bella thought Caprice's penchant for taking in strays was foolish and that her fashion sense was a horror. Caprice, who liked surprises and knew how to roll with the punches, believed Bella was too rigid.

"Has something happened to Mom or Dad, or Joe or the kids?"

"No, nothing like that."

"Then what's wrong? You look . . ." Caprice didn't quite have the word for it. Ruffled? Unnerved? Anxious? She settled for, "You look upset.

And what was that little flirty thing with Bob? What are you doing?"

"I'm just going to have coffee with an old friend. That's not a crime."

No, it wasn't. Still, Bob was an old flame, and she could imagine where a cup of coffee could lead when there were problems between Bella and her husband.

After a moment of silence, Bella sighed. "I need to talk to you about Joe. I don't know what to do."

"Where are the kids?" On a Thursday afternoon, Timmy should be at summer camp. But at four, Megan . . .

"Megan's with my neighbor. Nellie's really good with her, and in an emergency, she'll watch either or both of them for me."

"So this is an emergency?"

"It feels like it. I can't eat. I can't sleep. I'm so tired all the time."

"Did you say you talked to Mom?"

"Not about any of this. My marriage is too hard to discuss with her. With her and Dad married thirty-seven years and perfectly happy, I don't think she'd understand."

"Not perfectly happy. No marriage is perfectly happy. You know they argue now and then."

"Nothing like this," Bella concluded dejectedly.

Maybe not, Caprice thought. Their mom was a high school teacher, their dad a mason. Money had been tight with four kids and a house that needed constant repair. But most of the time Fran and Nick De Luca had agreed about their kids and, even more important, about family issues.

"So what's going on with Joe now?" He and Bella

had had a huge blowup at their mom's surprise birthday party six weeks ago. That was the day he'd found out Bella was pregnant. That day he'd also discovered his wife had told her sisters about it before she'd told *him*.

"He's hardly talking to me. He spends time fooling around with the car, puttering in the garage. He's also been away a lot at night. He comes home smelling like smoke. When I ask him about it, he says he's been out with the guys. I don't know what that means."

"Have you talked more about your pregnancy?"

"I talk, but he doesn't listen. I can tell. He just keeps saying we can't afford another kid. I just keep saying each child is a precious gift. He knows that. I can see it in his eyes when he looks at Megan and Timmy or plays with them. With our Catholic background, he knows there's no way I'd ever consider having an . . ." She stopped abruptly.

Bella couldn't even bring herself to say the word.

"I don't know what to tell you, Bee." In serious discussions, Caprice always fell back on her childhood nickname for Bella, who was the youngest. Her sister's name, Isabella, had been quickly shortened to Bella by everybody. But when they were little, Caprice's nickname for her seemed to give them an added closeness.

With Bella looking miserable, Caprice could only try to imagine how she felt. She and Joe had been married more than eight years, and for the most part, they'd been happy. At least Caprice and her family had thought that was true. Now it seemed as if her sister's marriage was falling apart.

"Is there anyone Joe might listen to? What if you sat down with Mom and Dad to discuss all of it?"

"That won't work. Joe would be defensive from the start. It's not just the fact I'm pregnant. He thinks I got pregnant on purpose. I mean, we got married because I was pregnant, and that was both our faults. We should have known better. He's always said we were going to get married anyway. But maybe since our wedding, there's always been a small part of me that doubted how he felt. And now . . . I don't know if he believes the antibiotic I was taking counteracted the birth control. I really think he believes I did this on purpose."

"He knew you were taking an antibiotic, didn't he? Did you talk about the consequences of having sex while you were on it?"

Bella blushed. "One night the kids were both at sleepovers and it just happened. I guess neither of us thought I'd be in the small percentage of women who would get pregnant." She paused and collected herself. "So . . . we're not talking. He doesn't want to find solutions. He just wants to be mad. Most of all, I think he's angriest because you and Nikki knew I was pregnant before he did."

"Have you considered going to counseling? Maybe a stranger to talk to would be best."

"We can't afford that. Our insurance doesn't cover it. I checked."

"You might have to afford it if your marriage is at stake. I thought you told Nikki and me you have rainy-day money stashed away that you earned making kids' Halloween costumes."

"But Joe doesn't know about that. The fact that I

have it stuffed in a shoe in the closet would make him blow another gasket."

If Bella wasn't going to listen to any of the advice she offered . . . "Why did you come to me today?"

Looking even more dejected, Bella answered, "Because I didn't know what else to do."

After taking a huge breath, Caprice blew it out. "All right. So here's what I suggest. Find a marriage counselor. You need a mediator. Use the rainy-day money. I can help you, too, but I know Joe wouldn't like that any more than the cash you've kept in that shoe."

Suddenly Juan Hidalgo came thumping down the steps, Eliza close behind him. Caprice's right-hand man had broken his ankle. Now it was encased in an unwieldy boot that looked like something an astronaut would wear on the moon. For six weeks while his broken ankle had begun healing, she'd used temporary help. But Juan managed most of the crews for her, supervised furniture arrangement from her floor plans, and was generally her go-to guy.

Now, however, she glared at him. That look made him slow his progress down the stairs. After all, he was also in physical therapy for that ankle.

"I'm okay," he assured her in response to the glare. Before she could scold him, he continued, "We're ready to move furniture from the second floor to the storage unit. I'm meeting the movers out front." Caprice was about to remind him to be careful again, but he was out the front door and into the July heat before she could. He could move faster on that boot than most people could without one.

Not slowing down herself, Eliza passed by her and Bella and returned to the living room. Caprice knew

Bob would shortly be moving his tarps and gear to another room—another glaringly purple room that was soon to be muted to cream.

"I feel like I'm in the middle of a cyclone," Bella muttered.

"You're in the middle of a house makeover. I guess you've never been on site while I'm working before."

"I guess not. Did Roz tell you I'm going to help get her store up and running?"

Caprice had helped keep her friend, Roz Winslow, from being charged in her husband's murder back in May. Afterward, wanting to change her life and needing a purpose, Roz had decided to open a fashion boutique in Kismet.

"Is Mom going to babysit Megan and Timmy?"

"Yes, she is. And when she can't, Nellie can. Roz said it will take a few months to get the store up and running, so most of my help will be behind the scenes. But she feels with my degree in fashion, I was the logical choice."

"You have told Joe about this, right?"

"Yes. And he growled something about not wanting favors from your friends. I got really mad and told him I married him instead of pursuing a career in fashion, so I'm well qualified to help Roz. He kept quiet after that."

Bella and Joe seemed to be digging their marriage into a deeper and deeper hole. If they didn't get help soon, there wouldn't be anything left to salvage.

The huge front door of the mansion burst open. Juan and two burly men bustled in. In their tank tops and jeans, and with their bulging muscles, they looked totally out of place in the marble-floored foyer with its two-story ceiling reaching into the second-floor gallery at the front of the house.

"I'd better go," Bella said, as Juan directed the men up the stairs. "I feel like I'm in the way."

Caprice wasn't going to admit that Bella was in the way. She would never do that. Family was everything to the De Lucas, even when they disagreed, even when they squabbled, even when they saw each other taking the wrong road.

"I don't know what to do to help you, Bella, but you can come to me anytime. You know that."

Bella gave Caprice an odd look, as if maybe she didn't know that, as if maybe Caprice's opinion mattered more than Caprice had ever imagined.

She gave Bella a hug and held on tight, the way sisters should. When she leaned away, she saw tears in her sister's eyes. Bella didn't cry easily, and Caprice suspected pregnancy hormones were at work.

"Are you and Joe coming to dinner at Mom's on Sunday?" No one missed dinner at their parents', not unless blood and a sudden accident were involved.

"Joe doesn't want to come."

"Then you and the kids come."

"He's never missed a dinner with Mom and Dad, not since before we were married," Bella said sadly.

"Try to convince him to come, Bella. Try to put everything aside for one day at least. Give yourself a break."

"I don't want everybody to gang up on him."

"We won't. I promise. Tell him that. Do you want me to talk to him?"

"Oh, no. I think he's still embarrassed about blowing up at you at Mom's birthday party."

She doubted that. Joe had just said what he was thinking—that he wanted to come first with Bella rather than her family always coming first. What a mess.

"Come on Sunday," Caprice said again. "Seth will be there." She knew her sisters were still curious about the handsome doctor, and dinner with their parents would give them the opportunity to get to know him better.

"Are you serious about him?" Bella asked.

"Trying not to be."

Bella shook her head. "I sure don't have any advice to give you about your love life right now."

That one statement proved Bella wasn't really herself. She was always ready to give Caprice advice, and anyone else who would listen, too.

After she walked Bella to the door, watched her go down the steps and climb into her car, which was parked in the circular drive, Caprice returned inside. She heard men's voices upstairs and lots of noise. Movers at work.

She headed back to the living room, needing to set up a schedule with Eliza. The real estate agent had mentioned wanting to shoot video and still pictures by the beginning of next week. Everything had to be painted, redesigned, and in place by then.

In the doorway to the living room, Caprice stopped cold because she heard Eliza say, "You have no right to ask Bella out on a date."

How awkward was this? But Eliza and Bob obviously didn't know she was there.

"What I do now is none of your damn business," Bob retorted with what sounded like menace.

Eliza must have heard menace too, because she

took a step back and looked as if she might burst into tears. Was that an act? Or did this multimillionaire entrepreneur really have feelings for this painter? Or . . .

Was she afraid of him?

Chapter Two

On the drive home that evening, Caprice made the turns to her neighborhood by rote, as Bella's problems tripped through her mind. She turned her sister's situation over again and again, but she didn't know what she could do to help. That frustrated her. Was Bella really going to have a coffee date with Bob?

As she turned onto her street, which was lined with decades-old elms and sycamores that shaded the sidewalk and front yards, she considered the interchange between Bob and Eliza. Were they dating? She was curious about that. Her family often told her she was curious about too many things. With forced conviction, she warned herself their conversation was none of her business. The last time she'd asked too many questions, she'd solved a murder and almost gotten herself killed!

As she neared her driveway, she breathed out a coming-home sigh because her house was a haven. Built in the early fifties, it was a Cape Cod style with a flagstone path leading to the front porch. Nestled between a crimson maple and a white birch, it was mostly built of brick. However, stone enriched the unusual arched door, and the copper roof above the porch was a distinct feature. Her home had a sturdy, warm, homey air that had attracted Caprice to it from the moment she'd seen it. The azaleas under the dining room's bay window had finished blooming long ago, but yellow and pink zinnias lined the gardens on either side of the porch, along with white begonias.

The tall privacy fence that stretched on both sides and surrounded the backyard was perfect for the peace and quiet she sometimes craved after a day of dealing with the suppliers, clients, and professionals she consulted. One of her guilty secrets was that she liked to garden in her bathing suit. At thirty-two, she was a bit shy about her body, which was about ten pounds overweight, and enjoyed the privacy of the fence as well as the tall poplars that practically hid it. She missed Dylan, the cute little dog that had found a home with her for a couple of months. They had played out here almost every day he'd been with her. But Roz had given him a home, and he was happy with her in her new town house.

Caprice pulled her restored yellow Camaro into her driveway, and the garage door slid up with creaks and groans. The paint had started to peel again. She really had to get a new one, or paint it once more before winter set in. From the garage, she stepped up onto a covered back porch and let herself in her back door. She had barely had time to set her purse on the counter and turn around when she heard a thud. Her cat had jumped from a perch on the turquoise-carpeted, floor-to-ceiling cat tree in the living room. Seconds later, Sophia, a strikingly

colored calico with long hair and a huge fluffy tail,
strolled through the dining room into Caprice's
retro-style kitchen. The appliances, all in a warm
buttercup color, harkened back to the fifties, as did
the antique maple table and the chairs with yellow-
braided seat pads.

After a long, soulful meow, Sophia hopped up
onto one of those pads and stared up at Caprice,
her golden eyes accusing her mistress of being gone
too long.

"I'm not late," Caprice protested, crossing to
Sophia and stroking the white ruff around her neck.

Sophia lifted her chin for an underside rub.

Caprice laughed. "You're not spoiled. Not much."

Sophia had been a stray when Caprice found her
shortly after she'd moved in. She'd considered the
cat a welcome-to-the-neighborhood present, and
they'd been best buddies ever since. Caprice had
named her for her Nana's favorite actress, Sophia
Loren. "I know you miss Dylan, but he's happy
with Roz."

For a few weeks in May, Caprice had also taken in
two kittens, but her brother Vince's law partner had
found them a home. She hadn't seen Grant for a few
weeks. She quickly reminded herself there was no
reason to see Grant. Really.

After dishing out some of Sophia's favorite canned
cat food, she bent down to place it on the mat on the
floor. She was straightening up when the cell phone
in her purse began playing the Beatles "A Hard Day's
Night." She opened the black-patent-leather vintage
handbag and fished out her phone. She smiled when
she glimpsed the caller ID. It was Seth.

"Home yet?" he asked.

His voice, which held just a hint of his Virginia roots, fired up hopes and dreams she'd thought she'd put permanently on hold after her last serious relationship.

"Just got in."

"I know this is last minute," he said, "but our coffee date seems like years ago."

"It was Monday," she teased.

"Yeah, seems like years ago," he repeated. "I'm almost finished here. The doc for the evening shift arrived, so how about ice cream at Cherry on the Top?"

"Ice cream for supper. Now that's an idea."

"I'll buy you a banana split with plenty of walnuts—protein, fruit, and dairy. What more could you ask for?"

She could ask for a lot more, but maybe she was afraid to. In the past, she'd been hurt by wearing her heart on her sleeve. Her high school sweetheart had broken off their relationship through e-mail. He'd had bigger ambitions than what Kismet offered. And then there had been Travis and his adorable daughter. After Caprice had fallen in love with them both, Travis had reunited with his ex-wife. She thought about the banana split Seth had suggested but, more important, the time with him. "Could be just what the doctor ordered."

"Rough day?"

"I'm sure not any rougher than yours."

"Meet you there in fifteen minutes?"

"Fifteen it is."

In fifteen minutes, she'd stare again into Seth's blue eyes and wonder if a thirty-two-year-old's dreams could actually come true.

* * *

"You're smiling," Seth said on Sunday as he wound his arm around Caprice's waist and led her up the porch steps to her parents' home.

Whenever Caprice walked into her childhood home, memories came rushing back. She had so many good reminiscences of delicious smells, of chasing Bella up the stairs, sneaking out onto her parents' balcony with Nikki, snitching Vince's favorite baseball so he had to track her down and then take her along to his game. Although they lived in Pennsylvania, the house was a California-style stucco with a red barrel-tiled roof that always needed repair. The house had been a fixer-upper. That's how her parents had been able to afford the property when they were building a family.

They'd fixed up the house little by little over the years, although they had kept basic features that were still high maintenance, like casement windows, the stucco exterior, and the roof. When Nana had moved in with them, they'd added on a suite for her. Caprice had good memories about that, too. She and Nana had enjoyed tea together since she was a kid. Every few weeks, she took an afternoon off and joined Nana in her parlor.

Caprice opened the screen door, and they stepped up to the foyer inside. "I'm smiling because, in a way, this will always be home."

To the left was a long living room, with a sunroom off that, and a library behind the living room with its own little balcony. Ahead of them was the dining room, which led to the kitchen.

A cuckoo clock struck five as they heard chatter coming from the kitchen.

Seth looked around and said, "This house *feels* like a home. I like that fireplace in the living room." He peeked through the archway. "What's the room beyond?"

"We've always used it as a library. Mom's an English teacher, and she's always kept it filled with books. She never forced us to read anything, but we saw her and Dad doing it a lot, and I guess we followed their example. Although most of his life Dad was a brick-layer and considered a blue-collar worker, he always liked reading about architecture, building things, and faraway places."

"You said your dad has his own company now?"

"For about the past fifteen years. And now that he's getting older, Mom doesn't like him going out with the crew as much, so he handles most of the pa-perwork."

Wonderful aromas wafted through the house. Impulsively, Caprice suggested to Seth, "Close your eyes."

"Uh oh. What are you going to surprise me with?"

"No surprise. Just a test. Close your eyes and tell me what you smell."

Seth did as she suggested and took a sniff. "Let's see—onion, garlic, tomato sauce." He took another sniff. "And something sweet and doughy."

"You're pretty good. Mom made her special recipe—her version of pasta fagioli. Nikki made a tomato and mozzarella side dish, and Bella prepared an artichoke salad. Vince is bringing wine."

Seth lifted the bag in his hand. "And you made bread."

"I did. We always coordinate. The sweet smells are from Nana's peach pies. This time of year, we can't get enough of them. Wait until you see Mom's tomato garden. She raises heirloom plants from seeds. I only have a few out back at my house, but she has about twenty-five of them planted. Nikki used her tomatoes in her contribution."

"Twenty-five plants? That's a lot."

"It is. Mom and Dad give some away. But the rest Mom and Nana freeze for the winter."

Seth studied Caprice curiously. "I didn't think families like yours existed anymore."

"Your family isn't close?"

"As a family doc, my dad was gone a lot. He missed most of my baseball games and other events."

"Did you miss not having brothers or sisters?"

Seth had told her a little about his background, that his dad had a GP practice in a small town in Virginia. His mom, a nurse, had worked with his dad. She suspected Seth had been alone a lot as a kid.

"I didn't miss having sisters," he said with a grin. "But, yeah, I guess I would have liked a brother to hang with. I had good friends, though. In fact, my best high school buddy had a family very much like yours—two brothers and two sisters, a mom who stayed home and baked cookies. The only difference was, he was Polish."

Caprice laughed. "And my mom didn't stay home. Once Bella started school, she went back to teaching and has been at it ever since. Come on, let's announce that we're here. Are you ready for this?"

"I handled your mom's birthday party just fine. I can handle this."

As she gazed up into Seth's blue eyes and studied his classically handsome face, she still didn't quite believe he was dating her. Could he handle her family and her life? Could she handle his erratic schedule and their interrupted dates?

He gestured to the dining-room table, beautifully set with silverware and crystal goblets, wineglasses, and cloth napkins, and gave a low whistle. "Someone went to a lot of trouble."

"Family dinners are important to Mom and Nana."

"Your Nana Celia's your dad's mom, right?"

"Yep. Mom lost her parents, so she appreciates Nana Celia even more. We all do."

Seth looked thoughtful as he followed her into the kitchen. The atmosphere there was absolute bedlam. Nikki was pulling the tomato, mozzarella, and oregano side dish out of the oven as Nana put finishing touches on a fruit salad. Bella was trying to keep eight-year-old Timmy and his little sister from poking their fingers into the peach pies cooling on the counter.

Her mom saw them first. She stopped what she was doing and enclosed Caprice in a huge hug. "Your timing is just right." She gave Seth a hug, too. "It's good to see you again. That spa day you gave me for my birthday was fabulous. That was a wonderful and thoughtful present."

"I heard Green Tea Haven was the best." He lifted the bag of bread Caprice had baked. "Where would you like this?"

"Right here," Nana said, pointing to a basket lined

with a linen napkin. She said to both of them, "Vince, Joe, and your dad are all outside. Your father wanted to show them the outdoor fireplace he finally got around to building."

"But it's time to eat now," Bella said. "Nikki, can you round up everyone?"

Nikki and Caprice exchanged a look. Bella liked to give orders. As the baby in the family, she pretty much always got her own way. She'd started out as cute as the proverbial button and had grown beautiful later to boot. Right now, since she was pregnant and going through troubles with Joe, they were all giving her some slack instead of arguing or rebelling.

Nikki went to the back door, opened it, put two fingers in her mouth, and gave a loud whistle. "Come and get it," she yelled.

Seth whispered into Caprice's ear, "This is going to be entertaining."

Caprice joked back, "Just be glad we don't charge admission."

His low chuckle urged her to think about what might happen later when they would be alone. Seth's kiss after their date at the ice cream shop had been everything she'd expected his kisses to be. But she wasn't sure she was ready for whatever came next.

As always, after her father gave thanks, dinner around the De Luca table was boisterous and lively—and downright funny at times. The food they all made was a unifier, a reason to sit together, satisfaction they could share. Her mom and Nana knew dinner was a blending experience, and that's why they always expected them all to be here. Family dinners were a tradition that Caprice and her siblings could rely on in rough times, in tumultuous times, and in sad times, as well as in happy times.

As Seth sat beside her and dug into everything on his plate with enthusiasm, finished his pie, and enjoyed the coffee, she felt something so right about his being here.

When dinner was over, the guys drifted toward the TV and the sports channel. They could be more of a hindrance than a help in the kitchen, and the women knew it, so they didn't complain as they cleaned up, stowed away food, and made packages of leftovers for everyone.

Caprice was slicing a piece of peach pie for Seth to take home that night when Bella tugged at her arm. "The kids are wrapped up in a board game. I need to talk to you. Come outside with me, okay?"

There was a sound of desperation in Bella's voice, and Caprice wondered how long she'd been holding in her emotions. She'd been quieter than usual during the meal, speaking only when spoken to. That certainly wasn't Bella. She had an opinion on everything under the sun. But now, it seemed that she didn't want to share an opinion with Caprice, but instead wanted to spill something.

It was quite easy to slip away. Caprice called to her mom, "We're going outside for a few minutes to check the tomatoes."

Nothing unusual about that. At this time of year, they had just begun to get big and ripen.

As soon as she and Bella slipped outside, Bella led her down an incline into the lower part of the garden. She really didn't want to be overheard. By Joe? Or by everyone else? Now Caprice was really getting worried.

She stopped beside a row of yellow tomatoes. "What's wrong?"

"So much that I don't even know where to start." Bella's voice was a little high pitched, and she was obviously close to tears.

Caprice wrapped her arm around her sister's shoulders. "Come on. Tell me."

"Joe didn't come home until after one last night, and he reeked of smoke. I pretended I was asleep because I don't know what to say to him anymore."

"You didn't question him about it?" Caprice tried to keep her tone as calm and reasonable as her question. She couldn't imagine why Bella hadn't asked him where he'd been.

"You just don't get it, Caprice. Maybe you have to be married to understand, but I've asked him before and he wouldn't tell me. I couldn't see that it was going to be any different now, and I just didn't want another argument."

If Bella wanted real answers, Caprice had a suggestion. "Have you gone through his pockets?"

Her sister actually looked shocked and slowly shook her head. "That seems like such an invasion of privacy."

"You can't have it both ways. If you won't ask him, you're going to have to find out another way. If he won't tell you, then maybe you need to invade his privacy."

Bella looked a bit embarrassed. "I did check his phone for any odd numbers, ones I didn't recognize. But I couldn't find a one. Anybody who called was one of his friends."

"What about text messages?"

"You know we're trying to cut expenses. Joe won't

pay for the text function. But that's not the only reason I wanted to talk to you. I . . ." Her sister confided, "I had coffee with Bob."

"You seriously did that? Bella!"

Her gasp of outrage had been a mistake. If Bella sensed that she was judging her, she'd clam up. Caprice took a deep breath and warned herself to go easy. "Okay, so you had coffee with Bob. Did you reminisce about old times?" Those memories could put distance between Bella and Bob, or bond them together more closely.

"Not so much. He really knows how to listen, like he really wants to know what I have to say. When I talk to Joe, it's like I'm talking to a door."

Right now a very closed door, Caprice suspected. "So what did Bob listen to?"

"I told him I want to sell the costumes I design on the Internet. He didn't laugh at me like Joe did. You know what he said?"

Caprice didn't like that excitement in Bella's tone one little bit. Excitement like that could be dangerous. "What?"

"He told me I always was talented, and I shouldn't give up on what I want to do. I'm going to see him again."

Bella's tone almost sounded defiant, and Caprice knew she had to be careful as she pulled out more details. "I can imagine having someone listen to you felt good, and that's why you want to see him again."

"You're exactly right. He has a board meeting at the community center next Sunday. I'm going to see him after the meeting. He's really involved there— painting murals on the walls with teens helping him after school. I already talked with my neighbor about watching the kids if Joe's not around."

"What if he is?"

"I don't know. I'll deal with that on Sunday. But he's there so rarely. I don't think it's going to be a problem."

"Can I tell you what I honestly think without you getting all upset?"

"I don't know because I'm probably not going to like it."

No, she probably wouldn't. "I think you're heading for trouble. What if Joe finds out you're meeting Bob?"

"Maybe he *should* find out."

The rebelliousness in Bella's tone signaled that she'd like Joe to be jealous, that she'd like him to show her he cared, that she wanted to know she was still loved. But, on the other hand, Caprice didn't believe Bella would really want to see the fireworks if Joe discovered her plans.

"You realize you could be purposely damaging your marriage?"

Suddenly, Bella's chin rose an inch or so. "I'm tired of feeling sad and bearing the brunt of Joe's resentment about my pregnancy. And I'm beginning to think . . ." Her voice trailed off as she got choked up, showing Caprice the hurt that lay beneath all the rest of her emotions.

"What are you beginning to think?" Caprice asked gently.

"I'm beginning to realize Joe married me in the first place because he *had* to, not because he *wanted* to."

Caprice was trying to decide the best way to respond

when she suddenly saw the tomato plants jiggle. Bella saw the foliage move and heard the rustle too.

"What is it? Do you think there's something in there?" She sounded almost panicked, as if a squirrel hearing their conversation would cause a scandal.

The tomatoes rustled more earnestly now.

Before Caprice could part the plants, two buff-colored paws appeared, then a wet nose and a scraggly head. It looked like a bedraggled cocker spaniel.

She automatically hunkered down. "Oh, my goodness. What are you doing in there?"

The dog was panting now, panting more than it should be.

"I don't believe this," Bella said mutinously. "We're having a serious conversation and we're interrupted by a . . . a . . . dog. You're a stray animal magnet!"

"Bella, I can't help *you* right now, but I can help her. She looks scared and dehydrated. Could you please get her a bowl of water while I see if she's okay?"

Caprice held her breath, hoping Bella wouldn't explode.

Chapter Three

Minutes later, Seth was the one who carried a bowl of water outside.

Bella hadn't exploded . . . simply stalked inside. Caprice shouldn't be surprised Seth had come to her aid. After all, a doctor was a doctor and . . . he was the kind of man who cared.

He spotted Caprice with the buff-colored cocker and hunkered down beside her, slipping the bowl in front of the dog. "She was under the tomato plants?"

"For cover and protection, I guess. Look at her. She's so thirsty."

"You've already decided this is a girl?" he asked with a smile, knowing that with the dog crouched down like that, they wouldn't be able to tell.

"She looks like a girl, and she feels like a girl. I mean her aura or something does."

He laughed. "That's a scientific approach if I ever heard one."

The cocker looked up at them with soulful, dark brown eyes, and Caprice knew the dog would be staying at her house tonight. In the garage, though, so

Sophia and the house didn't get infested with fleas. She knew the drill after taking in as many stray animals as she had.

"How old do you think she is?" Caprice asked.

"I'm no vet, but I'd say over a year and under five."

"She looks like Lady from *Lady and the Tramp*. That's my favorite Disney movie," Caprice confessed.

The dog stopped drinking, and Caprice reached out her hand so the cocker could smell it.

When it came to animals, Caprice followed her instincts.

The dog smelled her hand and then licked it as if she understood she'd found someone who could help her.

"Bella seemed out of sorts when she came in," Seth remarked.

"Our conversation was interrupted. But that might not have been a bad thing. Bella's headed in a direction I don't approve of. I'm trying not to judge her, but she doesn't want to give any thought to my suggestions, so there's nothing I can really do to help."

"Except listen."

"Yeah, I know. And I will. Still, this isn't the place to have the conversation we were having, not when someone is liable to come outside at any time." She looked toward the house, worried about Bella, yet knowing she couldn't help her at the moment. Maybe later, when her sister was in the mood to take advice.

Caprice checked her watch. "I'm going to call my vet. He has a small practice and often goes in to feed the animals himself on weekends. Maybe I can catch him."

"You're good friends?"

"After all the animals I've taken in, I'd say so. He's done me favors and I've done him a few. Sometimes somebody will drop off a stray at his practice. When he can't find them a home, he calls me. Let's see if she'll come out of the tomatoes so I can look her over."

Caprice stretched out her hand toward the dog again. "Come on, girl. We won't hurt you. Let's see how big you really are." She gently smoothed her hand over the dog's head, and the cocker didn't flinch from it. That was a good sign. She ruffled her ears, made more soothing noises, and took a step back, encouraging her.

Seth apparently understood one person at a time was enough for a frightened animal and quietly stepped back too. It didn't take long until Caprice had her arm around the dog. Soon she was running her hands over her, looking for problems other than the obvious.

"It's a she," she said with a grin.

"She looks like she's been outside for a while."

Caprice slipped her phone out of her lime-green Capris, scrolled through her contact list, and hit Call. She was grateful when she heard Marcus Lang's deep tone ask, "Hi, Caprice, what's up? Something wrong with Sophia?"

"Nope, she's good. But she may be in for a visitor. I found a dog."

"Of course you did," he said with a hearty laugh.

She could envision Marcus's black face in a wide smile, his laughter reaching his almost black eyes. He was big and burly but had gentle hands and a deep respect for animals. He'd earned his degree at

Colorado State and come back to Pennsylvania to practice. His family lived in York, but he'd decided to open his Furry Friends Animal Clinic in Kismet. There was another clinic in town. However, there, animals were treated more like numbers. Marcus treated them like people.

"What kind of dog?" he asked.

"A cocker. She looks like she's been outside for a while."

"I'm at the office now, catching up on paperwork. Do you want to bring her in?"

"That would be wonderful. You're wonderful."

"You and my mother think so," he said in a wry tone. "See you as soon as you can get her here."

After she ended the call, she asked Seth, "Do you mind dropping me and the pup at the vet's? If you get called away, Nikki can always come pick me up."

"No problem. Do you have any ideas on how to get her into my truck?"

"My guess is, she's starved. I'll find something inside, and we'll lead her with that. What do you think?"

"I think you've done this before."

"A few times," she admitted. "She looks like the kind of dog who should belong to someone. Marcus can check for a chip."

"A chip?"

"A computer chip that's inserted under the skin. Some owners have it done in case their dog or cat runs away. If someone takes the animal to a vet or shelter, they can scan for it. It connects animals to their owners. Hopefully she'll have one. Can you stay with her while I find something innocuous for her to eat?"

34   *Karen Rose Smith*

"And if she tries to run off?" he asked.

"You'll think of something."

He laughed.

Caprice's easy banter with Seth was one of the reasons she liked him so much. They could be light and funny and playful with each other, yet that spark was there. Roz had remarked that Caprice lit up like a Christmas tree when he was around. That lit-up feeling was so enjoyable, she didn't want to ever lose it.

Five minutes later, as she searched her mom's refrigerator for something for the cocker, like leftovers from the night before, Caprice's cell phone played from her pocket. She checked the screen. Eliza.

Eliza was one of those demanding clients who expected Caprice to be at her beck and call.

"Hello, Eliza."

"Where's Bob?" her client demanded to know.

"Bob? He was supposed to finish painting your house this afternoon." When it came to home-staging, Sunday could be a workday like any other. Caprice tried to keep the morning for church, and once a month or so she had dinner with her family, but most Sundays she was working in her office or scrambling to finish a project. Bob was one of those painters who didn't take any days off, though his crews did.

"You haven't heard from him?" Caprice asked.

"No, I haven't. What are we going to do?"

She'd planned to complete the staging tomorrow— have the furniture delivered from the rental company, move around what was already there. She'd also added hanging drapes, changing a few light fixtures, and mounting sconces to her to-do list. But

in order for all that to be done, the painting had to
be finished.

One of her main jobs as a home-staging professional was to quiet her clients' fears and anxieties,
as well as get the job done. She said calmly, "We have
plenty of time before the open house next Sunday.
I'll try to call Bob. But if I can't get hold of him, I
have someone else in mind who can help me in an
emergency."

And this was an emergency if Bob was missing in
action. Monty Culp, Roz's former gardener, had
helped her in a pinch before, and she hoped he
could help her again if she needed him.

After she ended her call with Eliza, she found
Bob's number. But her call to him went to voice
mail. She left a message for him to contact her as
soon as he could, and then she hung up. If he
didn't get back to her later tonight, she'd be on the
phone to Monty. Getting Eliza's painting finished
couldn't wait.

Her phone back in her pocket, Caprice found leftover chicken in the fridge. Minutes later Seth was
leading the cocker to his truck. She'd already said
good-bye and hugged everyone inside. They knew
the drill with animals. The fewer people around, the
better. She and Seth waved to her family, who stood
on the porch watching as they drove away, headed
for the veterinary clinic.

The cocker she'd found was pregnant! In a month
or so she'd have a litter of pups to care for along with
their mom . . . if she didn't find the dog's owner.

Caprice stood in her fenced-in backyard and

tossed one of the balls Dylan had left behind. It landed near a bed of fuchsia and white vinca plants that were thriving in the July heat. When the August humidity really set in, they'd be bushier and a few inches taller. Clumps of Shasta daisies bookended the vinca and gave Caprice an idea.

"I have a name for her," Caprice suddenly told Seth, who was working on cutting down a huge cardboard box so she could use it for the cocker's bed.

"I'm sure that, coming from you, it'll be original."

Caprice gave him a sideways glance and saw that he was complimenting her. She was used to Bella talking about her uniqueness as if it were a disease.

"She's sort of the color of my Shasta daisies. I'm going to call her Shasta. What do you think?"

"As I said—unique. I like it. I don't know any other dog with that name."

"Do you know any other dogs?"

He smiled and stood, holding the carton that was now about six inches high on the sides. "No, but I'm sure you'll introduce me to a few . . ." He stopped.

What had he been about to say? If he stuck around? If they continued seeing each other? If the stars lined up in their favor? But Seth didn't elaborate. In fact, he looked serious for a moment, but then the expression passed.

"I'll line this with those rugs you stacked in the garage."

"A towel on top," she reminded him.

"A towel on top. That garage is going to look like Shasta's own apartment soon. A good thing, too. After her pups are born, she'll need one."

Marcus had given her the rundown on everything she'd need in order to care for Shasta and deliver the pups. He was going to help with some of it. He knew a client who could lend her the right size whelping box, where the pups would be born.

She and Seth had moved any tools that could fall over and hurt Shasta into the shed in Caprice's backyard, where she kept her mower, a small hand tiller, and a step ladder. Caprice had some extra feeding dishes on hand, and she had laid down a place mat and put two bowls on it. Then she arranged a couple of old throw rugs and tossed toys onto them.

"This probably isn't how you expected to spend your night off," she said to Seth, as they started for the garage.

On the way home, he'd stayed in the truck with Shasta while Caprice had run into the discount store for an extra supply of paper towels, a collar, a leash, and a few dog toys. For the time being, she'd bought food from Marcus that was good for a pregnant pup. Tomorrow she'd visit Kismet's pet store, Perky Paws, to purchase a dog bed and other supplies for when Shasta came into the house.

"Maybe not exactly how I'd envisioned it," Seth agreed.

"Would you like a glass of wine? We could sit out on the porch for a while."

Even though the garage was cooler than the rest of the house in the summer due to its thick, cement-block walls and shaded windows, she wanted to make sure the cocker felt safe before housing her there for the night.

"I'll pass on the wine. Just in case I get a call. But soda would be good. Sitting on the porch with you sounds even better."

She liked the fact that Seth could roll with the

punches. With his career, he had to be an expert at doing that.

Once they were settled on the porch, Shasta lay near Caprice's foot. Next to Seth on a vintage fifties-style robin's-egg-blue glider, Caprice sipped her soda, then set it on a table beside the glider. Night fell with the swiftness of a thief stealing the summer day.

As Seth leaned over to kiss her, Caprice couldn't imagine a nicer way to spend the evening.

Baroque Bedazzle wasn't a common theme for a home-staging, but then Caprice's themes were sometimes very uncommon. She strove for high-end unique, and her clients knew it. That's why she had succeeded where others hadn't—why the houses she'd staged sold so quickly. Her open houses brought in home buyers from York, Harrisburg, Lancaster, Gettysburg, and now even as far as New Jersey and New York, Washington, D.C., and Baltimore. Her reputation was gaining steam, and she just wanted to keep a level head about it all.

At this Sunday open house, she had to keep her mind on what she was doing. It was hard to forget about last Sunday, when she and Seth had settled Shasta in and stolen time together. Yet by the end of the evening, she'd had the feeling Seth was holding back. She didn't know why. Maybe they'd fallen into their relationship too quickly.

But she shouldn't borrow trouble. Maybe he was just putting on the brakes and was cautious, like she was, because past relationships hadn't worked out . . . because they both wanted something more than an affair. She fervently hoped so. However, she'd had only a hurried phone call from him this week, and she was feeling . . . insecure.

Eliza, who was dressed in a purple-satin, dressy lounge outfit, sidled up to Caprice as guests began flowing through the double doors. "You've gotten their attention," she said in a low voice that included a bit of surprise that irked Caprice.

Of course she'd gotten their attention.

Immediately a new group of possible buyers commented about the pieces of furniture that resembled what French king Louis the Fourteenth might have used to furnish the palace at Versailles. Classical Baroque was impressive . . . over the top . . . dramatic. The style had begun to flourish around 1600 in Italy and then spread to most of Europe. The Versailles palace was one of the best examples.

A couple stopped and studied a foyer table with a rectangular top that rested on four cabriole legs. A carved flower basket was a centerpiece that connected thematically with the legs, and a gilded Capetian mirror hung above the table. The grouping gave the guests who entered the house a preview of what they were about to experience.

Most of the pieces of furniture belonged to Eliza. Caprice had just thinned them to make the rooms look posh and elaborate but not overcrowded. The two-drawer chest, the coffee table and side tables, the heavily carved and decorated armoires—all were quality pieces. For Eliza's penchant for purple, Caprice had substituted rich jewel tones in cranberry, hunter green, sapphire blue, and deep gold. In the bedrooms, tufted headboards and Louis the Fourteenth gold-leafed chairs looked as if they belonged. Caprice's furniture and color choices presented the house in magnificent splendor. She had made some rooms look bigger, others warmer.

"Those sconces you added to the upstairs hall this morning fit in perfectly. I'd buy them if I weren't hoping to move."

The hall had been a little dark, and while Caprice had no intention of lighting real candles in the sconce cups, flameless tea candles gave the illusion of flickering light.

"I know what I'm doing most of the time," Caprice said with a laugh, but her quip seemed to go over Eliza's head. "I still can't believe Bob left us hanging like that last Sunday. A quick call to apologize midweek, saying that he'd had to go out of town and he'd adjust his bill accordingly wasn't much explanation."

Caprice had switched to plan B and phoned Monty Culp, and he'd finished the job for them Monday. Bob's call after the fact with an apology hadn't been enlightening at all.

"Thank goodness your painter could take away Bob's tarps, pans, and brushes," Eliza said, wrinkling her nose at the idea of the house hunters seeing them.

Monty had assured Caprice he could stow it all in his garage. Bob was supposed to pick everything up tomorrow.

She thought about the fact that Bella was supposed to meet Bob tonight at the community center. Would he show up for that?

Eliza glanced toward the large dining room, with its humongous table and ornate, high-backed chairs.

"Nikki's food smells wonderful. I'm sure some of our guests came just for that."

Soon some of the open house guests would be sitting at that table, imagining themselves in this house as they sampled Nikki's food. Her sister had built a reputation as carefully as Caprice. But when they'd teamed up, her catering business had garnered considerable notice. The wealthy in the surrounding area often hired her to cater lobster and bison dinners, as well as wedding receptions.

"I sampled the cassoulet," Eliza said to Caprice. "It's mouth-watering. In fact, I think I'm going to snitch some with one of the baguettes and hibernate in my home office. I can close off that room, don't you think?"

"You might have someone knock."

"If someone who wants to buy peeks in, I won't care. But maybe I can get some work done."

At these open houses, Caprice's job was to oversee everything that was going on. After a few more words with Eliza, she decided to check on Nikki.

The kitchen was as elaborately baroque as the rest of the house. Everything about Eliza and her house shouted glamour, which was the exact impression she was going for. Most people would think the kitchen was the last place one could employ baroque design, but metallic glass paint and jewel-toned wallpaper could work wonders. The wallpaper had already been there, as had the ornate lighting fixture. Caprice had changed the hardware on the cabinets to a scrolled metallic design and hung window treatments that picked up the deepest emerald in the wallpaper. Shiny, ruby-red canisters hand-painted with intricate flower designs decorated the counter.

After consulting with Caprice, Nikki had decided to use sapphire-blue serving china and napkins. They were a dramatic contrast against the white linens spread on the table and sideboard, which held an array of warm buffet dishes, all with delicious aromas wafting from them. Nikki had prepared coq au vin; beef bourguignon; chips de citrouille (fried pumpkin slices), based on a recipe originating in the Perigord region of France; and chou rouge (braised red cabbage) from the Lorraine region. Nikki knew her foods, no doubt about that, as well as how to present them in the most pleasing way.

In the kitchen, a waiter served everything from baked apple Brie to marinated artichokes to cheese puffed pastry to crudités. Glancing around, Caprice found Nikki in an alcove near the pantry closet. She'd just stowed a few of her serving trays inside.

"You've outdone yourself again. The guests are gobbling down your food as if they can't get enough."

Nikki's brown brows drew together. "I just hope I don't run out of anything. This seems to be a bigger crowd than usual."

"Denise said she had tons of inquiries this time." Denise Langford was the luxury broker who often handled the houses Caprice staged. "Have you seen Denise?"

"I think she had some questions for Eliza, but I don't know if she found her." Nikki closed the pantry door.

"Eliza was headed for her home office. I'll tell her

Denise wants to see her. Have you heard from Bella in the last couple of days?"

"No, have you?"

"No, but there's a reason I haven't," Caprice said.

"Do I even want to know?" Nikki rolled her eyes.

"I don't approve of what she's planning to do."

"Is she thinking about leaving Joe?"

"I don't think so. Not quite that serious."

"So, spill. Tell me."

Nikki didn't have to wheedle much. Caprice asked, "Remember Bob?"

"Of course, I remember Bob. He broke Bella's heart. You hire him for jobs."

"Bella met him for coffee, and she's planning on seeing him again this evening."

Nikki gave a low whistle. "Old fires could reignite. Are they having coffee again . . . like in a public place?"

"I don't know. She said he had a board meeting at the community center. They're going to connect there afterward. Then I don't know what they'll do."

"You're worried she'll do something stupid."

"She's upset enough to do something rebellious. That's just as bad. And the more I think about it . . ."

"You want to stop her."

"I don't know about stopping her, but I feel I should do something. I think I might just go to the community center after we're done here and barge in on their rendezvous."

"She's going to hate you for that."

Would Bella hate her? Or would she thank her when she could see reason again?

Her ruminations about the best way to help Bella distracted Caprice as she mingled with prospective buyers, listened to their comments about the decor, and decided if she wanted to change anything for future house showings. Eventually she made her way to Eliza's office to tell her Denise was looking for her if the agent hadn't found her yet. This house was big enough to get lost in!

The door to Eliza's office was partially open. Caprice rapped softly and stepped inside.

The room was as ornately adorned as the rest of the house, but maybe a little less so since Caprice had staged it. They'd removed a bookcase and a curio cabinet to make the walking space more expansive. Caprice had arranged for the gold-trimmed white scroll desk to face anyone who came in. She'd also created a sitting area with Louis the Fourteenth chairs, an antique light fixture with jeweled cups, and a few more mauve and deep purple rugs to make the polished floors more hospitable. She'd let Eliza keep the deep-purple velvet drapes because, after all, this was her office, and she probably spent more time here than in the rest of the house.

Eliza looked up when Caprice rapped on the partially open door and walked in. "Did Denise find you?"

Caprice could see that Eliza's attention was elsewhere because she looked down again at the papers on her desk without commenting.

"Eliza?"

"I'm sorry. What did you say?" Her client's inattention was terribly unlike her. She was always sharp and seemed to be on top of everything.

"Is something wrong?" Caprice asked, stepping farther inside.

Eliza bit one of her perfectly lined and colored

full lips, hesitated, and then sighed. "I don't know when I'm going to be moving to L.A."

The first question that came to Caprice's lips was—*But you do still want to sell the house, don't you?* However, she didn't ask it because Eliza was worried about something, and Caprice sensed it would be better to find out what that was first.

"Are you afraid the house won't sell quickly?"

"No, not that." She glanced at the cell phone on her desk as if she might have received a call. "My investment backing for Connect Xpress in L.A. has fizzled, and now I don't know if I can open the business there."

"Were you getting a loan through the bank?"

"Oh, no. I'm using private funding with a partnership agreement. Jeff Garza was going to invest."

Caprice recognized that name. "Doesn't he own a security systems company?"

"Exactly. He's involved in a lot of community organizations, too."

"He's on the board of the community center, isn't he?"

"Yes. He's heading up the fund-raiser to bring more improvements to the center."

"My mother served on the board with him."

A wry smile crossed Eliza's face. "And probably didn't like him very much?"

Diplomatically, Caprice didn't answer. Her mom had commented more than once that Jeff Garza was opinionated and arrogant.

Eliza shook her head. "That's okay. A lot of people don't. They say he's a control freak. But he was a willing investor, and they're not always easy to find.

I want to franchise Connect Xpress someday, and I need a wealthy, connected partner to do that."

"So he's pulled out altogether?"

"No, not altogether. Apparently he made some bad investments, and he wants me to give him a month to see if they'll improve. I know it will take at least a month for the house to sell and for me to settle on it. My concern is—what if he pulls out after that month?"

"You could look for other investors in the meantime."

"I could. That's what I was thinking about when you came in. I'm even considering flying to L.A. with whatever proceeds I make on the house to try to find investors there. It's a dilemma. But I'll figure it out."

Eliza was a savvy businesswoman, and Caprice knew that she would solve her problem. It didn't sound as if she was giving up the idea of selling the house.

Just then there was a rap on the door, and Denise peeked in. "Am I interrupting?"

"No, especially not if you have good news for us," Caprice quipped.

Denise laughed. "No, we didn't sell the house yet. But we have three very interested prospects. I've made appointments with them to come back for a second look later in the week. They all feel the real estate market is at a critical point, and before it takes off again, they want to take advantage of it. The one gentleman didn't have his wife with him, so, of course, he wants to bring her along to see it."

"I'll coordinate my schedule to make sure I'm not here for the showings," Eliza assured her.

While Caprice was interested in the buyers, she

knew she could do more good circulating while Eliza and Denise compared their schedules.

She'd started to move toward the door when Denise stopped her. "I wanted to talk to you too. If the planets line up right, I could have a hugely famous client on my list."

"Would I know him or her?" Caprice asked, curious.

"I can't say until the party has signed on. But I did want to tell you to take extra care with the Sumpter estate."

In Caprice's mind, the Sumpter estate was everything an estate should be. Two stories and sprawling, it had a pool with a pool house and was surrounded by black wrought-iron security fencing. Colin Sumpter, who had already moved to Italy, had decided on a Wild Kingdom theme for the open house the following weekend.

The fact that Denise was telling her to take extra care was a bit insulting, but she said lightly, "You know I always take care with every house I stage—big, small, or in-between."

Denise looked a bit chagrined. "Yes, I know you do. And I think the Wild Kingdom theme is going to be fantabulous. Still, I just wanted you to know that if I sign this party on, he or she might stop in at the open house. Tell Nikki, too, so she's prepared."

Like Caprice, Nikki always tried to be prepared, but Caprice didn't mention that. Instead, she was intrigued by the prospect of someone famous dropping in. A corporate mogul? A politician? A fashion designer? And if any of the above, why would they come to Kismet?

* * *

Caprice was still pondering that question when she pulled into the community center's parking lot a few hours later. She'd stopped at home to check on Shasta and let her romp in the backyard while she'd changed into a Beatles T-shirt, red denim pedal pushers, and flip-flops. Sophia had meowed several times when she'd opened the bedroom door. The feline was totally put out with her because she'd had to spend another few hours in the bedroom while Shasta had the run of the downstairs.

After giving Shasta and Sophia food, water, and a little attention, Caprice had decided to leave them in the house together. After all, she wasn't going to be gone that long, and they did have to learn how to get along. When she was at home with them, they each found their own space and didn't bother each other. Hopefully they'd do the same while she was gone.

The community center was located just outside the downtown area, within walking distance of the stores, restaurants, and professional buildings. It was also near two complexes of low-income apartments, each consisting of about fifty units.

The building that housed the community center had once been a warehouse, but it had been renovated twenty years ago. It needed renovations again. Fund-raising, apparently led by Jeff Garza, was going on to make that happen. A chain-link fence surrounded the outside basketball court. Inside were a game room, an arts and crafts room, a couple of offices, and a meeting room. Her mother had said something about the storage area and the rooms beyond the game room still being in a state of flux. That area was near the back door and didn't concern

Caprice as she entered the game room and spotted the partially completed mural on the wall.

The room had recently been given a fresh coat of beige paint. There were finished murals on two walls. One that depicted teenagers standing in a group talking caught her attention. It was detailed and artistically done. A third mural was sketched on the wall on the far side of the room. She supposed each wall would have a mural of its own. The work there was good, and she caught sight of a couple of the kids studying it with interest. Two other boys were duking it out at the pool table, and teens at card tables played cards or used electronic devices. This was a place for kids to come so they weren't lonely. Here they could escape their family life . . . or the lack thereof.

Caprice wasn't sure where she was going to find Bella. Her sister had told her she'd be meeting Bob here around eight-fifteen, after the board meeting. It was almost eight-thirty, so maybe they had already slipped away. Caprice hoped not.

She didn't know any of the kids in the room, so she headed for the desk, where a supervising adult was on duty. The woman wore a name tag—Reena Baublitz. She looked to be in her forties. A brunette with her hair cut in an up-to-date, chin-length wedge, the woman sat at the desk with a laptop open in front of her. Every once in a while she looked over the groups in the room, then went back to what she was doing.

Caprice decided Reena might have some answers for her.

When Reena saw Caprice approach, she asked, "Can I help you?"

"I hope so. I'm meeting my sister here, Bella Santini. She was going to speak to one of the board members after the meeting broke up."

"Oh, the board meeting was finished . . ." Reena checked her watch, ". . . a half hour ago. They all scattered afterward. I guess they're anxious to get back to their families on a Sunday evening."

Caprice took out her phone and brought up a picture of Bella and showed it to Reena. "Have you seen her?"

"Yes, I did. Just a few minutes ago. I thought she was the mom of one of the kids in the arts and crafts room. We keep the young ones separated, you know, from the older ones. Projects work out best that way."

Caprice could see Reena was going to march into the pros and cons of that method and was about to interrupt her when a scream rent the air from somewhere beyond the game room.

Bella! No, couldn't be.

But then a second scream followed, and Caprice knew she'd been right. That was her sister's scream.

Although Reena and the kids in the room seemed to freeze, Caprice took off, heading toward the blood-curdling sound. Was someone trying to hurt Bella . . . kidnap her . . . mug her?

As her mom had told her, the area beyond the game room was indeed in the midst of renovation. Plastic hung from the four walls. But the back door led outside. That door was hanging open.

Again she heard Bella's voice as her sister yelled, "Help. Someone please help."

Now Caprice heard people running behind her, but she didn't care. She only had one thought. Get to Bella.

When she ran outside, she stopped short at what she saw. Green paint spilled across the asphalt from an overturned can. In the midst of that paint, a man lay, his head bashed in and bloodied.

Bella knelt beside him, crying, saying over and over, "He doesn't have a pulse. I can't find a pulse." She was struggling with the body, trying to turn it over, apparently intending to attempt CPR.

As soon as Bella pushed the man to his back, Caprice recognized him. Bob Preston lay there in the puddle of green paint, and he looked . . . dead.

Chapter Four

Caprice speed-dialed Vince.

Before he even had time to ask "What's up?" as he usually did when he saw her name on his screen, she said, "Bella needs you at the police station. Hurry."

An officer was helping Bella into a patrol car, bloody clothes and all.

Caprice was about to be isolated and questioned by a detective. Her fingerprints were already on file with AFIS—the Automated Fingerprint Identification System—since she'd stumbled into another crime scene. After one look at Bella, the officers at the scene had decided to take her to the station for what Caprice knew would be an interrogation—not merely questioning. She also guessed, as had occurred in the spring when she'd happened onto the murder scene, that her car, as well as Bella's, would be impounded. There would be warrants issued, and the cars would be towed to the station's garage and searched.

"What happened?" Vince inquired sharply, all lawyer now.

Caprice quickly told him.

"Are you okay?" he wanted to know.

"I'm fine. But I heard some chatter. Detective Jones will be questioning Bella, and he's ruthless. I know what Roz went through."

Detective Carstead was striding toward her, and she had to end her call.

"I'm leaving now," Vince assured her. "Call someone for yourself. You shouldn't be alone."

"I'll call Nikki to pick me up."

Detective Carstead had been respectful before when he and Caprice had encountered each other in a similar situation, and he was respectful now. He'd already verified the fact that she'd come into the community center a few minutes before she'd heard Bella's scream. As he stuck to the basic questions, she didn't give him more than he asked for. She simply told him what had happened, what she'd heard, what she'd seen, and what she'd found.

"Did you know the deceased?" he asked, studying her closely.

Detective Carstead might not be as aggressive as Jones, but he was sharp. Before the evening was over, he'd know she contracted with Bob and his crews to paint for her. So she didn't hesitate to say, "I often worked with him. I stage houses, and he often painted for me before a staging."

"Did you know him on a personal level?"

She remembered their last bantering conversation. "Bob was personal with everyone. He was a great conversationalist. He could get anybody to talk about anything. But he didn't give much away."

"Why do you think that was?"

Considering her dad, Vince, and Grant, she asked

the detective, "Aren't most guys that way? They talk about sports, not about their childhood."

Carstead almost smiled. Almost. He was in his late thirties, with black hair and very dark brown eyes that didn't miss much. He asked, "Did you and Preston ever see each other socially?"

"Do you mean did we date? No."

"How did your sister know him?"

No one had said she had. But the police would find out details soon enough. "She went to high school with him." Caprice wasn't going to say any more than that.

Would Vince let Bella explain her recent relationship with Bob when Detective Jones questioned her? That was hard to surmise.

After the detective put his notebook away and told her she could leave, Caprice thought about calling Joe. But she didn't know how Bella would want her to handle this, so she didn't. Without hesitation, she phoned Nikki.

When Nikki's cobalt-blue sedan slowed at the curb in front of the community center, Caprice was standing outside the perimeter of the crime-scene tape.

After she climbed into Nikki's car, Nikki shook her head. "Déjà vu."

Nikki had picked her up at the last murder scene she'd happened on.

After Caprice had fastened her seat belt, Nikki took off with a squeal of tires. She said nonchalantly, "All the cops there are too busy to keep track of me speeding. How was Bella?"

"Very pale . . . a little green . . . still covered in paint and Bob's blood."

Nikki gave Caprice a sharp glance. "You're not thinking that—"

"No, of course not. From what I could see and hear, the police didn't find the murder weapon. The murderer must have made off with it. I don't think Bob was murdered all that long before Bella found him."

"She'd better tell them about her and Bob before they find out and think she's hiding something. What did you tell them?"

"Just that they were high school classmates. Really, what else was there to say? They had once been a couple but that was years ago? They'd had coffee a few days ago?"

"That would be enough for a detective to make a connection."

"That's why I didn't say anything more than I had to. If it's all going to come out, Bella needs to tell it, not me."

"If Vince got there in time, he'll tell her to be quiet."

"I know what he's going to tell them—charge her or let her go. She'll probably faint if he says that."

"Where's Joe in all this?"

"He doesn't know yet. That's going to be one weird conversation, no matter who tells him."

"It should be Bella."

Her silence told Nikki she agreed. But shoulds and woulds and ought-to's didn't matter much when emotions were high and a crisis imminent.

Nikki's heavy foot sped them to the police station in record time. Night had fallen, and the halogen lights surrounding the parking lot blazed.

After Nikki parked next to Vince's sporty luxury

sedan, they approached the building, which had been refurbished not so long ago. The double glass door pulled hard, but Caprice yanked at it, eager to see Bella.

Caprice walked right up to the officer at the desk. "I'm Caprice—"

"De Luca," the officer finished. "Yes, I know. Detective Jones said you'd probably show up. Right over there."

He pointed to a bench that Caprice remembered being as uncomfortable as the bench that had once sat outside the principal's office at her Catholic school. Although Caprice settled there, Nikki didn't. She tapped her foot. There was no point asking the officer at the desk how long this would be. It would take however long it would take. Detective Jones was a pit bull and wouldn't let go until he got answers that led him one way . . . or another.

When Detective Jones escorted Vince and Bella into the reception area, they all looked as if Armageddon was only minutes away. Bella was wearing a Tyvek jumpsuit and some kind of paper booties. They'd obviously confiscated her clothes as evidence. No one spoke. Jones gave Caprice a penetrating look, then turned on his heel and went back through the doorway that opened onto a hall, bordered by offices that led . . . to the jail.

Although the station wasn't cold, Bella wrapped her arms around herself. "Can we go home?"

Caprice went to Bella and gave her a huge hug. "We'll talk about this when we get back to your place. Did you call Joe?"

Bella shook her head and tears welled up in her eyes. "They took my phone."

"You consented to give it to them before I arrived," Vince reminded her.

Bella lowered her voice to almost a whisper. "There were two calls from Bob when we set up times to meet. I forgot about those when I gave them the phone. But it doesn't matter because I told Detective Jones I was there to see Bob about developing an online business."

Caprice must have had a blank look.

Bella reminded her, "My costumes for kids."

"Come on," Vince said before either of them said anything else. "Let's get out of here. This isn't a place to have this kind of discussion."

Outside, Bella rode with Vince, probably because she didn't want to answer more of Caprice's questions. After they all arrived at Bella's house and she unlocked the door, they went inside.

Caprice handed Bella her own phone. "Call Joe."

"I have to change out of this thing," Bella said, eyeing the phone as if it could bite her.

But Caprice just held out her phone, and finally Bella took it.

"What about the kids?" Nikki asked.

"They're still with my neighbor. I'll call her, too, and see if she can keep them a little while longer."

Nikki jumped in. "Do you want me to take them overnight? They haven't spent any time with me for a long while, and I can get them to school in the morning."

But Bella shook her head. "No. I'm going to need to be around them. I don't know what's going to happen next."

Although Caprice wished she could overhear the phone conversation between Bella and Joe, she didn't know what Bella said to her husband because she went to her bedroom to make the call.

Vince shook his head. "She might need a criminal attorney. I can protect her rights, but only so far."

"They're not going to charge her," Nikki said, seemingly sure of it.

"There's no way to know," Vince said.

When Bella returned to the living room twenty minutes later in shorts and a tank top, her hair was wet. She'd obviously taken a shower. Without makeup, this was an Isabella Santini whom Caprice rarely saw. Bella was usually primped and perfect. Now she looked beaten.

"What exactly did you tell Detective Jones?" Caprice asked her.

"I told him what happened. He kept asking me about it over and over again, six ways to sideways."

"Did you tell him that you and Bob were involved at one time?" Caprice prodded.

"No, I didn't. When he asked me how I knew Bob, I told him we went to high school together. I explained we ran into each other while you were staging Eliza's house and decided to have coffee and talk about the idea of my costume-making business. And tonight we were going to discuss it further. Why should I tell him any more than that?"

"Why, indeed?" Vince muttered. "Because there are people in Kismet who know your history with Bob, and I'm sure some of them will be only too glad to enlighten the detective. It might not happen for a few days or a week, but it's going to happen. Caprice knows how relentless he is."

"Especially when he's after one particular suspect. If he sets his sights on Bella—"

"We don't know that he has," Vince warned her. "Don't borrow trouble. Where was Joe?"

Bella looked confused for a moment. "I don't know. He's on his way back from somewhere."

"From a smoky place where he's been spending all his time?" Caprice asked. "What did he say?"

"I just told him something had happened and he had to get right home. I didn't explain. I couldn't. Not over the phone."

"You think it's going to be any easier in person?" Nikki asked, being the forthright sister she was.

"I don't know, Nik. I just know I couldn't do it over the phone."

Through the screen door, they all heard Joe's van pull into the driveway. They all heard the driver's door slam. They all heard his footsteps as he approached the front door.

He impatiently burst inside, asking Bella, "So what's going on? As usual, I see your family's here, and they know before I do. Did you miscarry?"

Caprice saw her sister's spine straighten and her chin go up, defiance back in her eyes. "You'd like that, wouldn't you?"

"Bella . . ." he said, exasperated.

As if she couldn't hold it in any longer, she blurted out, "I went to the community center to meet Bob Preston. I found him murdered, and the police think I did it."

Caprice was beat by the time Nikki drove her home.

"Do you want company? Do you want to talk?" Nikki offered.

But Caprice shook her head. "Not tonight. Maybe tomorrow."

With understanding, Nikki reached over and gave her a hug.

A few moments later, after unlocking her front door, Caprice waved good-bye to her sister. However, as she opened the door, she suddenly remembered she'd left Shasta and Sophia both roaming free together for more hours than she wanted to count. A light on the timer beside her sofa had switched on at nine o'clock. The first disruption she glimpsed was the throw rug from the entrance way curled up and rolled. The fringes went every which way.

She called, "Shasta! Sophia!" and went into the living room. Immediately she heard doggie nails on the hardwood floor, and Shasta ran to her from behind the multicolored striped sofa.

"What were you doing back there?" Caprice asked her, noticing the dog looked almost as fearful as the day they'd found her. But then Caprice spotted the reason why. The lava lamp was tilted over onto the side table next to her huge, dark fuchsia chair. A ceramic dish she used to hold a sachet of rose petals lay in pieces on the floor, shards here, there, and everywhere. The little gauze bag was torn apart. Grateful that the dish had contained rose petals instead of something harmful, she shook her head. Affirmations on small slips of paper had also spilled from the brass silent butler that was lying open on the floor, but Caprice wasn't troubled by the mess. When a person had pets, a person expected messes.

"I can see the two of you got into trouble. But that was my fault. I was gone too long. Come on, girl. I'm going to let you outside for a run, and then I'll see if I can find Sophia."

Shasta scampered around Caprice now, obviously happy to see her. She seemed to be gaining a little more weight each day.

"At least I fed both of you before I left. I'll find you a snack when you come in, okay?"

Shasta gave a bark as if she understood it all.

In the kitchen, Caprice found the napkin holder on the floor, the napkins scattered in a path across the sunny, yellow and white linoleum. Water puddled around Sophia's water bowl as if the pair had run through it. Really, as messes went, this wasn't too bad to clean up. Of course, she hadn't found Sophia yet.

As she flipped on the back porch light and let Shasta outside, she wished Bella's mess wasn't so . . . messy. Joe's reaction to Bella's summation of the crisis had been sputtering disbelief. She and Nikki had left so he and Bella could consult with Vince alone. If only Joe wasn't so touchy about the fact that Bella's family sometimes knew more than he did. He didn't have any brothers or sisters, so he had trouble understanding the bonds between Bella, Nikki, Caprice, and Vince. He and Vince got along okay, but he and Caprice had clashed more than once. Most of the time, Caprice knew she should just keep her lips zipped. But that was hard when she wanted the best for Bella and her kids.

Caprice threw Shasta's ball several times, ruffling her fur each time she retrieved it. The night was absolutely balmy. It was a shame it had been marred by murder.

Murder. Bob Preston's head bashed in. Bob was dead.

Her chest tightened as the repercussions of the events of the evening washed over her. Her eyes burned as she remembered Bob's teasing, his goal-oriented work ethic, his charm. Maybe she'd been in shock since she'd heard Bella scream and was now coming to grips with it all.

After Shasta romped around the yard and did what she had to do, Caprice cleaned up and let her inside. Tonight she sought comfort in her surroundings—her retro kitchen, her pets, and everything she appreciated most about her life. She poured dog food into Shasta's dish for a snack, hoping Sophia would appear when she heard the *ping-ping-ping* of the little bits falling in. But the cat didn't appear, so Caprice went looking.

After a thorough search of the living room and dining room hiding places, even the wash basket in the downstairs bathroom, Caprice headed to her office. Shasta bounded after her, but she held up her hand and ordered, "Stay," at the threshold. Shasta whined but stayed. Whoever had owned Shasta earlier had trained her well. Caprice wondered if the fliers she'd left with Perky Paws and Marcus and had posted on the bulletin boards in the grocery and drugstores would bring results. If not . . . like it or not, Sophia and Shasta would be house buddies.

Inside her office, Caprice checked the usual spots where Sophia might nap—her desk chair, on top of the printer, and atop a stack of manila folders on the floor. However, she didn't find her feline friend.

The cat could be sprawled on her bed up in the bedroom. However, noticing the closet door wasn't altogether closed, she opened it further and peered inside under her winter coats.

There was Sophia . . . snuggled on top of an old blanket, but facing the inside wall.

Shasta still whined at the doorway.

Hunkering down, Caprice petted Sophia. The cat turned, and her golden eyes glared at Caprice reproachfully.

"Well," Caprice said. "Did Shasta want to play and you didn't?"

After another look that told Caprice that Sophia had been disturbed from whatever she'd wanted to do, the feline scratched her ear a few times, yawned, and stretched in the ultimate cat stretch that Caprice always envied. With a shake of her head, she scooped Sophia up into her arms and nuzzled her white ruff, cooing to her a bit.

Sophia began purring.

Caprice's cell phone suddenly played "A Hard Day's Night." Checking it, she saw the call was from Bella.

She placed Sophia on her desk chair and asked her two pets, "Are you two ready to be friends again?"

Shasta trotted over to Caprice's chair, sniffed at Sophia, then circled the chair. When Sophia hopped down, tail high in the air, Shasta followed her . . . without chasing her.

When Caprice answered her call, Bella said, "Detective Jones phoned. I have to be at the station tomorrow at 9:00 a.m."

Caprice didn't like the idea that Bella was probably Detective Jones's prime suspect. But after all, she'd had blood on her hands. "Vince is going with you?"

"Yes, but . . . Detective Jones wants to see Joe, too." Bella's voice broke.

Caprice's throat tightened in fear for her sister and brother-in-law. "Do you know why?"

"No. Unless he found out about my history with Bob."

"You should have told him," Caprice scolded again.

"Well, I didn't," Bella snapped.

Caprice could just see Bella planting her hand on her hip.

"He might think Joe had a motive, too," Caprice suggested.

"What do you mean 'too'?"

"I mean in addition to whoever else had a motive. He hasn't found one for you yet, and we can hope he doesn't."

Bella went silent until finally she explained, "Vince thinks we should ask Grant to go in with Joe, but Joe doesn't want him there. Caprice, I'm scared."

"I know you are, but the best thing you can do is convince Joe to let Grant help him."

"Maybe you could talk to Joe?"

"Like he ever listens to me."

"This time he might. You were involved in this kind of thing before. And Grant helped, didn't he?"

Yes, Grant had helped. But she and Grant had a tenuous friendship that went back to her brother's law school days, when Grant had been his roommate and Vince had brought him home on weekends. Caprice had had a crush on him. However, Grant had gotten engaged and then married, and Caprice had turned off that crush and any attraction she'd felt. She hadn't seen him for years until he'd returned to Kismet to be Vince's law partner. There was a sad story behind that, and Grant didn't talk about it.

But that was part of the problem. They didn't talk about the child he'd lost or his subsequent divorce because the wound might never heal. She doubted if Grant would agree.

"You know I'll talk to Joe if it'll help."

"Hold on a minute. Vince left, and Joe's getting ready to go over to Nellie's for the kids, though I hate to bring them home into this tension."

"That tension could be there for a while, Bee."

"What am I going to tell them? I doubt we can keep this from them. It will be on the news."

"You and Joe won't be, not unless—"

"Go ahead and say it," Bella said morosely. "Not unless one of us is charged." She sighed. "I'll get Joe."

Not two seconds later, Joe was on the other end of the call. "So you were there."

"I was there."

"Bella says she knelt down beside him to see if he was still breathing."

Caprice hadn't intended to go over all of this again, but if Joe needed to verify what Bella had told him, she would do it. "Yes, that's how she got blood on her."

"But his head was bashed in."

"That's right." Caprice tried to put the pictures out of her head, tried to forget about seeing Bella covered with paint and blood.

"Vince thinks Jones found out about Bella and Preston dating years ago and that's why he wants to talk to me. What do you think?"

"I think Detective Jones is a good detective."

"We can't pay for a lawyer."

"Joe, I don't know if you can afford to be without

one. Grant will probably tell you, and I'm sure Vince already has, that if the police are seriously looking at you as a suspect . . . or at Bella, you'll need criminal defense attorneys. But Grant can help protect your rights. He did it for my friend, remember?"

"Yeah, I remember. The thing is, if Vince calls his partner in for me, that's going to be purely business."

She wasn't sure what Joe was getting at, so she kept quiet until he continued.

"Maybe if you give Grant a call, he'll consider doing it as a favor?"

Sometimes she wanted to throttle Joe Santini. Sometimes she wondered what her sister saw in him. But no matter what, he was her brother-in-law.

"What makes you think Grant will do this as a favor to me?"

"Because he helped you before. Because I see the way the two of you . . . talk. You're friends or something, and you've known him almost as long as Vince has."

"Not as well."

"The last thing I want to do is ask you for a favor," Joe said angrily. "If you can't do this, fine. I'll go in there myself. I don't have anything to hide."

"Where were you tonight?"

Silence met her question. She didn't press further for an answer, but she did say, "You can bet Detective Jones is going to ask you that, and if you don't have a good answer, you really will need Grant there."

Her brother-in-law still kept silent.

"I'll give Grant a call, but you'd better tell Vince I'm going to do it."

"He already thinks I'm a cheapskate. But I'll tell him."

Since they *were* talking, Caprice decided to fish a little more. "Joe, did you know Bella was going to meet Bob?"

"No, I didn't. How would I know? Are you going to tell me how long this has been going on?"

"Bella will tell you. And, Joe, nothing was going on. They just met up and talked."

"Yeah," he said morosely, and Caprice felt sorry for him. As if he could sense that, he mumbled, "I'm giving the phone back to Bella, and . . . Thanks, Caprice."

That thank-you was big for Joe. He had pride and a lot of it.

"Do you want me to call you after I speak with Grant?"

"Just tell him to give me a call if he's going to do it."

He was assuming that Caprice could convince Grant Weatherford to take up his cause. Could she?

After a few last words with her sister, Caprice walked into the living room to keep her eye on Shasta and Sophia while she speed-dialed Grant's number. She'd needed it handy not so long ago.

As his cell phone rang, Caprice saw Shasta had settled on the sofa, while Sophia sat watchfully on the afghan Nana Celia had crocheted that was thrown over the sofa's back. Ready to leave a message for Grant on his cell and try his town house number, she was surprised when he answered right before the call went to voice mail.

"Did you have another family dinner that got out of hand?" he asked wryly.

Grant had attended their family dinners many times. "Family dinner was last Sunday," she answered reasonably. Then a thought occurred to her, and she felt her cheeks flush. "Am I interrupting something?"

After a heartbeat of silence, he responded, "Just replays on the sports channel. What's going on?"

He sounded concerned, as if he was wondering if one of her family might be sick or something. This was a whole lot worse.

"I have a favor to ask." After all, the last time they'd talked, they'd decided they were "friends."

"You have more kittens you want me to place?"

Grant had helped her find a home for two strays. She wondered how that divorced, single mom next door to him was faring, or if she and Grant were connecting. Hence her question about interrupting something. After a mental shake, Caprice reminded herself that was none of her business.

"I need your help for Bella and Joe." Before he could ask more questions, she jumped right in. "The police want to talk to Joe tomorrow and he needs someone to protect his rights. Bella found Bob Preston dead outside the community center. The police could think Joe has a motive."

Grant must have heard something in her voice besides her obvious concern. His deep baritone got a little deeper and a little more probing. "*Bella* found Bob Preston's body?"

"I, uh, I found her with Bob Preston's body."

"Don't tell me you're involved in another murder investigation."

"All right, I won't tell you that," she retorted.

There was that old tension between them again. It
never took much.

"I can't believe you're involved in another murder."

"It's not like I went looking for it. And that's not
the point. The point is, Bella was kneeling in a
puddle of paint beside Bob, blood on her hands,
when the police arrived. She and Bob dated when
she was in high school. They thought it was serious."

"I remember Vince telling me that when he suggested Preston's company paint my place."

"Did they?"

"No. I decided to do it myself. But I don't understand why the police are going to question Joe if
Bella found the body. Unless . . ."

Swiftly, Caprice told him what had happened
when she was preparing Eliza's mansion for an open
house. After that, she told him about Bella's coffee
date and her scheduled meeting with Bob at the
community center.

Grant whistled through his teeth. "I knew Joe and
Bella were having trouble after that blowup at your
mom's birthday party, but this is beyond trouble. Just
what does Joe expect me to do for free?"

"Just be there tomorrow."

"Your family has meant a lot to me over the years,
Caprice. Sure, I'll help out. But tell me one thing."

"What?" She felt as if she were walking into some
kind of trap.

"Are you going to stay out of this murder like you
should, or be foolish again and try to get to the
bottom of what happened?"

She heard the judgment in his tone, at least that's
what she thought it was. "This is my sister and her
husband, Grant. I'll do whatever I have to do."

"That's what I was afraid you'd say," he muttered. "I'm going to tell you the same thing this time that I told you the last time. Stay far away from the police station. Stay far away from the investigation."

"And what if I don't take your advice?"

"Then we'll both be sorry."

Chapter Five

When Grant crossed the threshold into Bella and Joe's house the following morning, the living room went silent. Not that there had been much conversation before her brother's partner's arrival, Caprice thought. The tension between Bella and Joe was as thick as any tomato sauce she'd ever reduced.

Immediately Grant assessed the situation. He glanced at Caprice but spoke to Joe. "I think we should go over a few basics before we see the detective."

"Why don't you go into the kitchen," Bella suggested.

Caprice knew that with Vince advising Bella and with motives for murder in question, Grant would want a private session with Joe. Taking advantage of that, she'd have one with Bella.

After Joe and Grant sank down on chairs at the kitchen table, she pulled her sister to the farthest corner of the living room . . . away from the kitchen. "Tell me you and Joe talked more about all of this."

"I can't tell you something that didn't happen," Bella snapped.

Caprice reacted to her sister's snippiness. "What do you two do, just sit and stare at each other?"

"No. We go to separate rooms. We take care of the kids. We glare, not stare, at each other."

To her dismay, Caprice didn't know a better way to handle this . . . a better way to get to the bottom of it. So she just went at it. "Has Joe given you an explanation for where he goes at night?"

"He doesn't explain anything. He never has. Not unless he's trying to pretend he knows everything about everything."

"Bella . . ." Caprice wanted to be understanding, she really did, but this kind of back and forth wasn't going to cover any ground.

As if Bella realized that too, she looked away, down the hall to the kids' rooms. They weren't there. Timmy and Megan were having pancakes with their neighbor Nellie.

Maybe Bella was remembering happier times with their children . . . her other pregnancies. "I don't know why Joe won't tell me. Maybe he's having an affair." Her voice caught on the word.

Most of all, Caprice wanted to wrap her arms around Bella. But she had the feeling her sister would push her away. Bella was trying to be strong and not break down. Affection could make her break down, whereas anger and resentment could very well shore her up.

"So exactly what is his alibi? What's he telling Grant?"

This time Bella's gaze swerved toward the kitchen and she sighed. "He says he went for a drive. But he also says he didn't stop anywhere and that he doubts if anyone saw him." She took Caprice's arm and pulled her a little bit farther down the hall. "I found something, though."

Maybe they *were* going to get somewhere. "What?"

"You suggested I go through his pockets, so that's what I did. I found an e-mail coupon from Holly-wood Casino. It was sent to his work address."

North of Harrisburg, the casino was a playground for senior citizens who had a penchant for slot machines, as well as for more serious gamblers who headed for the poker room and the blackjack tables. The casino was part of a complex that included Penn National Race Course.

"Have you ever gone there with him?" she asked.

"We drove up there a couple of times after the casino was added to the track. But that was a long time ago, and we haven't been back. At least I haven't."

But possibly Joe had.

Bella's eyes were so troubled because she'd obviously been living with that realization since she'd found the coupon. "I looked through the top dresser drawer too, and his underwear drawer. But I didn't find anything else. I write all the checks for the bills, and I pay our credit cards online. There haven't been any strange charges. But . . ." She sighed again. "I'm not naive. He could have a credit card I don't know about. I have a couple that he doesn't know about."

So much for one hundred percent disclosure in marriage, Caprice thought. When had Bella and Joe's communication started to break down? Or maybe it had never been built on a solid foundation from the beginning. Was an unexpected pregnancy ever a good foundation to marry? She supposed it could be if two people really loved each other, if those two people were really ready to get married. Had Bella and Joe been ready to get married?

Caprice didn't know if she was helping the cause of their marriage or just helping the cause of the investigation when she asked, "Does Joe have any place else he spends a lot of time . . . where he might stash something?"

"Like what?"

"I don't know. Anything he wouldn't want you to see."

"I can check the top shelf of the bedroom closet. The kids couldn't reach that if he was worried about them finding a secret stash. The only other place might be . . ." She thought about it. "Possibly the garage. I never go in the garage unless I'm getting into the car or out of it. I suppose he could have a strongbox on his tool shelf that I don't know about."

"If it's a strongbox, you won't be able to open it."

"That depends. I'm good with a hairpin."

All at once, Caprice was looking at her sister in a new light. Maybe she wasn't all just pretty curls and perfume. Maybe because Joe was rigid and somewhat controlling, she'd defiantly adapted to her life with skills Caprice didn't know she had. On the other hand, she might have also learned to lie a little too often. Caprice really didn't want to think that. There was a big difference between little white lies and monumental ones.

"Have you and Joe had problems only since you told him you're pregnant, or did they start before that?"

"Every marriage has problems," Bella said, defensive again. "Even Mom and Dad don't always get along."

"But they always make up," Caprice reminded Bella, knowing it was true.

Yes, their parents had sometimes disagreed, but after the disagreement . . . her mom would make a frocia, one of her dad's favorite meals, and he'd open a bottle of one of their favorite wines. They'd negotiate over that meal, and then they'd turn in early. As Caprice had gotten older, she'd realized what that meant, even if she didn't *want* to realize what that had meant.

"I'm not trying to pry, Bella, really I'm not. I'm just trying to figure out if Joe . . ."

"Has kept his vows?" Bella asked. "I think he's the kind of man who does. That's why I married him. That's why I've stayed with him, even when we aren't getting along so well."

"I want you to think about something, Bee, and think about it really hard. Was he acting differently before the news of your pregnancy? Did he come home smelling like smoke then?"

"Everything's becoming all muddled together."

"I know. But this is important."

Bella closed her eyes, as if she was trying to remove herself from the present situation so that she could go back. "Last winter I got really worried one night when the roads were icy and he was terrifically late. He said he had a client meeting. I really didn't think too much of it because then there was Valentine's Day and he sent me flowers. Joe doesn't usually buy me flowers."

A guilt present? Compensation to make up for

whatever he was involved in? Whether it was another woman or something else. Unsettling as the realization was, Caprice wasn't sure if she knew Joe well enough even after all these years to decide whether he'd break his vows. Could anyone really know someone else?

"There are tons of questions we need to have answered here, Bella. Where was Joe last night if he didn't go for a drive? If he was with another woman, is he afraid to say so because he doesn't want to lose you? If he wasn't with another woman, then where was he? And then there's the really important question."

"More important than any of those?"

"The most important question. You might be the only one who can answer it."

"What?"

"Do you think Joe could hurt somebody? If he found out about your rendezvous with Bob, could be he jealous enough to kill him?"

Before Bella could recover from the shock and horror of Caprice asking that question, they heard chairs scraping against the linoleum in the kitchen. As the two men entered the living room and she and Bella did the same, Caprice noticed the sharp contrast between Grant and Joe.

Grant wore a charcoal suit, a pale gray shirt, and a red-black-and-gray patterned tie. He was the epitome of the thirty-something professional. No one would ever guess by looking at him the tragedy he'd been through. He never spoke about his divorce and the loss of his child. His guard was usually up. Her best friend, Roz, insisted there were thumping vibrations in the air when she and Grant were in the same room. Her mother had told her that she treated Grant with kid gloves. Not so much anymore. Not so much since the murder investigation they'd gone through together in May.

But thumping vibrations?

That was just from the strain that was created because the two of them disagreed about a lot. They didn't think the same way. They often seemed to be at odds. Yet she also realized she'd trust Grant with her life.

When she looked at Joe, she saw a man who wished he could wear jeans and a T-shirt to work every day. She saw a man who wanted to come first and foremost with his wife over and above her family. She saw a man with traditional values who'd never before seemed to be hypocritical about any of them.

But was he? Did he have a mean streak, instead of just a short temper? Did he do more than raise his voice when he grew angry?

She and Bella heard Joe say to Grant, "I can't pay you very much. We're strapped right now, and with the baby coming, we only have some savings from . . ." He stopped. "It's from presents her family gives us."

Caprice heard the near-resentment in Joe's voice.

She heard even more when Joe added, "We use it for the kids when doctor visits get out of hand. That kind of thing."

Caprice saw Bella's chin go up and her shoulders square. She wasn't sure what was going to come from her sister . . . but something was.

Bella cut in. "I have money saved."

Joe looked as if she'd just dropped a bowling ball on his foot. "What?"

"I have some money saved. All those costumes I've

been sewing at Halloween the past couple of years, they're not all for our kids. Maybe you didn't notice what I was working on, but I sold them to other moms. I've been stowing the money away. It's in a shoe up in my closet, up in *our* closet. I know it's probably not enough, but it can get Grant started."

Grant's gaze met Caprice's, and they both remembered her phone call to him. Now he said, "I know money is something we all have to think about, but for this morning, let's just put it aside." He checked his watch. "We don't want to be late for that appointment with Detective Jones at the station, and I'm sure Vince will already be waiting there. If we go past this initial representation, then we'll discuss money and payment. All right?"

Caprice could have hugged him. Because he was doing such a nice thing for her sister, of course.

Of course.

This time Caprice sat on that hard bench at Kismet's police department for three hours. Three hours.

She didn't have to be here. Grant had told her she *shouldn't* be here. But she had to show Bella and Joe some support. Especially Bella. She was pregnant, for goodness sakes. With all this stress, who knew what could happen.

When Vince, Grant, Joe, and Bella emerged from the hall and spilled into the reception area, Caprice wanted to run to them. But she didn't. She waited. Joe and Bella looked wrung out. Vince and Grant just looked serious. No one spoke until they all went outside.

Then Caprice demanded, "So tell me what happened."

"No charges . . . yet," Vince added, simply giving her information she already knew. After all, they had all left the station without anyone being handcuffed and detained.

Joe shook his head. "They just kept going around and around and around in circles. I answered the same questions at least thirty times."

"You were consistent," Grant said.

That didn't tell Caprice anything. She didn't know if consistent was bad or good, though it obviously meant the police hadn't caught Joe in a lie.

"My history with Bob came out," Bella said in a small voice. "They knew bits and pieces. I had to tell them we were serious once." Her eyes met her husband's, and she looked so regretful.

If Detective Jones knew all about Bella and Bob, then they could ascribe a motive to either Bella or Joe. Caprice had to dig up more information about Bob. She had to find out if there were others who might have a motive for killing him. Detective Jones had been shortsighted once before, and chances were good he would be again.

"Was Chief Powalski there?" Caprice asked her brother. The chief of police and her dad were friends, and Mack had been like a favorite uncle to her and her brother and sisters. He'd helped Caprice on her last case, but she didn't know what would happen now.

"He was there," Vince said. "But he's not involving himself in this. He knows us, so he can't."

Maybe he couldn't be involved himself, but just maybe he could watch over them all.

"I have to call Mom," Bella said anxiously. "I spoke with her early this morning so she didn't find out I was involved in this from someone else. She said to call her when I was finished here. But I'd rather make the call when I get home."

As a high school English teacher, her mom enjoyed her summer break by spending more time with Nana, gardening, and, this summer, cataloging recipes on the computer. So many of Nana's recipes weren't specific about measurements. Her mother was trying to nail them down so anyone could make them.

"I can drop you and Joe off at your place, then Grant and Vince can get back to their office," Caprice offered.

"And what are *you* going to do?" Grant asked her, glancing at her psychedelic van, painted in swirling colors and large flowers. It was parked beside his silver SUV.

She knew why he was asking. He expected her to get into trouble. She just might. But she didn't have to tell *him* that. "I have to go home and let Shasta out."

"Shasta? You took in another stray?" The censuring note had left his voice, and he even sounded a little amused.

"I did. She's a cocker spaniel, and she's pregnant. So I don't like to be away too long at a stretch. I have a video conference at two, and lots of paperwork to finish. I had an open house yesterday, and I have to make follow-up calls about that."

Grant eyed her speculatively. "And then?"

She might as well tell him, because eventually he'd find out she wasn't going to leave this case alone. "I might take a look around the community center."

"Caprice, it's a crime scene. Stay away from it." His voice was hard.

Vince, Bella, and Joe were all looking their way, obviously interested in the interchange.

With others watching, she kept her cool and refused to let her usually long fuse ignite. "I know it's a crime scene, and I wouldn't even consider crossing the yellow tape. But there's a basketball court outside of that tape. I expect there'll be some teenagers dribbling and shooting baskets there, out of curiosity if nothing else. The center will probably put one of its counselors outside just to watch over them."

"And just why do you want to talk to the teenagers?" Grant seemed to be holding onto his temper, too.

"Because some of them might have been working with Bob on the mural. Some of them might have heard things. I want to give the police suspects other than Bella and Joe."

Vince stepped in now. "Detective Jones won't appreciate your interference again."

"I solved his case for him the last time." When Vince was about to protest, she held up her hand. "I won't do anything he wouldn't approve of. Really. I'm just going to talk to some teens." When Vince and Grant exchanged looks, and their mouths went taut with everything they weren't going to say,

Caprice motioned to Bella and Joe. "Come on, I'll get the two of you home."

Then maybe Bella and her husband would talk. Maybe they'd draw closer instead of pulling farther apart.

The first thing Caprice did when she returned home was find Sophia again. Giving both her and Shasta the run of the house last night and this morning might not have been the most intelligent thing she'd ever done. But she didn't feel it was fair to lock Sophia in the bedroom and give Shasta free rein. On the other hand, she hadn't wanted to put Shasta in the garage when she didn't know how long she'd be gone.

The only evidence that the two might have had another chase was the scrambled throw rug. Other than that, nothing was broken. Nothing was scattered. Nothing was where it shouldn't be. However, once more she found Sophia in the closet.

Staring down at her, Caprice asked, "Are you going to do this every time I leave? A nap's one thing, but holing yourself up in here is another."

Sophia looked up at her with eyes that said, *You let that creature loose again.*

"You need to make friends," Caprice told her. "Shasta could be around for a long time, let alone her pups."

She crouched down and gave Sophia a good, long petting session while Shasta sat outside the office door, waiting and whining a little.

Finally Caprice stood and told her cat, "I'm putting food out in the kitchen, and Shasta will be outside playing for a while. So stop pouting and come join us when you're ready."

Sophia blinked, crossed her paws, and didn't look as if she were going to move anytime soon.

With a shrug, Caprice took Shasta to the back door and let her outside. When she'd dropped Bella and Joe off at their house, they'd both seemed shell-shocked. The silence in the van had been uncomfortable and scary. Caprice wanted them to hug each other and support each other, but . . .

She'd brought in the stack of mail from the mailbox attached to the brick outside the front door. As Shasta wandered about the yard, Caprice stood at the doorway and watched, absently sorting through the envelopes. She stopped when she came to an official-looking one with the return address *Women for a Better Kismet.*

She'd spoken to the group a couple of times since she'd been home-staging, and had attended their monthly meetings when she could. She often made contacts there. She also enjoyed the rapport from the mix of stay-at-home moms and professional women who just wanted to make their town a better place. Usually notices of meetings arrived in her e-mail. Maybe this was about plans for something special they'd organized.

But as she opened the envelope and read the letter inside, she realized this event was a done deal. She was nominated to receive an award! She was familiar with the yearly banquet at the Country Squire Golf and Recreation Club on the edge of Kismet. It was an event that raised money and helped spread the word about the group. But this year, it was going to be a very special event for her. She'd been nominated for the organization's Woman of the Year Award for her achievement in developing her small business into a success, for her work with stray animals and for her assistance to the police in solving the Ted Winslow murder case. The winner would be announced at the banquet. How exciting was that?

Without any hesitation, she found her phone and speed-dialed Nikki. She was sure her mom would be tied up on the phone with Bella for a while.

A half hour later, still tossing a ball for Shasta, Caprice ended the call with her sister and found she was both happy and sad. Nikki had been so excited for her, and Caprice was sure she'd spread the news. But they'd also talked about Bella, and Caprice was genuinely worried. They all were.

But worrying just took her in circles, so she decided to do more than worry. After her video conference, she was heading to the community center. Grant had his reservations, and she knew they were valid ones, but those reservations weren't going to stop her. She had to help Bella.

Around four o'clock Caprice parked about a half block from the center. She walked down the opposite side of the street, passing the downtown park. This year the center was planning on holding a fundraising day there. Had the plans for that been derailed because of the murder? The board would have to decide.

The day had grown quite a bit warmer. After spending the afternoon in her air-conditioning, Caprice worked up a sweat quickly as she hurried across the street and down the broken pavement toward the community center's basketball court.

Yellow crime scene tape still surrounded the building and parking lot. Caprice knew the York County forensic team would finish as quickly as it could because manpower to keep a crime scene intact was expensive.

A basketball game was in progress, and lots of dribbling and guarding was going on. Groups of girls bent their heads together along the perimeter, watching the game. Well, not watching the game, but watching the guys play the game. She spotted an older gentleman who looked to be around her dad's age in a polo shirt and khakis with a whistle hanging around his neck. If she tried to talk to the kids, he'd probably disapprove, so she might as well just introduce herself and go from there.

Approaching him, she stood beside him and watched the game. "It's a good thing these kids have the community center so they can let off some energy."

"Wish I had some of that energy," the man muttered and turned to her. He asked, "Are you one of the volunteers?"

She held out her hand. "Caprice De Luca."

He extended his hand to shake hers. "Elias Treadwell. Everyone calls me Eli."

"It's good to meet you, Eli. To answer your question, no, I'm not one of the volunteers. But . . . my sister found the man who was murdered here."

"Bella Santini."

"You know her?"

"I know her in a roundabout way. She made costumes for my grandkids for Halloween last year. She and my daughter sometimes carpool. I spotted Bella one afternoon last week when she stopped in here to talk to Preston."

So Bella had seen Bob other than for their coffee dates?

"Bob was here working on the mural?" Caprice guessed.

"Yes, it's something the kids enjoy doing with him. At least those who don't like basketball so much."

"I was hoping to talk to some of the kids who worked with Bob on that mural. Do you think that's possible?"

Eli studied Caprice and, putting two and two together, came up with the right combination. "Is your sister a suspect?"

"The police have questioned her, like they've questioned everyone. But I am worried about her. I thought a little additional information might not hurt."

"I watch those cop shows on TV, and you're probably right." He pointed to a boy standing by himself. Eli nodded to him. "That's Danny Flannery. He was working with Bob on the mural, but . . ."

"But?" Caprice prodded.

"He actually got into a fistfight with Bob and threw a couple of punches. Bob just mostly defended himself, but I think Danny was intent on doing damage."

"They had a fistfight here?"

"Yep. No one knows what it was about. Danny wouldn't say, and neither would Bob. He was suspended from the center for a while because of it."

"When was this?"

Eli thought about it. "A couple of months ago. He and Bob have hardly talked since. You might want to start with Danny."

A few moments later, Caprice wasn't sure what angle to take when she approached Danny Flannery. Then she decided honesty was the best course. Why would he talk to a stranger otherwise?

The boy's expression was sullen and his body language defensive as he leaned against the fence, baseball cap backward and slightly askew, and oversized T-shirt drooping practically to the knees of his worn jeans. He looked a little rough, and Grant's warning still rang in her head. But fear wasn't an emotion she wanted to lay claim to, not when Bella and Joe's future could be in jeopardy.

She smiled and asked the teenager, "Is basketball not your game?"

He narrowed his eyes. "What's it to you?"

Maybe she had to tell him exactly what she wanted. Maybe she had to be careful how she did it. But she intended to get a few answers from Danny Flannery . . . today.

Chapter Six

Caprice studied the teenager and suddenly realized the designs on his T-shirt and those on his sneakers were hand-painted. Acting on a hunch, she asked, "Did you paint your T-shirt and sneakers?"

His eyes widened as if he hadn't expected anything like that. "Yeah," he answered warily, looking over her tank top, which sported a huge decal of a white Persian cat, and then the fifties-style pedal pushers she'd found at her favorite vintage clothing shop, Secrets of the Past. "But you didn't paint yours," he muttered.

She laughed. "Nope, I didn't, but I wish I could. I hear animals are tough to sketch or paint."

"That depends," he said with a shrug. "Furry ones are the worst, but they can be done."

Talking about art was obviously a lot different than talking about basketball. "Are you helping with the murals on the game room wall?"

"I was." He jutted his chin toward the building. "I

was banned from there for a while, but I've been helping to finish them."

Danny was tapping his foot, bursting with indignation about his work being interrupted. That indignation had apparently made him spill something he might not have spilled otherwise.

"Caught smoking or something?" she asked easily.

He eyed her again and asked, "What's it to you?"

Dropping all pretense, she said flatly, "My sister found Bob Preston's body."

His eyes widened and his mouth dropped open. "You're kidding, right?"

"No." She took out her phone and quickly found a picture of Bella. "If you spend a lot of time around the community center, maybe you can tell me if you've seen her here."

At first Danny looked as if he didn't want to get involved, but then innate curiosity must have made him reach for the phone.

Studying the picture, he gave a quick nod. "Yeah, I've seen her around. Were your sister and Preston hooked up?"

"Old friends," she answered easily.

But Danny narrowed his eyes, and he could see through that evasive answer. "Friends with benefits," he mumbled.

Caprice was about to protest in outrage when he went on, "He always had a couple of women hanging around. I saw him with a blonde with long, red fingernails and dressed like she didn't belong in Kismet."

That could be Eliza, Caprice thought. She always dressed impeccably in expensive clothes, and long red fingernails were usually part of the outfit.

"There was a redhead, too. She met him out back last week. Bob was a popular guy." There was resentment and bitterness in Danny's tone, and Caprice wanted to get at the reason why.

"So what did you and Bob fight about?"

He didn't seem surprised that she knew. Maybe there had been many witnesses. "Nothing."

If he thought that was going to end their conversation, it certainly wasn't. "*Nothing* shouldn't have started a fistfight."

Avoiding her gaze, Danny said in a low voice, "We just disagreed about something."

"Do you take swings at everybody you don't agree with?"

She'd apparently gone too far, because Danny said, "It's none of your business."

It was her business if this teenager had killed Bob, but she wasn't going to out-and-out say that. Eking out information little by little was probably the best way to go. It wasn't the fastest, but it was often the surest.

She switched the course of their conversation. "The murals are looking good. Do you think they'll let you finish the last one?"

"I don't know. Bob was in charge. I already did most of it." He hastened to add, "Bob was just sort of there. He didn't actually do most of the sketching and painting."

That might be true, but from what she understood, Bob was getting the credit for the murals. Is that why he and Danny had fought?

Danny pushed himself away from the fence. "I gotta go. Nothing's happening here."

She wondered what he expected to happen here

when he didn't play basketball and couldn't go inside because it was a crime scene.

Without another word to Caprice, or anyone else hanging around, Danny sauntered past a group of girls and off the property. When he hit the street, he jogged across and kept jogging.

Caprice wondered if he was running from her or running away from something he'd done. Hopefully, she could soon figure that out.

Caprice hadn't seen or heard from Eliza, and she wondered how her client was faring since Bob's murder. If they had been dating . . . if they had been close . . .

She would be passing Connect Xpress on her way home. She might as well stop in and see if Eliza was there. Caprice knew her house with its freshly painted walls and de-cluttered look didn't feel like home to Eliza anymore. People liked their belongings around them—memorabilia, pictures, and furniture that carried memories of regrets as well as good times. Caprice understood that she was messing with people's lives when she staged a house because it wasn't exactly "them" anymore. It wasn't exactly "theirs" anymore. And that was really the whole point. All Caprice wanted to do was invite newcomers in, newcomers who would want to live there and make that home theirs.

Even though Eliza was eager for her move to L.A., she'd had trouble with the whole staging concept. But, again, that wasn't unusual.

Five minutes later, Caprice drove past the building where her brother lived, an old school now transformed into condos. Downtown Kismet's charm was rooted in its early 1900s heritage. Red-brick buildings were trimmed in white around windows and eaves. Oval signs on wrought-iron brackets hung in front of many businesses.

She drove another block, past a deli where Vince often bought takeout and an old movie theater that ran marathon film fests, mostly on weekends. It was a masterpiece of old movie decor inside. In the oldest part of Kismet now, she passed Cherry on the Top and, a few storefronts down, Secrets of the Past. Glancing at the arts and crafts mall on the other side of the street, topped by the Blue Moon Grille, she spotted the driveway for Connect Xpress. Unlike other shops, its red-and-black sign looked almost garish on the front of the building. Huge, it was topped by halogen lights that illuminated the store-front at night.

No one could miss it. That was for sure.

Instead of parking in front of the building at a meter, she swerved into one of the spaces perpendicular to the side of Connect Xpress. After she climbed out of her van, she locked it. A few seconds later, she was opening the heavy glass door and stepping inside the video-dating business.

The reception area carried through the red and black theme with two leather couches, black enamel tables, and dark red carpet that was so plush her footsteps were soundless. Usually, though, someone was at the counter, ready to greet anyone who walked in. Caprice knew the setup because Eliza had shown her around when they'd had one of their meetings here about her house. There were two taping rooms in the back and an office area that veered down a hall to the right.

As Caprice walked that way now, her sandals clacked slightly on the hallway tile.

She called into the office. "Is anyone here?" Taking a few more steps, she glimpsed someone sitting at a computer at a long station that accommodated two other desktops. She supposed this was where the editing was done on the videos that Connect Xpress recorded.

The redheaded young woman at the computer didn't notice Caprice and didn't answer. She was just sitting there, staring at the monitor.

"Excuse me," Caprice said, a little louder.

The woman looked up, obviously startled. Her eyes were red, and so was her nose. She looked as if she'd been crying. "Can I help you?" Her voice was thick, and she cleared her throat.

"I'm looking for Eliza. Is she here?"

"No, she said she wouldn't be in today, and I . . . I shouldn't be. It's not as if I'm getting anything done. The guy I was dating . . ." Her voice broke and she turned away.

Caprice's radar went on alert. Danny had said Bob had also met with a redhead.

She approached the young woman and sat at a chair at the computer station next to her. "I'm Caprice. You seem really upset. Is there anything I can do?"

"I'm Jackie," the woman told her. "There's nothing you can do. My boyfriend was . . . Bob was . . . killed."

Caprice took another good look at Jackie, with her red hair and very blue eyes. Was this the woman

Danny had spoken about? For Caprice, the shock of Bob's death had been swallowed up with Bella's involvement in it, but now she felt the reverberations and sadness of it. She could only imagine what Jackie was feeling if she'd been close to Bob.

"I knew Bob. I stage houses and often used him and his crews. I'm sorry you lost him."

"We'd been dating a couple of months, and I really like . . . liked him," she corrected herself. "He made me laugh, and he acted as if he cared about me."

"Bob could make anybody laugh. He was a charmer, too."

"I know," she admitted. "I'm the one who shot his video here."

"Do you mean a dating video?"

"Yeah. Do you want to see it? That's what I was watching."

Caprice knew Bob didn't have any trouble getting a date. Had he wanted to expand his dating pool? "Bob shouldn't have had any problems getting a girl to go out with him. As you said, he was fun."

"So good looking too. I couldn't believe it when he looked my way."

"If you'd like to show me his footage, I'd be glad to watch."

Jackie moved the mouse and the screen saver went off. The video was right there. She pressed the arrow to start it.

Sitting on a high stool, Bob smiled into the camera, looking like a model for a TV ad in a crew-neck sweater and khaki slacks, so different from the attire she usually saw him in—a T-shirt and jeans.

She heard Jackie's voice as she suggested, "So tell me what you like to do on weekends."

"I like to go dancing . . . or canoeing. As long as I'm doing something, I'm good. I work out at the gym. Been a member of Shape Up for years."

One thing Caprice knew—Bob liked to keep moving.

"I work out there, too," Jackie murmured. "That's where the two of us really got to know each other."

The gym. Another place to explore where she might find Bob's friends . . . or foes.

"Tell me about your family," Jackie's voice prompted from off camera.

And Bob did, explaining that he was an only child and his parents had been older. He mentioned they had passed away, and he sometimes missed not having any family. But he had lots of good friends.

Jackie stopped the video as if it was too painful for her to watch. "He did have so many friends," she said. "He was always getting a call or texting some-one."

She said to Jackie, "Bob and my sister were sup-posed to have coffee together the night he died. Did you know that?"

"Really?" Jackie asked, looking startled.

"They ran into each other and had coffee last week, too. They were catching up with old times."

"How did they know each other?" Jackie asked casually, but Caprice knew the question wasn't casual. If Bob had lots of friends and Jackie sus-pected he might not be seeing her exclusively . . .

"They knew each other in high school. They were pretty serious at one time."

"What happened?"

"Oh, I don't know if I should say. Bella was in school in Philadelphia, and a long-distance relationship is tough."

"Did Bob go out with someone else?"

Caprice kept silent.

"I know he had a reputation. I knew that before I started dating him. When we were out together, sometimes I saw him looking at other women, but I didn't want to believe he'd cheat on me. I can't believe he cheated on me."

"My sister's married, so I really think they were just catching up."

Jackie's eyes were stormy, and that pretty blue maybe wasn't so innocent after all. What if she'd found out Bob was supposed to have coffee with Bella? What if she wasn't surprised at all by the information Caprice had given her?

Jackie was at least five-eight. In her Connect Xpress shirt and shorts, Caprice could see that she was fit. Could this pretty woman wield a murder weapon in jealousy?

Caprice guessed anything was possible. Someone killed Bob, and Jackie's motive stacked up in the same way Bella or Joe's would. She'd have to check out the gym and see if she could find out anything there.

She'd learned a lot today. She'd go home to her pets and take care of work that was mounting up. Also on her to-do list was to post a photo of Shasta on her Web site and send notices to the radio station, the *Kismet Crier*, and the free community paper.

Tomorrow she'd continue her investigation. Tomorrow she also should probably consult with Vince and Grant about what she'd learned. After a few more minutes of conversation with Jackie, and with another expression of her condolences, she left the woman at the computer again, suspecting Jackie would be running that video again and again and again.

In love . . . or with regrets?

The following morning after breakfast, Shasta wanted to sit at Caprice's feet and be petted more than she wanted anything else. Better than anyone, Caprice knew she not only needed food and water, she needed attention. For however long she'd been on her own out in the big world, she hadn't received it.

Finding photos she'd taken of Shasta on her computer, she chose a few she liked and wanted to add to a page on her Web site. She sent them to her Web mistress, along with copy. Afterward, she thought about everything she'd learned about Bob and possible suspects. She really should talk to Grant or Vince about what she'd discovered. The thing was, Shasta seemed particularly needy today. Pregnancy hormones?

Picking up the phone on her desk, she called Grant's and Vince's receptionist/secretary/Girl Friday while she played with Shasta's ears and petted her. She and Giselle were more than acquaintances and less than friends, but they had a good relationship. She asked if either Grant or Vince were free.

Giselle said easily, "Grant is free for the next hour."

"So if I just show up, he'll let me in?"

"I'll make sure he does. Lawyers need breaks, too."

"This is business," Caprice assured Giselle.

"Even if it wasn't, I'd let you in."

Caprice envisioned Giselle, with her spiked gray hair and stylish glasses, winking at her. After Caprice ended the call, Shasta whined at her feet. The dog was well behaved. Caprice considered something she might not usually consider. Just maybe Giselle would let the *two* of them in.

Fifteen minutes later, with Shasta following happily on her leash, she climbed the steps to the first floor of an old house turned into professional offices. Vince rented the first floor for his law practice. A staircase in the foyer led to the second floor. She bypassed that and opened the door into Vince's space.

Giselle sat at her desk and waved to Caprice. She'd spiked her hair with enough gel to make it stand up straight. Today she wore rectangular blue eyeglasses and had lined her eyes with the same blue. Even though she was fifty-four, she was fashion-conscious.

Whenever Caprice walked into Vince and Grant's reception area, she had to shake her head at the decor. Vince believed in being practical. A wool rug covered the floor, and he'd ordered nondescript chairs from an office supply store. A chrome lamp sat on an objectionable laminated table. Caprice knew she could make this area in this old house look elegant and welcoming. But Vince wanted no part of her ideas.

Giselle suddenly spotted Shasta. Her eyes widened, and she said, "What a cutie. Is it friendly?"

"She's everybody's best friend." And to prove it, Shasta went over to Giselle for a head rub.

The office manager laughed, then murmured,

"This ought to be interesting. But . . . nothing ventured, nothing gained!"

Proverbs were part of Giselle's personal philosophy, and she often quoted them. "Did you tell Grant I was stopping by?"

"I didn't get a chance. He's been on the phone. But I'll buzz him now."

Hardly two seconds after she'd pushed the button, Grant opened his office door, stepped into the reception area, and spotted Caprice. Then he saw Shasta.

He didn't even blink. Dressed in a navy suit, with his steel-gray tie straight, he was nothing if not unflappable . . . at least usually. By now, Vince would have been exclaiming that a dog didn't belong in his office. But Grant just motioned her into his.

Unlike Vince's office, Grant's had character. It hadn't been professionally decorated either, but he obviously had good taste. Positioned facing his desk were two wine-toned leather club chairs with brass fittings. A painting of the Grand Canyon was centered on one wall, accompanied by two sand-art plaques with Native American motifs. His desk, like Vince's, was a laminate, but his wine-colored leather blotter complemented the chairs. The pencil holder on his desk was a nice piece of pottery hand-painted with images of wolves.

Instead of going to the chair behind his desk, he sat in one of the chairs in front of the desk and motioned to Caprice to do the same.

When she did, Shasta rubbed up against his leg and plopped at his feet. Grant shook his head and gave Caprice an I-can't-believe-you look. "You had a good reason for bringing your new stray dog to my office? Does she need a lawyer?"

Shasta raised her head and looked up at him with adoring eyes. He reached down and scratched her behind her ears.

Caprice already knew Grant was an animal lover. He just didn't admit it. She wondered again how the two stray kittens—Creamsicle and Stripes—he'd helped place were doing with his divorced next-door neighbor. She decided not to ask.

"I didn't want to leave her alone. She's still settling in, and she's pregnant."

"Pregnant?"

"It happens," Caprice said with a shrug and a little smile.

"I don't have a lot of time, Caprice, so you'd better tell me why you're here."

Yes, Grant was a get-to-the-point kind of guy. "I thought you might want to know what I found out about Bob, or rather his murder."

Grant's lips thinned in disapproval that she was snooping. But instead of scolding her—because he apparently knew that wouldn't do any good—he asked, "You have suspects already? I should have known you'd find alternatives to Bella and Joe."

"The important thing is that the police find an alternative. And, yes, I have. It turns out Bob has kept up his lady-killer ways. He was dating Jackie Fitz, who works at Connect Xpress."

"And how did you find this out?"

"Nothing illegal. I stopped in to talk to Eliza, and Jackie was there watching a video that Connect Xpress had taped of Bob. She was really upset and crying. She had real feelings for him."

"That's a big jump to being a suspect. You think she could have murdered him?"

"It's possible. If she found out he was having coffee dates with Bella." She hurried on, knowing her time was limited. "Then there's this teenager at the community center who had a fight with Bob. Danny was working on the murals with him at the center. He wouldn't tell me what they fought about, but he was suspended for a while because he took a few swings at Bob."

"Motive?" Grant asked.

"That I'm not sure about. One thing I discovered was that Bob took credit for Danny's artwork."

"In less than twenty-four hours you've come up with two suspects. I wonder how well the police have done."

"If they focus just on Joe and Bella, they won't be looking any further. You know Detective Jones."

Silence filled the small office until an awkwardness fell over her and Grant. He shifted in his chair, gave Shasta another pat, then cleared his throat. "Vince told me you and Seth Randolph officially are an item."

Official was an odd word to use. So was *item*. "He joined me for one of our family dinners, and we meet for coffee as much as we can. But you know a doctor's schedule."

"Actually, I don't."

"He's on call a lot. Some days he might work a twelve-hour shift."

Grant just cocked his head and nodded, but she wasn't exactly sure what that meant. She and Grant had sort of become reacquainted friends during her last sleuthing adventure. Sometimes when they were together, she remembered the crush she'd had on him when Vince had brought him home on weekends from law school, and the way she'd buried it once Grant had gotten engaged and then married. When he'd moved to Kismet to join Vince in his law practice, he'd changed—had become guarded and distant—a different man than the more relaxed college guy she'd met when he'd been Vince's roommate.

Had he asked about Seth to make small talk? She couldn't read his expression or the look in his unfathomable gray eyes.

Tension always seemed to permeate their relationship.

Uncomfortable with it, she knew the time had come for her to leave. When she stood, Shasta did too. "I don't want to take up any more of your time. Since you're advising Joe, I thought you should know what I was doing."

"And what's next?"

"I'm not sure. Bella doesn't think Joe's being straight with her. I'd like to find out where he's been spending his time."

"If I tell you to be careful, will you listen to me?"

"I'm always careful."

His chiding look made her shrug, and she went on. "I try to be. I'm not sure what my next step is going to be. You know me—go with the flow."

"And get washed down the river," Grant muttered.

She wrinkled her nose at him and led Shasta toward the door.

He rose and followed her.

Shasta went over to his feet, looked up at him again, and gave a yip.

"She likes you."

He didn't comment on that and instead just asked, "Do you think she was on the streets long?"

"It's hard to tell. But she has the sweetest disposition, and I think someone loved her."

Grant gave Caprice an odd look.

She became so uncomfortable, she blurted out, "If no one claims her, are you interested in a pup when her litter arrives?"

Without hesitation, Grant shook his head. "I don't have the time a pet deserves."

"You could make the time. Your office isn't that far from your town house. You could drive home at lunch to let a dog out."

"Don't start weaving my life for me, Caprice. I keep my life simple now."

Yes, he did. And he never talked about what had happened, a crisis that had brought loss and grief into his life in more ways than one.

As Shasta once again rubbed up against Grant's dress slacks, Caprice suggested lightly, "Think about it."

She didn't give him time to say he wouldn't because she left his office, waved at Giselle, and led Shasta outside.

Chapter Seven

When Caprice returned home, she decided to take Shasta for a walk. In spite of the heat, the two of them could use it. They were returning from an around-the-block stroll when she spotted her elderly neighbor kneeling on a garden pad alongside her house, her straw gardening hat shading her from the sun. She wore a wildly flowered cotton blouse and striped seersucker pants. Caprice didn't hesitate to see what she was up to.

"Hey, Josie," she called as she approached her. "You shouldn't be out in this heat, should you?"

"I'm just pulling a few weeds, making sure everything is shipshape."

Now Caprice was concerned. Josie had often spoken about selling the house and finding a condo or something involving less maintenance.

"Have you decided the yard's too much for you and you want to sell?"

Josie rose to her feet from her kneeling position. "Oh, no. Decided not to. Had a long talk with my kids. I'd have to give up too much to move. My gardening keeps me nimble. I like walking around this neighborhood. I like my independence. And the truth is, I don't particularly want someone watching over me, not yet. So we're going to do a couple of things. My son's going to buy one of those medical alert devices. You know, you can hang it around your neck or carry it in your pocket. Then if you fall, you just push the button, and there's three people on a list. The service calls each one of them, and if they can't get anyone, they call an ambulance."

"That sounds like a wise decision." Her Nana Celia had one of those.

"And I'm having a security system put in the house. Just a precaution. After all, there have been two murders in Kismet since spring. I didn't know the first victim, but one of Bob Preston's crews painted my house. They did a good job. I just hate to think of someone I knew being killed."

Caprice understood exactly how she felt. When she thought of Bob, she just couldn't fathom the fact that he wasn't around any longer.

"In fact, I was going to call his company again to paint my shed," Josie went on. "Do you think someone in his business is going to keep it going?"

That was a good question. Kent Osgood, Bob's right-hand man, could probably take over the handling of the crews. It depended on the wording of Bob's will, and if Kent would have to buy out the business.

"I could just call Kent Osgood," Josie said. "I have one of his business cards. One day when he was working here, he gave it to me, and he said he also painted small jobs when he could after hours. So I could call him, couldn't I?"

So Kent took jobs on his own. She hadn't known that. She'd always dealt with Bob when she contracted with him. Was Kent trying to undermine Bob's business so he could go out on his own? Or was he just trying to earn extra money?

She thought about the best way to talk to him. The trim on her back porch really could use a coat of paint. After all, she had her neighbor's recommendation to call him.

"I have trim on my porch that should be painted. Do you have Kent's number handy?"

"I sure do. It's on my refrigerator. By the way, you don't have blueberries in your yard, do you?" Josie asked, changing the subject.

"My mom does, but no, I don't. Why?"

"Because I have a bush that's loaded with them, and I just don't have time to pick them or do anything else with them right now. You're welcome to them."

"Thank you so much for offering. I have a recipe for blueberry bread they'd be yummy in. I put it together when Mom started growing blueberries."

"You'll have to give me your recipe."

"Of course. And it makes two loaves. Since I'm using your blueberries, you can have one of them."

"No, dear. A whole loaf will go to waste. My doctor says I can only have a small piece of a goody like that now and then. If it were up to him, I'd become a vegetarian."

Caprice laughed. "I guess we all should, but what fun is there in that? After I bake the bread and it cools, I'll bring over one slice. How about that?"

"Now that sounds perfect. I have some quart

boxes on my back porch. Just help yourself. I'll get
Kent's number."

Caprice had a full afternoon. She had to visit
Older and Better, the antiques shop, to find some
rustic accents for a luxurious log home she was staging at the end of the week. But she couldn't turn
down fresh blueberries, and picking them would give
Shasta even more time to romp around.

After Josie went inside, Caprice took a quart container from her neighbor's back porch and went to
the blueberry bush. Shasta darted around Josie's
yard, never going very far afield.

Caprice's box of blueberries was almost half full
when Josie came outside again holding an index
card. "Here's Mr. Osgood's number. It's different
from the one I call for Mr. Preston."

She wondered if this was Kent's home number.
She was going to find out. Tucking the card in her
pocket with her phone, she continued picking
berries from the bush until she'd picked two quarts.
She left one quart with Josie, who could just wash
them and enjoy them au naturel. They were supposed to be chock-full of antioxidants.

Josie's smile was wide and her thank-you genuine
as she waved and watched Caprice take her quart of
berries to the gate in her fence with Shasta at her
heels. After she closed the gate and reached her
porch, she made a quick decision. Sitting on the
fifties-style glider, she pulled out her cell phone.

Then she dialed Kent's number.

Older and Better was one of Caprice's favorite
haunts. It was located on the outskirts of Kismet, and

she often stopped there on her travels to and from Harrisburg or on a jaunt down to Lancaster. Maybe she just enjoyed getting lost in the past. Maybe the glassware and old furniture brought back memories of being a little girl. Everything in Isaac's shop told a story, and she loved to listen to those stories.

As usual, Isaac Hobbs was in his shop. He practically lived there when he wasn't on a buying trip, though his main assistant, Julie Ann, as dedicated to his antiques as he was, kept a close watch when he wasn't around. Today, however, he was.

He smiled when the front door creaked open and a little buzzer went off.

Today Caprice was interested in rustic but well-made furniture that might look a little distressed, but not too overused. Sometimes she just rented pieces from Isaac for the length of a staging. Other times, she bought a table or a chair, Waterford cordials, or an antique Victrola cabinet and kept them in her storage shed, ready for when she might need them.

Isaac looked up from a glass case that held antique jewelry, smiled, and waved for her to come closer. "Just the girl I want to see. You're going to want to see this ring."

Uh oh. She admired old jewelry, and Isaac knew it. She'd spent hours examining pieces in his shop. She'd bought Nana a 1940s brooch for her birthday last year. But rings? Rings could be her downfall. Today she was wearing a gold initial ring that her dad had given her one Christmas. She also wore a mood ring. They were coming back into fashion. Antiques endured. Fashions were cyclic, but classic was always classic.

"You aren't going to tempt me, are you?"

"From what I hear, you're making good money these days."

"Excuse me?"

"Hey, I'm just telling you what the scuttlebutt is. You stage a house and it sells, even in this market."

She *was* doing well, and sometimes good old Catholic guilt kicked in and she felt like maybe she shouldn't be when so many others weren't. But as her mom often told her, guilt was meant to push you toward the positive. So she did what she could to help others, especially her furry friends. Still, she didn't know if she liked the idea of anyone talking about how well she was doing.

"You're not going to give me names, are you?"

"Nope. I have a confidentiality agreement with my customers. You know that."

Isaac was sort of like the bartender at a tavern. He listened to everybody, took it all in, and kept it to himself. Most of the time, anyway. Unless it was public knowledge. She was counting on some of that public knowledge today, along with finding furniture for that log home.

"So what do you have to show me?" she asked, really interested.

He slid a ring from a black velvet box. This particular ring appeared so delicate and fragile in his big calloused hands. It was a beautiful pearl, about nine millimeters, set in a white gold band channeled with garnets. It was delicate and feminine and striking. She didn't have any pearls in her jewelry wardrobe, not rings anyway. For handling animals and moving furniture around, she needed pieces that could withstand bumps or a good washing with a bar of soap. Pearls couldn't.

But that didn't mean she couldn't admire them. That didn't mean she couldn't look at this ring and wonder what she could wear with it the night of the awards dinner.

"It's beautiful, Isaac. What's the price tag?"

"Three hundred dollars."

No, that wasn't exorbitant. But in spite of what she made or didn't make, she wasn't careless with her money. She always thought about need versus want, and this was certainly something she wanted but didn't need.

"Try it on," he encouraged her.

She knew she shouldn't. And miraculously, as if it were made for her, it slid right onto her finger. She sighed. "Well, of course it fits."

Isaac laughed. "Why don't you drop a hint to that doctor you're dating that you'd like it. Christmas isn't that far away."

Christmas and Seth. Those two words seemed to go together so well. "I don't know if we're that far along yet," she said honestly.

"I heard somebody saw you two smooching outside of Cherry on the Top."

She felt heat crawl up her neck. Kismet was the ultimate small town. Nothing went unnoticed—not her yellow Camaro, or her practically psychedelic van, or the penchant she had for taking in strays. She moved her hand this way and that so the ring would catch the light shining through the window.

"I didn't come in here today to look at rings," she said, looking at it anyway.

"How often do you buy what you actually came in here for and not something else?"

Now it was her turn to laugh. "I need occasional

tables, maybe a coffee table. I'm staging a log house in Reservoir Heights."

Reservoir Heights was one of the ritziest areas of town. Her best friend Roz had lived there before her life had changed. The houses were magnificent, each somehow unique and built on enough property to give them an estate feel.

"If you can't find anything in here, you can check the storage rooms. I bought furniture at two public sales last weekend and filled them up pretty well."

Last weekend brought back memories of what had happened to Bob. When she thought about Bob, Caprice felt a tightness in her chest and fear that Bella could be charged with his murder.

She slipped off the ring and handed it back to Isaac. "So have you heard any scuttlebutt about my sister?"

Isaac focused his attention elsewhere and took his time settling the ring in the little black velvet box.

"Isaac?" she asked.

"How about some coffee?"

It was July and Isaac's air-conditioning unit was running full force. Coffee wouldn't be her beverage of choice on a day like this.

But Isaac talked better over coffee, so she agreed. "Coffee it is."

He kept two chairs behind the counter for this exact purpose, a tête-à-tête with a customer or an old friend. Isaac was older than her parents, but she still felt he was a friend.

He poured two mugs of coffee, and after he'd added milk and sugar to Caprice's from a small refrigerator under the counter, he handed it to her. The walnut captain's chairs they sat in were surprisingly comfortable with their red-and-black-plaid cushioned seats.

"Some people think she might have done it, others don't," he revealed with a shrug. "But the flagrant rumor going around is that she had an affair with him."

"Oh, Isaac. It's not true."

"I'm old enough to know rumors can have a spark of truth, but not much else."

"They were friends," Caprice explained lamely.

"Old friends, right? She used to date him."

"Do you have a good memory, or did someone dig that up too?"

"It doesn't matter, does it?"

"No." She took a few swigs of stale coffee and didn't make a face, even though she wanted to. "Did you know Bob?"

"I knew him some. He painted this place a couple of years ago. A few months ago, Kent Osgood painted my kitchen after I had a leak in an upstairs bathroom. Bob stopped by the day he was working and helped him finish up."

"Did they seem to have a good working relationship?"

"Seemed so to me. They laughed and joked like guys do, talked about baseball teams. I think Kent was five or six years younger than Bob, but I got the idea they did some stuff together outside of work too. You know, like an Orioles game or a nightcap at Susie Q's."

Susie Q's, a sports bar near the community center, was frequented by a lot of the single men in town. Her brother told her guys often stopped in there for happy hour just to get a glimpse of the skimpy outfits the waitresses wore.

"You're looking for another suspect, aren't you?" Isaac asked over the rim of his mug.

"I'm considering who might have had a motive to kill Bob."

"Is Bella really in trouble?"

"We don't know yet. I'm hoping not."

"Lucky you have a lawyer in the family."

Yes, it was, and Joe was lucky that Grant was on his side.

"Have you heard many rumors about Bob himself? Maybe stuff he was into? Stuff he shouldn't have been into?"

Isaac thought about it and shook his head. "Not really. I was a little surprised about the rumors about him and Bella, though. He's dating a pretty redhead."

"You mean Jackie at Connect Xpress?"

"Oh, so you know about her."

"I get around."

"So you do," he acknowledged with a wry grimace. He motioned to the case with the pearl and garnet ring. "Can't talk you into that ring?"

"Not today. And I'd like to chat longer," she said. "But . . ."

"You've got animals and work, and maybe a hot date?" he asked with a wink.

"Seth works almost as much as you do. That doesn't leave a lot of time for hot dates."

"Tell him about the ring," Isaac advised her. "I'll keep it in my safe instead of in the case for a while."

"Isaac—"

"I rotate my inventory. You know that. No reason it has to go in the case this month. After all, garnets are January's birthstone. And the pearl? Well, June has passed, hasn't it?"

She laughed and set her coffee mug on the side table. "Come on. Let's get started looking at the furniture. I have a feeling this could take a while."

And it did. It was almost 4 p.m. when she left Isaac's. She adjusted her Bluetooth earpiece, dialed Bella's number, and headed home. Caprice thought Bella's phone was going to go to voice mail, but her sister answered.

She didn't say hello, but rather opened with "Mom told me you're up for an award. Congratulations."

There wasn't much oomph behind Bella's good wishes, and Caprice absolutely understood the reason. In Bella's situation, how could she be happy about anything?

"Thank you. I'm up against some great women. But it's an honor to be in the running."

"That's a politically correct statement if I ever heard one," Bella said. "You can save that for the press. You want to win, I know you do. You've got a competitive streak, just like Vince."

That was possibly true, but she wouldn't admit it. "So how are you and Joe?"

"It's so quiet in this house, my ears are ringing. If it weren't for the kids, I don't know what I'd do. He thinks I had an affair with Bob."

"Oh, Bella. Why won't he believe you?"

"Because I often tell little white lies so he doesn't disapprove. Or I just don't tell him things at all—like about the pregnancy, at first, and the money in my shoe. I mean if he were perceptive at all, he would have realized I wasn't making all those kids' costumes just for the fun of it. But he never even asked, and that's because he's not interested in what I do."

Caprice didn't argue with her sister because she knew in part that it was true. Joe cared about what Bella did only as it affected him. Weren't most people like that? Weren't most husbands like that? She hoped not. Come to think of it, her father wasn't like that.

Seth wouldn't be like that.

Don't even think it. You're not anywhere near thinking about him as husband material.

Bringing her attention back to the situation at hand, Caprice asked, "Did you talk to Joe about that coupon?"

"No. It's just too tense here, Caprice. If I ask him about that, he could blow up and walk out."

"But he wouldn't stay gone."

"You seem to be more sure of that than I am."

"He's not going to throw away all the years of marriage he has with you."

"I'm not so sure of that, either. Maybe he never really wanted to get married in the first place. Maybe my pregnancy then was a trap, like this one is now."

Bella was going down a really negative road, and Caprice didn't know how to turn her around. "Do you want me to come over? We could cook. I could play games with the kids."

"That sounds nice, but having you here could ruffle Joe's feathers even more."

Caprice wanted to shake some sense into Bella's rooster. Maybe he needed a few head feathers clipped. "Can I give you some advice?"

Asking permission might not help because Bella didn't take advice easily. However, she didn't seem to know which way to turn and maybe she would listen today.

"What is it?" Bella asked warily.

"You can't live your life for Joe. Maybe part of the problem is that you've always tried to please him. Right now, you have to do what's going to make you feel better and what's going to keep your kids protected and happy."

Silence stretched for at least five seconds as Caprice veered into her neighborhood.

"I make life convenient for him," Bella said weakly.

"Yes, you do. But life isn't convenient right now for either of you."

"I can't talk to him," Bella erupted. "He has this frozen expression on his face, and his shoulders are all rigid and his hands are balled into fists."

"Then write him a letter. But whatever you do, think about your happiness and the kids, and whatever's going to get you through this. If he's not going to support you, you still need support. I'm here, Bella, and so are Nikki and Vince, Mom and Dad, and Nana."

"Oh, Caprice."

She heard Bella's voice break. She hadn't intended to make her sister cry, but she had to know she was loved. "Take care of yourself and call me if you need me."

"I will."

Caprice ended the call and knew she couldn't just sit around and watch everything fall apart, not when her family was involved. She'd go home, give Shasta a few runs around the yard, feed her and Sophia. But then she was headed to the casino. It occurred to her that nosing around was one of the things she did best.

*　*　*

Two hours later, Caprice had found a slot in the parking garage of Hollywood Casino. She'd devised a plan on her way here. First, she needed a member's card. All casinos had them now. She doubted if there were casinos in which patrons still used actual coins in the slot machines.

Before she'd stepped into the elevator, she could smell cigarette smoke along with lingering perfume. She knew both would be strong downstairs. She piled into the elevator with two couples who wore smiles and were chattering among themselves. One couple looked to be about as old as her parents. The second couple might just have topped the forty-year-old hill. The casino really was a playground for all ages.

She'd heard that during the day it was mostly the over-fifty crowd who enjoyed the bells and whistles the casino had to offer. But at night, the casino drew a mixed crowd.

After the ride down, the elevator door opened. Walking through the casino entrance, Caprice spotted slot machines. The cushioned seats at each machine were emblazoned with HC on the back. The machines made a *ding-ding-ding* sound while music played in the background and conversation swirled all around.

Caprice looked up toward the ceiling, two stories above. Fake trees with lighted globe lights reached upward. Straight ahead, she saw a towering statue of a galloping horse and rider. To her left, more slot machines dinged.

A security guard stood at this entrance, and

Caprice asked, "Can you tell me where I'll find the service desk?"

The guard motioned straight ahead and told her she couldn't miss it.

No, she couldn't.

She didn't have a long wait because the process was efficient, and soon she had a card on a bungee-like cord. This card would enable her to earn reward points that she could use for everything from restaurant meals to gift shop goodies. The pamphlet she'd received with her card told her she could also go online and check not only her reward points but also what she'd won and lost—for tax purposes, she imagined.

There was a lot to explore. She had a plan, but before she decided what she was going to do next, she toured the place. The noise and lights and music were exciting. All persuaded adrenaline to flow. The geometrically patterned, jewel-tone carpet was eye-catching, as were the blinking lights and revolving, color-rich icons on the slot machines. She passed not only blackjack tables, but roulette, Texas Hold'em, and baccarat too. The room where the live poker games took place looked to be a serious endeavor.

She'd never particularly liked slot machines. Playing them, she felt as if she were throwing her money away. So she watched those playing, took a spin around the gift shop with its retro memorabilia, and just generally found her bearings. She didn't imagine that the pit bosses and the managers would like anyone asking too many questions, so she would have to be careful. There were lots of security cameras, after all, and she imagined everyone was watched closely.

She had to think like Joe. No small feat.

Although there were nonsmoking sections in the casino, the distinction was pretty much a moot point, considering that the smoking sections were right beside them. If Joe's clothes had picked up the smell of smoke, this was a place where it could certainly have happened.

She ignored the entrance that led outside to the racetrack and concentrated on the bar, which was as intriguing as the rest of the facility. High tables dotted the area, and ESPN was projected onto the domed ceiling.

Caprice felt the need to take some kind of action. It was time to do something.

She checked the casino register for the types of machines and found what she was looking for—the section featuring poker machines. For some reason, she imagined Joe might play there when he wasn't headed for the more serious tables. He liked poker and often sat in on her dad's games. If he was working up the nerve to drop some real cash, he might settle at those machines first . . . or after. It was a long shot, but she believed in long shots.

Considering Joe's stinginess, she was sure he would play in an area where drinks were served to patrons while they gambled. That narrowed down where Joe might sit to play.

Taking out her phone, she scrolled through photographs, found the one she wanted, and marked it so it was handy. Then she extracted the bills she'd brought along to stake her. All the poker machines were occupied in the section where drinks were served, so she wandered to another section and smiled when she saw the Kitty Glitter slot machine. It was empty.

What, no one here likes cats? She herself didn't care much for numbers, bills, sevens, and gold bars, let alone cherries. But this machine, with its pictures of breeds of cats and so many ways to win, attracted her.

She started with a dollar bill. What could she say? She wasn't a big spender, not on slot machines. On her fifth push of the button, she won two dollars and forty cents. She was really getting into the spirit of it, was even two dollars ahead, when she knew she had to move. She needed to sit at one of those poker machines for a while, so one of the attendants would bring her drinks and she could chat her up. After all, that's why she was here.

She wandered about for ten minutes until one of the poker machines opened up. She slid onto the seat, intending to stay for a while. She played slowly between button pushes, reflecting on the tables she'd found at Isaac's and where she'd place them in the log home. The attendant for her section brought her one soda, then a refill. And still Caprice played, slowly and carefully stretching out her funds. Each time the attendant brought her a drink, Caprice made small talk about the weather, about the crowd, about the music. From her badge, Caprice could see the server's name was Pauline. The third time Pauline delivered a soda, Caprice was more than a woman sitting at a slot machine. They'd become friendly.

"Can I get you another drink?"

"I'm going to have to find a bathroom soon, but I don't want to give up my seat," Caprice joked.

"You should have brought a partner along. Then you could switch off."

"My brother-in-law often comes here." She slipped her phone out of her pocket and easily found the picture. Before Pauline could slip away, Caprice showed it to her. "Do you recognize him? He might even be here. With all the noise in here, he can't hear me ringing his phone."

Pauline glanced at the photo of Joe and Timmy standing in their backyard. Even before Pauline said anything, Caprice noticed an expression of recognition on her face.

She shrugged. "I don't think he's here tonight."

"But he comes in other times when you're working?"

Pauline eyed her suspiciously. "Why do you want to know?"

"The truth is, my sister thinks he's having an affair and I think he's gambling. I'm not sure which is worse, but I'd just like to know."

Pauline looked uncertain.

"I won't say how I found out," Caprice said. "I just need a little ammunition to give my sister so she can ask the right questions. You know what I mean?"

"Let me get this soda for you. I'll be back," Pauline said, and Caprice wasn't sure she would be. However, after she delivered her tray of drinks, Pauline brought Caprice hers. Setting it down, she said in a low voice, "I usually work evenings. He comes in a couple of times a week."

That's all Caprice needed to know.

Chapter Eight

Caprice brought her van to a squealing stop a half block from Bella's house. There was a patrol car parked in front, and the forensics vehicle was in the driveway. Bella had called her this morning practically screeching in panic.

Bella and Joe stood on the front lawn with a grim-faced Vince. To her surprise, Joe was the one who told her what was going on in even, calm terms.

"Detectives Jones and Carstead are in the house. They had a warrant. They're searching for the murder weapon and anything else to incriminate us."

Although Joe's voice seemed calm, Caprice heard the tension in it, saw the creases in his forehead, spotted the tense line of his shoulders. She looked to Vince for further explanation.

"He's right. They're going through the garage with a fine-tooth comb. They also went through his toolshed. The van will be next."

Bella and Joe were standing about ten feet apart, one on either side of Vince. They weren't looking at each other. They weren't united in any way. They were like pillars in the sand, beaten by waves, leaning in opposite directions, away from each other.

She had to help them somehow. She was pretty sure Bella didn't want her marriage to fall apart. If her sister didn't want it, Caprice didn't want it for her, either. Joe might be a pain in the butt sometimes, but he was Bella's pain in the butt, and a good dad to Megan and Timmy when he was with them.

An hour later, the police vehicles were gone. Bella rushed inside the house to see what kind of mess had been made, and Vince went with her. Joe was slow to follow.

Caprice decided talking to him first might be the best way to go. Instead of rushing in with Bella, she stood beside her brother-in-law and just waited.

"They took two pairs of my shoes," he muttered.

"Maybe there were footprints at the scene."

"They took a couple of tools, too."

"Will they find anything when they analyze them?" she asked softly.

"No!" Joe answered hotly. "They won't find anything. I didn't do it."

She waited a beat, then revealed, "I know you've been gambling at Hollywood Casino."

Joe's head swung around, and all of his attention was riveted on her. "Just how do you know that?"

"Does it matter?"

His lips thinned into tight lines, and he dug his hands into his jeans pockets. He was all defiance and defensiveness and irate indignation, though Caprice had the feeling that something else was underneath all of that.

"Joe, talk to me."

"Why should I? You'll just spill everything to Bella."

"Maybe *you* should be spilling everything to Bella. Secrets between you right now can be as damaging as anything you're not telling the police. Don't you see that?"

"*She's* been keeping secrets."

"You mean saving money for a rainy day?"

"I mean dating an old flame."

"She had coffee with him."

"Yeah, and what was she going to do the night he was killed?"

"Did you ask her?"

He stared at Caprice for a long time as if daring her to back down. But then he was the one who did. He looked down at the grass under his feet. "No. Maybe I don't want to hear what she was going to do."

"Joe, Bella is pregnant with your baby, a baby she thinks you don't want."

When he started to sputter, she held up her hand. "I'm just telling you how she sees this. You've been away late at night, and you come home smelling like smoke, and maybe liquor. I don't know. Have you told her what you've been doing?"

"I can't."

"You've been seeing someone on the side?"

"No!" he erupted again. "Of course not. My vows to Bella mean everything, and you should know that after all these years."

"If *she* doesn't know it, how could *I* know it?"

He closed his eyes and shook his head. "Things have gotten so messed up."

"What things?"

He sighed with a resignation that seemed to make his whole body sag. "I went to the casino one night with some guys from work. It was a few months ago. I didn't tell Bella because she and I hadn't gone out in a long time. Money was tight. I didn't want to get into a fight."

"Peace at all costs always costs a lot," Caprice murmured. Joe and Bella had been trying to keep the peace—and damaging their marriage while doing it.

"No lectures, okay? I don't have to tell you any of this."

"No, you don't," she shot back. "But since the police issued a warrant to search your home and car, my guess is they'll be taking you down to the station to question you again. Do you really think all this isn't going to come out? Wouldn't it be better if you and Bella talked first?"

"I'm telling you, she's not going to want to know that I've been losing our money." He glanced up at the house as if his wife might have heard him.

"A lot?" she asked.

"Enough. That night when I went to the casino with the guys, I won three hundred bucks. Three hundred extra dollars that we could toss into the kitty for food or clothes or a higher electric bill."

Caprice guessed what was going to come next.

"So I thought, like a stupid idiot," he went on, "if I could win three hundred dollars, I could win more. Right?"

Caprice didn't say a word. She didn't have to because Joe answered his own question.

"Well, I didn't. I lost little by little. So I ratcheted up the stakes. Instead of just video poker and blackjack, I got a seat at a poker table. I lost two hundred dollars, then four. I won back fifty. So I tried to win back more. I kept going back because I thought I could at least break even. Bella wouldn't have to see I'd taken a cash advance on a new credit card. She wouldn't see that I filled up the van with half a tank of gas instead of a whole tank, to use that money at the casino. The whole thing just snowballed. She told me we were having a baby, so I tried even harder to win."

"But you couldn't."

"No, I was just a sucker who didn't stop soon enough."

"How much did you lose?"

He eyed Caprice now as if she were a judge who was going to bring down the gavel and sentence him.

"Five thousand dollars."

Caprice breathed a little sigh of relief. Five thousand dollars was nothing to sneeze at, but hopefully five thousand dollars wouldn't make them lose their house, either.

"When you married Bella, didn't we all make you feel as if you were part of our family?"

"Yeah, I guess you did," he muttered. "But you're all so tight, sometimes I feel left out too."

"I'm sorry about that, Joe. That's never been our intention. You do know, don't you, that sometimes Vince feels left out too, because Bella, Nikki, and I talk? Because we usually tell each other everything?"

"Vince doesn't care what anybody thinks about him. He knows no matter who he dates or what he does, you'll all stand beside him."

"And you don't feel like that?"

"Especially not now, not with the police questioning me as if I'm some kind of criminal."

"They're questioning Bella, too."

"Yeah, but you don't believe she did it."

She could ask him the question again, but she didn't know if she should. Maybe that would put an even deeper wedge between them. Had Joe just been driving around the night Bob was murdered? Had he been headed for the casino?

"I didn't kill him," Joe said as if she *had* asked again what was uppermost in her mind.

Birds chirped in the trees. The sound of a chain saw hummed in the distance.

Caprice lightly touched Joe's arm. "Let's go inside. You and Bella need to have a long talk, don't you think?"

Joe's shoulders drooped. "I don't know how we're going to afford raising another kid."

That was a very big question. But an even bigger question was whether the police considered Bella or Joe to be prime suspects.

Just what would they do if one of them was arrested?

Caprice couldn't stop thinking about Joe and Bella as she left them alone and stopped at her house to make sure Shasta and Sophia were copacetic. They must have had a morning run because the throw rugs were again ruffled and the silent butler she kept on her coffee table was almost tipping over the edge. But other than that . . .

Sophia gave her a wide yawn, and Shasta looked up at her angelically.

"Okay, one run around the yard, then I have a house to stage. My assistant can't do it all."

Juan was overseeing the delivery of the furniture and the incidentals, but Caprice wanted to be there for placement and to see what they might still need.

A half hour later, she drove into Reservoir Heights, as always admiring the view. The lots were two or three acres, some placed around the reservoir with a view of the lake-like setting. When she was a half mile from the log home, she saw it on the crest of a hill. It had a dramatic, lodge-like look and contained five thousand square feet of amenities. Terraced into the hill, the dining room had a view of the reservoir through floor-to-ceiling windows. The front of the house looked as if it were built on log pillars, and a deck surrounded the entire first floor. The basement level included a three-car garage, a workshop, a large game room, and three bedrooms.

After she pulled into a parking area alongside the house, she mounted the rustic cedar stairs, stopped at the landing to look out over the view, then continued up to what was considered the first floor. A Native American patterned rug hung over the deck's banister, and the sliding glass doors stood open. She stepped inside and considered the beautiful home, which had been vacant for two months because its owner had taken a job in Arizona and moved his family there.

One of this home's strongest attributes was the open concept of the great room, dining area, and kitchen, which had a large breakfast nook. The dining room and great room featured cathedral

ceilings that soared above a native rock fireplace.
A winding log staircase led to the second floor.

Caprice knew lofts were a waste of space, but she
really did like them. They added drama to the small-
est A-frame. This was by no means an A-frame. This
type of home was better suited for a family with
tween to teenage kids, though the office near the
master suite on the second floor could be developed
into a nursery. The three bedrooms in the basement
provided privacy older children might like.

Her theme for this house was Rustic Chic. It definitely was that, even with an unfinished staged look.

Juan descended the stairs from the second floor.
He must have heard her van. "The master suite is
finished. That lodgepole pine bed you found was
perfect. I didn't know how that red, white and blue
quilt you picked out would look on the king-size bed,
but it worked. I should have trusted your eye."

"Sometimes I need more than one set of eyes,"
Caprice joked. "And you're it."

She glanced around the great room, furnished
with a multicushioned blue and red denim couch, a
couple of primitive antiques she'd found at Isaac's, a
few occasional tables, and a bookcase that was delivered this morning. "I haven't been to my storage
compartments yet for accessories. I'll do that this
afternoon. Do you think we have enough furniture?"

Two monstrous faux-suede-covered chairs formed
a grouping with the sofa. A heavy pine chest acted
as the coffee table. The sturdy oak dining table, with
its pedestal and benches and an accompanying large
hutch, filled just enough space in the dining room.
Glancing at the walls, she decided Juan had done a
fine job with a framed print of stampeding horses, as

well as a metallic hanging of cattails swaying in the breeze.

"I don't think you need me," she said as a compliment.

"More furniture for downstairs is coming in about half an hour, and you didn't give me a floor plan for that. The rest is exactly the way you designed it, so don't try to be all humble on me. It won't work. I heard about that award you're up for."

"Now how did you hear about that?"

"I was in touch with Nikki about what she's serving on Sunday. She told me. She's so proud of you she could pop."

"I'm just as proud of her. She always makes these stagings a real party. This one's going to be a down-home feast, very different from what we usually do. I think her special recipe for baked beans is even on the menu."

"Along with corn bread, chili, grits, meat loaf, and mashed potatoes," he added. "She's going rustic with the hors d'oeuvres for this one too. Something about a dip of cheese with ground beef, and bread sticks to eat it with. But she's using imported ales and lager, along with wine developed right here in the Susquehanna Valley."

Caprice gazed around the space. "Sometimes I wonder how we'll be ready on time, but we always are."

"Yep, we always are."

Before Juan could head upstairs to whatever he was doing before she'd arrived, she said, "Can we talk about Bob?"

Juan studied her for a moment, then sank down onto one of the suede-like chairs. "Sure, we can. But

I'm going to rest this ankle while we do, if you don't mind."

She didn't mind at all. In fact, if he needed more help, she wished he'd ask for it. But he wouldn't. That was Juan.

"You know I don't mind. Do *not* overdo it."

"About Bob," he said seriously. "I know Bella found him."

"You've been around him the past couple of years. Tell me what you thought of him."

"You want an objective opinion?"

"Something like that."

Juan shrugged. "He was an okay guy. He was a woman's guy."

"What do you mean?"

"You know the type. They can get along with any woman, can charm them, flatter them, make them feel special. I bet he never had a turn-down date in his life."

Maybe not a turn-down date. But Bella had turned him down when she'd found out he'd been unfaithful. Had that always rankled with Bob? Had he wanted to try to get even for that by charming her again now?

"What do you know about Kent Osgood?"

"I'm sure I don't know much more than you do. He turned up in Kismet about a year and a half ago around the time Bob decided to add another crew and go after more lucrative painting jobs. From what I've heard, he and Kent became friends and then partners."

"Partners?"

She hadn't known Kent was officially Bob's partner. Could that be a strong enough motive for murder? "Kent's going to paint the trim on my back porch day after tomorrow."

"You suddenly needed a back porch trim? Something tells me you're looking into Bob's murder, and you'd like to get to know Kent a little better."

"But you're not going to tell anybody else that's what I intend to do, right?"

Juan grinned. "Wouldn't think of it. Are you doing this for your sister?"

Yes, she was. She was doing this for Bella.

On Friday morning Caprice was on her phone with Roz when Kent Osgood drove up in his truck.

"The painter's here," she told Roz. They'd been discussing plans for the fashion boutique Roz intended to open.

"And you think he could be a suspect?" Roz asked, sounding worried.

"It's possible. If he is Bob's partner, maybe he inherits the business. And don't tell me to be careful. He's going to be painting the trim on my back porch. I've got my cell phone in my pocket, and Josie is right next door."

"And you really think you'll be able to meet me this afternoon, to talk about the space and displays and everything else?"

"I explained exactly what I wanted him to paint, and he says he should be finished in a couple of hours. I spent most of yesterday at the log house with the real estate agent, taping video, and shooting photos for their Web site. Almost everything is ready for Sunday. I'll stop in at your new space after Kent leaves."

"Sounds good. Keep Shasta at your side. She'll

protect you. I know Dylan would drag me out of a burning building if he could."

Caprice laughed at that picture. Dylan was a ball of fur and weighed about ten pounds. But he was loyal, and Caprice knew Roz was right.

Caprice met Kent at the curb. After their phone conversation, she'd e-mailed him photos of what she needed to have painted. He'd e-mailed her back a ballpark estimate that she'd okayed. Now they exchanged pleasantries and he shook her hand. Kent looked to be younger than Bob, maybe in his midtwenties. He had sandy blond hair and green eyes, and loose-limbed movements that told her he might have been an athlete in high school. The day was already hot, and he wore a tank top and jeans.

Releasing a ladder from the rack at the back of his truck, he hefted it up and carried it as if it weighed very little. Caprice had surmised right away from their phone conversation that Kent, unlike Bob, wasn't a talker.

At her back entrance, he said, "This is a cinch. I'll be done by midmorning."

Small talk obviously wasn't his forte, but she needed him talking to find out anything.

Hearing them at the back door, Shasta began barking.

"You've got a dog," he said offhandedly as he raised the ladder and propped it against the side of the porch.

Animals always made conversation easier.

"I do. Actually, I found her a week before Bob's murder. She's helped to distract me since."

Which was absolutely true.

At the mention of Bob's murder, Kent frowned,

and she thought his complexion might have gone a little paler.

She'd expressed her condolences on the phone but said again, "I'm sorry you lost him. His murder must have been quite a shock."

"It was."

He adjusted the ladder behind two peony bushes.

"Have you heard anything about the funeral?" Caprice asked, thinking the body might have been released by now.

"He's going to be cremated," Kent answered, thin-lipped. "There won't be anything else."

Since Bob didn't have family, would those arrangements be left to his partner?

"My sister told me Bob didn't have any family. His parents are gone. No brothers or sisters. He knew so many people."

Kent didn't say anything to that.

Shasta's barking broke the silence. She heard voices close by and she wanted out.

"If I'm inside with her, she won't bark and she won't bother you."

Although Kent hadn't seemed interested in their conversation, Caprice felt him watching her now as she went up the steps to the porch, crossed it, and opened the door. Maybe in a little while she could offer him a glass of iced tea and urge him to talk. But before she could slip inside, Shasta bounded out. Seeing Kent, someone new who might play with her, she scampered down the steps and rounded his legs.

Caprice was going to catch Shasta by her new collar, but Kent waved his hand at her and said, "Let her be. She's fine. Is she friendly?"

"Yes, she is, though she still gets startled if you

move too fast. That probably comes from being on her own for a while as a stray. She's pregnant."

He stooped down to pet the dog's head.

"Pregnant." He eyed the dog thoughtfully. "If you want to leave her out in the yard while I'm painting, I don't mind."

"She might get in your way."

"I doubt that. I'll keep the paint can closed and just use the tray. But it's up to you."

"It wouldn't hurt to leave her out here a while, especially while you're doing the upper section."

He gave Shasta another pat.

She looked up at him, tilted her head, and barked, and then ran off across the yard.

"When is she due?"

"We don't know for sure. But my vet thinks in a few weeks."

"Are her pups spoken for?"

"Not yet. Are you interested?"

"If I can afford one."

Caprice wasn't going to charge, not to find Shasta's babies good homes. And it all depended upon if she found Shasta's owner. If she did, the pups were theirs.

Would Kent Osgood give a pup a good home? Caprice hoped Bob's murder would be solved by then, because she wouldn't give one of Shasta's pups to a suspect in a murder investigation.

Caprice allowed Shasta to stay in the backyard while she went inside. But she didn't go far. She wanted to use Josie's blueberries while they were fresh. Since the recipe she'd developed made two loaves, she'd keep one, giving a slice to Josie, and the other she'd take along for Seth tomorrow night.

She was looking forward to their date but afraid to look forward to it too much. An emergency could pop up at the clinic and Seth could be occupied. Or he could be called away. But that was the life of someone who dated a doctor.

And if they went beyond dating?

There would be time enough to think about that later.

Checking on Shasta, seeing that she was nosing around and not getting into trouble, Caprice set her oven at 350 degrees. Baking would make the kitchen warm, but she'd turn on the air before she left for Roz's. Glancing into the living room, Caprice saw Sophia perched on one of the shelves of her cat tree, sitting in front of the open window. She enjoyed watching the birds, butterflies, and bees, meowing every once in a while as if she wanted to tell Caprice about them.

After washing her hands thoroughly, Caprice pulled out her colander and carefully removed any stems from the blueberries before dropping them in it. Then she rinsed them thoroughly, allowing them to drain while she pulled together the other ingredients. What she liked most about this recipe was the fact that she could dump everything into one bowl, then mix it up. Taking pecan pieces from her freezer—she kept an assortment of nuts there for recipes—she dumped some into her lime-green chopper. The chopper whirled until she had a cup of finely chopped pieces.

Placing her mixer bowl front and center on the counter, she found sour cream in the refrigerator and scooped four tablespoons into the bowl. She added flour, sugars, baking powder, eggs, and milk.

After measuring out four teaspoons of vanilla, she mixed it all for about a minute and a half until it was smooth and no flour remained on the bottom or the edges of the bowl. She quickly stirred in the pecans and then carefully folded in the blueberries. They would burst inside the bread while it baked, sending their fruity flavor throughout.

After pouring the batter into two foil baking pans she'd greased and floured, she popped them in the oven and set the timer. Pulling her tablet computer from its charger on the counter, she sat at her kitchen table, checking her list for Sunday's open house, making sure she hadn't forgotten anything. But every once in a while, unbidden, Bella's scream re-echoed in her head and she relived finding Bella with Bob's body. It would take a while for those pictures to fade . . . a long time.

She glanced outside where Kent was working. The baking blueberry bread filled the house with a wonderful aroma. When the timer rang, she tested the bread with a toothpick, found it had baked just right, and set it on a wire rack to cool. Ten minutes later, she removed one of the loaves from its pan.

Although she'd offered Kent a glass of iced tea and a slice of warm bread, he'd declined, said he was fine, and continued painting. He obviously wanted to be left alone, except for Shasta. It wasn't unusual for some animal lovers to prefer their furry friends to humans.

Was he a viable suspect? She just hoped the police were looking further than Bella and Joe.

By the time the blueberry bread had completely cooled, Kent had finished outside, packed up, and left. Caprice wondered if he was always stoic and always quiet. Maybe he was just the type of man who didn't have much to say.

She'd have to ask Josie about that.

After her morning in the yard, Shasta was ready for lunch and a nap. Caprice smiled as Sophia deigned to join her in the kitchen, munching on dry food while Caprice grabbed a serving of pasta salad from the fridge. Fifteen minutes later, she was out the door and on her way to see Roz.

Most locations in Kismet were only five to ten minutes away. Caprice drove to a section of town that had recently been labeled Restoration Row. She should have realized when she saw the address, 11 Bristol Row, that she'd be headed to the street that the town council and a group of investors had taken over. Located there were some of the oldest row houses Kismet had to offer. The city council had arranged with investors to buy the rundown properties, then restore and refurbish them so that this lagging section of Kismet would attract a higher caliber of renters, as well as more businesses. Brick facing had been utilized halfway up the facades of the houses, and gray siding with black shutters hung on the upper half. Trees had been planted at intervals along the street, and old-fashioned lamplights looked like the gas lighting of old. The houses all had similar porches with steps and black aluminum railings.

Caprice wasn't sure what she thought about the street. It was a uniform look, and she preferred neighborhoods with individual, unique houses. But the refurbishment certainly was an improvement over broken and boarded-up windows, crumbling steps, and peeling paint. Apparently Roz was renting one of these buildings for her fashion boutique.

A public parking lot situated at the end of the street had meters. Caprice dropped in two quarters, hoping that would do it. She'd have to come out and feed the meter again if she was here longer than a half hour.

When strains of "A Hard Day's Night" came from her purse, she dug into it for her phone. She had a text from Vince.

Where are you?

She quickly typed in, **At Roz's store.**

He just texted back, **Stay there until I get there.**

How did he know where the store was? She replied with a frowny face icon. He knew she didn't like to take orders. What was buzzing around in his mind this morning? If he drove, he'd be here in two minutes. If he walked, it would be closer to five. His office wasn't very far away.

Putting Vince out of her mind for the moment, she went up the three steps. She didn't know whether to knock or just open the door. Finally she settled on both. She rapped a few times and opened the door.

Bedlam met her. She heard hammering on the second floor. Workmen in hard hats and heavy boots were working near sawhorses in the interior room. Roz, ever fashionable in a pale green tank top, matching slacks, and sandals, waved from her position at their side, excused herself, and came toward Caprice, her gold earrings swinging. She was beautiful in a model kind of way, and Caprice wondered if she'd ever get married again, especially after what she had experienced in her first marriage. Caprice knew a hurt heart didn't heal quickly.

Hers still had wounds from Travis. Divorced men were dangerous in more ways than one. If they couldn't forget their first marriage, they still might have feelings for their ex. She'd never forget about that, just as she'd never forget about her first serious relationship and how Craig had broken her heart by e-mail. She was happy now, so she guessed everything had turned out for the best. However, pain lasted as long as the memories. That's why she hadn't been involved with anyone before Seth for a long while.

"Don't you just look too cool, in tie-dye spaghetti straps and a fuchsia skort. I don't know, Caprice, that's not quite vintage."

Roz was teasing her about her penchant to buy vintage clothes at Secrets of the Past. But it was a little harder to wear vintage in summer, though she'd kept up the theme with her tie-dye.

She motioned to the workmen and the noise upstairs. "You're really getting things done."

"I am. *We* are." She laughed. "It's exciting. Once it's not dangerous here, I want to bring Dylan with me so he's not alone at the town house."

"You could get him a friend," Caprice teased. "In fact, remember, I'm going to have pups in a few weeks."

Roz shook her head. "A pup is a big responsibility, and with the business opening, that might be a little too much. Can you take a look around and work up some ideas for displays for me?"

"I bet you already have ideas."

"A few. Let me tell you about them."

So she did while she took Caprice on a tour of the downstairs and the upstairs.

"I know having two floors is a little unconventional, but I can specialize that way. I can use one room upstairs just for evening wear, while another could be purses and shoes. The great thing is that there's a back stairway, too, so I can put in a chairlift and have a ramp going outside. Anyone who wants to shop here can."

"You're barring no expense." Roz was a rich woman, but Caprice knew she wasn't doing this just to make money.

"I want to make women feel special, to help them to look good. I might even bring a cosmetologist in once a week and do workshops. What do you think?"

"I think you're brimming with ideas, and all of them are good."

"And you'll work up a design for me? I need to know the best way to position racks, how big I should make the dressing rooms."

Just then the front door opened without a knock, and Vince stood there, looking formidable. Caprice's inner "uh oh" alert bonged because she knew he was here to see her.

Still, in spite of his expression, Roz said pleasantly, "Hi, Vince."

The creases on his brow eased a bit as he returned, "Hi Roz. I'll have those papers drawn up for you by next week. I need to talk to Caprice, if you don't mind."

"I don't mind."

As Roz moved away toward the back of her boutique, Caprice asked her brother, "Just what do you have to tell me that you couldn't tell me over the phone?" Then she swallowed hard. "Is it Bella? Joe?"

"No, not in the way you mean. I needed to see you face-to-face. I heard you hired Kent Osgood to paint the trim on your back porch. Since when did that trim need painting?"

"Since I wanted to refresh it."

Vince grunted. "You pummeled him with questions, didn't you? About Bob and their relationship."

Now she did feel a bit guilty. "I asked a few questions, not many."

"I'm going to tell you this once, Caprice, just once. Stay out of it, or you're going to make everything worse for Bella and Joe."

Chapter Nine

Ever excited about her date with Seth on Saturday, Caprice tried to keep busy in her home office before he arrived. There was always work to do, but right now she couldn't concentrate on it. The investigation into Bob's murder revolved like a merry-go-round in her mind, as did her worry about Bella and Joe.

When Sophia sauntered into the room to investigate what Shasta was doing, Caprice pushed her wheeled chair back, held out her arms, and twirled. "What do you think?"

Sophia didn't seem impressed, so Caprice held her arms out and did it again. Shasta barked and took a few steps back as the chair moved a little.

"Shasta approves," Caprice told her feline.

At Secrets of the Past, she'd purchased a vintage-style sundress for tonight that was printed with big yellow, pink, and purple flowers. It was designed with a full skirt that she hoped didn't add more pounds visually. Even though she was about ten pounds overweight, her waist was one of her good features.

This dress emphasized it. She'd bought yellow pumps to go with her yellow-vinyl vintage bag.

Her doorbell rang and she jumped up, scaring both Shasta and Sophia, who scattered.

"Sorry, girls."

Both cat and dog were already roaming the living room when she opened her front door to Seth.

He smiled at her, one of those bone-melting smiles. At least *her* bones melted. He was wearing black cargo pants and a pale green polo. If a man could be considered yummy, he certainly was tonight.

She opened the screen door, and he didn't hesitate to come in, crouch down, and pet Shasta.

"She's looking good."

Seth didn't look into her eyes as he usually did, and Caprice wondered what was going on.

But then he stood, took Caprice's hand, and pulled her into a quick kiss. "I missed you."

The words certainly sounded sincere, and now he did look at her from head to toe. Then he grinned. "You're going to be the prettiest date at the Blue Moon Grille. I even think we're going to have a full moon tonight."

The Blue Moon Grille had an outside deck, but it was always well-populated.

"We might not be able to get a table, not on a night like this."

Seth gave her a wink. "I just happen to know someone who works there. He put our name on a reservations list. We're good."

She certainly hoped they were. This relationship was so new she was concerned something would mess it up. Maybe *she'd* mess it up. Her sisters constantly told her she sabotaged new relationships because she was afraid of getting involved with anyone again. She usually pooh-poohed that and told them she was just busy. But deep down she knew there was truth in it.

Seth asked, "Do you have to let Shasta out before we go?"

"No. I took her for a walk and we played a bit. She just went out by herself after I got dressed. She was outside a lot today. And yesterday, I had the back porch trim painted, and she got friendly with the painter."

Seth narrowed his eyes. "Did this painter work with Bob Preston?"

"Well, yes, he just happened to."

Seth shook his head. "I'm not going to say it."

"Good."

She picked up her purse from where it lay on the seat of the high-back mirrored hall bench, where the foil-wrapped loaf of blueberry bread also sat. She picked up the loaf as well.

Seth opened the door for her.

They were companionably quiet on the drive to the Blue Moon, which was a bit unusual because they always had a lot to say to each other. But Seth seemed to be in a reflective mood, and she remembered the last time she saw him, the way he'd held back when he'd kissed her. Her sixth sense told her something was going on, and her sixth sense was rarely wrong. Her Nana Celia had helped her develop it.

From the time she was a little girl, when Nana would see an expression on her face, she'd asked, "What's your stomach telling you?" It had taken Caprice a while to realize exactly what Nana was talking about. But soon she'd learned to follow the stomach quivers, the sighs that came from deep within, the little warning bells that rang in more than her head.

Nana's coaching over the years had paid off. So, now, she didn't know what to expect tonight. Not at all.

The line at the Blue Moon Grille stretched through its reception area on the first floor of an arts and crafts mall and practically out the front door. But Seth wasn't daunted by it. He took her hand and led her to the hostess.

"Reservation," he said. "For the deck. Seth Randolph."

As a doctor, Seth had to be confident in his diagnoses and in his decisions. He seemed to treat the rest of his life with that same confidence. That was one of the qualities she admired about him. There were so many others.

Always a gentleman, Seth let Caprice precede him up the stairs that led to the second-floor dining area and the deck outside. The chatter in the main dining room was loud around the bar and at the tables. They were glad to escape through sliding-glass doors to the outside deck, where the hostess showed them to a corner table. Caprice liked that idea because they wouldn't have other patrons at their sides or at their backs, just in front of them. Those corner tables were a little more quiet and hard to reserve. There was a vase of wildflowers on the table, which was surrounded by two black wrought-iron chairs that might have been uncomfortable but weren't because cushy cushions had been tied to the rounded backs and the seats. The glass-topped table held two white place mats, silverware, and crystal.

Caprice motioned to it all. "Thank you for this. It's lovely."

"I wanted to bring you someplace nice where we wouldn't be interrupted."

As he held her chair for her and she sat, she looked up at him over her shoulder. "So we won't be interrupted tonight?"

She knew Seth couldn't always control that. Sometimes, whether he was on call or not, when an emergency popped up he had to go.

"There are two doctors covering tonight, and no one is supposed to call me."

She laughed. "You must have bribed them."

"You, Miss De Luca, are way too smart for your age. I promised them tickets to Orioles games."

"You certainly do have connections."

"I meet a lot of people in the course of a day, and not just patients. Patients have friends and families. Some of them are grateful for what we do. They give me their cards, and they say 'If ever I can help you in any way' . . . So once in a while, I make a call."

"That's nice."

He could see she meant it.

She went on, "Maybe we should just go back to using the barter system. It would be a lot friendlier and a lot fairer, don't you think?"

"If someone changed my oil, I could give him a physical for free."

"Or if someone gave me blueberries, I could bake blueberry bread and return the favor. I made a loaf for you. That's what I left in your car. Put it in the refrigerator when you get home."

"I think I like this bartering. Just what would you and I barter?"

"Maybe if you use your imagination . . ." she teased.

"Oh, no. You're not going to give me a kitten for taking your temperature."

Now she really laughed. "You've got my number."

Seth smiled, then looked away, and she wondered if she'd said something wrong. But the waiter came to take their order.

"No expense spared tonight," Seth said. "Order whatever you want, from soup to nuts."

"It's a good thing I joined the gym last month."

"You mentioned that. Are you using weights?"

"No. Mostly I'm swimming. It's the one form of exercise I actually enjoy. The problem is finding the time to do it. Lately I don't get there till around seven in the evening. Lap swimming is from seven to eight."

Caprice started her evening with a strawberry daiquiri. The bartender used fresh strawberries, and that was rare. She knew the price reflected that, but Seth had said to spare no expense tonight. They ordered two plates of appetizers—fried cheese sticks and an artichoke, cheese, and spinach dip that was warm and served with toasted rounds. Nikki made a similar dip, and this was almost as good.

Over the best ribs in town, glazed by a blackberry barbeque sauce, they laughed, licked sticky fingers, and shared a monumental dish of steak fries dripping with cheese. It wasn't long before Caprice was telling Seth everything she'd found out about Bob. He listened well, asked perceptive questions, and didn't wag his finger at her, maybe because he was an investigator at heart. After all, he had to solve the puzzle of people's illnesses. He took a look at all the information she'd gathered and linked it together in pretty much the same way she had. This early, no one person was an obvious suspect, if you didn't believe Bella or Joe did it.

Seth shook his head when she brought up that point again.

"Granted, I haven't known them very long, but you've told me a lot about your sister Bella, and how the two of you grew up with Nikki and Vince. She might *think* about murdering somebody, but she'd never do it. Joe I really don't know as well. But the few times I've talked with him, he seems like a solid guy. He wants what's good for his family, even though he might not know the best way to get it. I don't think he'd put himself or them in jeopardy by doing something so stupid."

"Now that he's explained about his gambling," Caprice said, "I don't think so, either. I haven't heard from Bella since the police searched their house, so I don't know what happened after he told her."

"But you'll be calling her soon to find out."

"I have to nudge sometimes. That's what sisters do."

"I think it's great your family is as close as it is."

Was he telling her the truth? Could he ever be part of a large family like hers?

This time their conversation slowed to a stop because a guitarist strolled around the deck. Caprice recognized the folk melodies, beginning with "Blowin' in the Wind."

She leaned close to Seth, asking him, "Did you ask him to play that tonight?"

"Could be I told him to stick to the sixties and seventies. I know that's some of your favorite music."

Dusk had fallen, and the moon was already a

whitish-silver ball hanging in the black sky. Caprice didn't know if she'd ever been anywhere as romantic, if she'd ever been with anyone as romantic. Seth wrapped his arm around her shoulders and pulled her close for a kiss. They were in their own world, surrounded by the falling night.

Nevertheless, when he leaned away, he didn't look happy.

"What's going on, Seth?" she asked quietly, needing to know.

"I have something to tell you. The truth is, I don't know how you're going to react."

She definitely didn't like the start of that. "Do you want to tell me here, or do you want to tell me in private?" Now she was feeling a little scared.

He must have decided "here" was as good a place as any because he said, "I've applied for a one-year trauma and surgical critical care fellowship at Johns Hopkins in Maryland."

Her stomach jumped. "One year starting when?"

"Starting in September."

"That's only a month off."

"I know. Someone dropped out of the program. I read about it and applied. I'll find out soon."

Baltimore wasn't that far away—about an hour and a half tops. But Caprice had been burned by a long-distance relationship once before. Still, she cared about Seth a lot.

Seth took her hand again. "It might not come through. If it doesn't, nothing will change. But if it does . . . then we'll both have a lot to think about."

Yes, they would.

Seth must have seen the disappointment in her

expression, and maybe more. He asked, "Do you want to go, or do you want to stay?"

Caprice was all about enjoying the present moment, as much as any she might forfeit or gain in the future. "That depends," she said, shoving worry onto the back burner for later. "Are you going to share a piece of that chocolate cheesecake the Blue Moon is known for with me?"

"I'll do better than that," he said, standing. He held out his hand to her. "Will you dance with me?"

She took his hand, stood, and went to the postage-stamp-size area of the deck where a few couples were dancing. When Seth took her into his arms, she chose not to think about tomorrow.

Caprice waited in the garden behind Saint Francis of Assisi Catholic Church on Sunday morning for her parents to extricate themselves from their many friends. She really should get going. She had an open house to see to.

But after Mass, her mother had leaned over and whispered in her ear, "I have some news you'll want to hear. Meet me near Saint Francis."

Saint Francis was one of Caprice's favorite saints. Maybe her love of animals had been nurtured through her mom's and Nana Celia's stories about the saint, and his connection with furry creatures. The statue of him had been in the center of the garden in the back of the church for as far back as she could remember. It had been refaced and refurbished like so many things about the old church. But it had withstood the buffeting of time.

The rectory's housekeeper saw to the bright

flowers that surrounded it during the growing season. Right now, the saint, the bird on his shoulder, and the little bunny at his feet were surrounded by red and white geraniums.

She often stood out here after an early Mass feeling the morning breeze on her face, sitting on the concrete bench near Saint Francis, thinking about all the things one should think about after church and before the day shifted into high gear. She wondered if Joe and Bella would be coming to a later Mass, or if they weren't venturing out today. Nikki and Vince often attended Saturday night services to keep their Sunday free. But Caprice enjoyed this early-morning quiet and the well wishes of friends and parishioners she'd known all her life.

Caprice's mom, dressed in a pale blue summer skirt and blouse, left the group where Nana and her dad were still talking to friends. She sat down next to Caprice on the bench. "I know you need to get going, but I thought you might be interested in what I found out."

Suddenly her mom was on her feet again, waving to a woman who'd come out of the back of the church. She called, "Melinda," and motioned the blonde to join them.

Caprice recognized Melinda Barnhart, the director of the community center.

"I was talking to Melinda this morning before church," her mom explained. "She told me that Bob was excited about a new project he was involved in, some kind of smartphone app."

It seemed funny to hear those words roll off her mom's tongue, but more and more people her age were becoming tech-savvy. As a teacher working with teens, her mother prided herself on knowing the latest lingo.

After Caprice and Melinda exchanged a greeting, Fran directed Melinda, "Tell Caprice what you were telling me."

Melinda glanced around to see if anyone else was listening. "Bob told me to keep the news under my hat, but now that he's dead . . . It's such a shame. He was such a friendly young man. He related so well to the kids."

"So you and Bob were close?" Caprice asked, unsure where this was headed.

Melinda thought about it.

"Not close as in good friends. But . . . he lost his mother when he was a teenager. When we were working with the kids, he talked to me about that a couple of times, explaining how he understood where they were coming from, especially the sullen and alienated ones. Apparently he'd gone through a stage like that himself. So I guess in some ways, though I hate to say it because it makes me feel old, he looked on me as a mother figure. He often asked my advice when working with the teens and ran ideas by me before the board meetings."

"I see," Caprice said, and she did. She didn't know what she'd do without her parents. If she didn't have them, she'd always be trying to fill the void. Maybe Bob had done that too.

Her mother seemed to know what her daughter was thinking because she squeezed Caprice's arm as if to say, *I'm always going to be around, one way or another.*

Melinda saw the gesture and smiled approvingly. She went on, "Anyway, Bob told me about this phone app he'd invented. Apparently it was going to be hooked to sales in a chain of home-improvement stores. You could go to the app and take a picture of a color you'd like to see in a paint. The color of that object would be digitally matched and transferred to the store for paint preparation. He'd confided he'd be receiving a tidy sum for the deal."

After Caprice thought about that for a moment, she asked, "Did he say what he was going to do with the money?"

"No, he didn't. But he was excited and more than a little happy about it. Who wouldn't be? He gave the impression it could fund anybody's retirement, but he didn't say specifically that's what he was going to do."

"Did he mention if anyone else knew about it?"

"No. And because he asked me to keep it a secret, I assumed nobody did."

That was an assumption Caprice couldn't make. A tidy sum from a phone app could be another motive for murder. Just who would gain from it? Who would have gained from it if Bob died?

Those were questions Caprice was going to find the answers to.

It was almost nine o'clock that night when Caprice's doorbell rang. Sophia was sprawled across her lap as she stretched out on the sofa, reading through a few articles she'd printed out about the latest trends and decorating innovations. Shasta lay on the floor beside her, and every once in a while, Caprice dropped her hand and petted her head, thinking about the log home's open house and how well it had gone. Denise was pretty sure an offer would come in tomorrow.

Shasta seemed to be on alert moments before the doorbell rang. Sophia, on the other hand, complained with a loud meow when Caprice nudged her up so she could answer the door. She switched on the porch light and peered through one of the four small glass windows set into the door. She couldn't have been more surprised. Grant stood there.

When she opened the door, he didn't smile a "hello." He simply said, "I'm concerned about Joe and Bella. Can we talk?"

She might have expected this visit from Vince, not from Grant.

"Sure, come on in. Has something happened?"

"Not specifically."

He stooped over and patted Shasta, who was already rubbing her head against his leg. Grant wore a chambray shirt with the collar open and his sleeves rolled up. His jeans appeared to have seen many washings.

"What does 'not specifically' mean?"

He didn't answer her. He didn't give Shasta another pat. He did ask, "When is she due?"

"My vet says probably a few weeks."

"How many pups will she have?"

"She could have five or six."

"If you don't find her owner, do you think you can find homes for all of them?"

"I *will* find homes for all of them, though I might keep one."

"And Shasta?"

"Well, of course and Shasta. I'm still hoping her owner might see one of the flyers I made and pinned

on bulletin boards in grocery stores and places like
that. I also placed a notice again in the community
paper."

"But you'll keep her if you can't find where she belongs."

"We've already formed a little family here. No,
Sophia's not really happy about it, but she'll adjust.
Pets aren't really that different from people. It just
takes time. Would you like something to drink?"

"Actually, I would. The temperature out there isn't
dropping much."

"I've got fresh-squeezed lemonade or iced herbal
peach tea."

"Lemonade."

"Oh, and I made blueberry bread. Would you like
a slice of that?"

"Sounds good."

As she led Grant through the dining room into
the kitchen, she wondered if Seth was eating *his* blueberry bread. It seemed a little odd that she was giving
it to both men right now. Not really odd. A coincidence.

She shook off any thoughts of comparing the two
men. There were no comparisons to make. Grant
was here on business. Mostly business.

After she filled the lime green and fuchsia-striped
glasses with ice and poured the lemonade, she
placed one in front of Grant on the table.

He took a few swallows. "This is great, thanks. It
tastes like my mom's."

"Is that good?"

"It brings back memories of when I was a kid."

He didn't talk much about anything personal, so
she waited, seeing if he'd open up more. Taking the

blueberry bread from the refrigerator, she cut off two slices, put them on a napkin, and set them in the microwave.

"It's better warmed up. It will go great with the lemonade. Trust me."

He gave a shrug, and thirty seconds later, she placed a slice in front of him.

"One thing I don't understand about you," Grant said seriously, as if she were a terrifically complicated puzzle, "and there are a lot of things . . . is how you can take an animal in and then give it away. I mean I saw you give up those kittens. That was hard for you. Certainly you're going to get attached to Shasta's pups. Then you'll have to give them away. Doesn't that sense of loss do something to you?"

She wondered exactly what he was getting at. Maybe not *her* sense of loss as much as his.

"What you're really asking me is do I get over it. Not exactly. But knowing the animals I've placed in good homes are happy is the important thing for me, not what I feel when I let them go. And I tell myself, I have to let them go."

"You can tell yourself that over and over again, and still not believe it. Not where it counts."

He sounded almost resentful about that fact. Was he thinking about his ex-wife . . . his daughter?

Before she stopped herself, she asked, "Do you ever see your ex-wife?"

"I didn't mean to get into that kind of conversation," he muttered.

When she remained quiet, he took a few more swallows of lemonade, then he said, "No, I don't see her."

But did he still have feelings for her? Caprice had

been involved with a divorced man, and she'd gotten burned badly. She'd fallen in love not only with him, but also with his child. When he'd returned to his wife, both relationships had fallen apart.

Maybe Grant hadn't really let go. Maybe that bond of losing a child would always tether him to his ex-wife.

He stared down at the blueberry bread and the way the blueberries had puffed in the oven, spreading their sweet goodness throughout the bread. When the bread was warm, the blueberries tasted even better, and so did the pecans. He tore off a corner of the bread and popped it into his mouth, maybe hoping to end the conversation.

He chewed and then smiled. "You do know how to bake."

"I was taught by the best. Nana and Mom also taught us that no matter what happens, we can be stronger and do better because of it."

He leaned back in his chair, and his expression didn't become grim, as she thought it might. It became almost amused. "Are you giving me a lecture?"

"Would it do any good if I was?"

"Probably not."

"So are you going to tell me why you're concerned about Bella and Joe?"

"I can't explain specifics, but I can tell you I've heard rumors. There's talk about an arrest warrant."

"Do they think they've found evidence from what they've collected?"

"That's possible."

"Which one's in more danger?"

"I can't really say."

"No, you can't say. But Joe's your client, so Joe has to be the person of most interest."

"I didn't say that."

"Oh, Grant, quit it. You don't have to be secretive with me. If Bella had the problem, Vince would have already talked to me."

"I looked into Kent Osgood," Grant said. "He is what he seems. He's from Allentown. He lived there all his life. He took vocational courses in high school, and when he got out, he started apprenticing on a paint crew. He worked in a home-improvement store for a while, but then decided he liked to paint."

"Why did he come to Kismet?"

Grant shrugged. "He never knew his dad. His mom died with complications from lupus a couple of years ago. He wandered a bit, but he came here because he said he liked the looks of the town online. He figured people here valued good work, and he knew he was a good painter. Bob hired him on, and the rest is history."

"What about Danny Flannery? Did you talk to him?"

"If you can call what he and I did talking. He's a teenager. I couldn't engage him in chitchat or conversation about Bob. He clammed up tight."

"So what's the bottom line?" Caprice asked. "Why did you come over?"

He looked her squarely in the eyes, hesitated a few minutes, then finally revealed, "The murder weapon was a ball-peen hammer. Can you imagine Bella swinging one of those? I'm hearing that Joe is the one without an alibi. He also had a strong motive and the opportunity. So I'm here to tell you, we could be in this for the long haul. Joe could be arrested, and I want you to be prepared."

How could she ever prepare for a member of her family being charged with murder?

Chapter Ten

Some nights Caprice just grabbed a quick supper, which meant thawing a wedge of lasagna she'd frozen and mixing up a salad, or grabbing a container of White Rose Dairy strawberry yogurt from the refrigerator and sitting at her desk with it while she worked. Healthier than ice cream, right?

Sophia definitely agreed. Shasta thought anything Caprice ate was a treat for her too.

After a peek into the fridge on Monday evening, Caprice grabbed an egg and a dish of steamed broccoli. All right, she'd eat healthy. Well, sort of healthy. A frocia would be perfect. Her dad liked it made with asparagus, but Caprice wasn't picky.

As she whipped the egg with a fork, she thought about the top suspects for Bob's murder. There was Jackie, Bob's girlfriend. There was Danny, an angry teenager. Possibly Kent, who had recently become Bob's partner, but that wasn't common knowledge. Why? Because it had happened recently, or for some other reason? Then she considered Joe. She just couldn't believe her own brother-in-law was capable of murder.

When Caprice had whipped the egg into a froth of foam—she wielded a wicked fork—she set the small bowl on the counter. She was rummaging in the cupboard for a cast-iron pan when her cell phone played its Beatles' tune.

Shasta barked, a new habit that was supposed to alert Caprice to the call . . . or else Shasta was a connoisseur of Beatles' music.

With the frying pan in one hand, she picked up her phone from the counter with the other. It was Bella.

"How are you?" Caprice asked.

"I need you. Can you come to the urgent care center? Mom's phone is going to voice mail, and Joe isn't answering either."

"Take a breath and tell me what's going on."

"It's Timmy. He got hurt playing baseball. Seth sent him to X-ray, and he's trying to schedule us an appointment with an orthopedic doctor."

So Seth was on duty this evening. She pushed their last conversation out of her head, as she'd been doing ever since he'd told her he might be leaving Kismet. Her heart was heavy with the idea just when she'd been feeling so hopeful.

Timmy. Her focus should be on Timmy. "I'll be right there."

She didn't know what else to say. Bella had experienced her share of stress lately, that was for sure.

Five minutes later, she'd warned Shasta and Sophia to behave as she locked the door and headed for her Camaro, no worse for the wear after being impounded.

This time of day, the Kismet urgent care center was parked up and busy. The center needed two doctors on a shift at a time, but Seth had admitted they didn't allot funds for two. Is that why he was considering taking a fellowship? Because the job here was too hectic?

The scene inside the waiting room was controlled chaos. Every seat was taken. Three patients were lined up at the registration window. How was she going to get back to Bella and Timmy?

Bella must have understood the situation and known when to expect Caprice because she popped out of the doorway that led back to the exam rooms and motioned for Caprice to come with her.

Caprice rushed over without hesitating. "Where's Timmy?"

"He's back here with the nurse. Seth is going to put a temporary cast on his arm. It's a madhouse today. Of all days . . . I could have taken him to York Hospital, but I knew this would be faster. Maybe I should have gone there. I couldn't get hold of Joe."

Bella was working herself into a state, and she had every right to. But soon she'd be crossing the line into tears, and Caprice knew Bella would hate breaking down here. So she wrapped her in a hug right there in the middle of the hall. De Lucas believed hugs were almost as good as food.

A nurse flew by. Loud voices sounded from another cubicle, but Caprice paid them no mind.

Finally Bella pushed away. "I'm all right, really I am. I have to be. The kids need me. Come on, Timmy will be glad to see you. I'm probably making him more scared than he already is."

When they reached the cubicle, Seth was there.

He'd encased Timmy's arm in a plastic cast. "There's your mom now. I told you she wouldn't desert you. It looks as if she brought reinforcements."

His gaze met Caprice's, and Caprice knew from the bottom of her Capezios she didn't want him to leave Kismet. But she might not have any say about that. She would, however, have some say over what would happen if he did leave, and what she'd do about it.

Caprice went over to Timmy and smoothed his hair from his brow. "Hey there, big guy, what happened?"

She could see the lines of tears on his cheeks, and his uniform was streaked with dirt.

"I slid into third base. I stole it, but my arm bent under me in a bad way."

"It could happen to anybody stealing a base," Caprice told him seriously. "Does it hurt?"

He looked her straight in the eye and then said what his dad would probably have said. "Not much."

However, she could tell that wasn't true. He was pale, and having X-rays taken for something that hurt was no fun.

Seth turned to Bella. "I need your permission to talk to you about Timmy with Caprice here."

"Of course, you have it. She's my emergency number, along with my husband."

Seth nodded.

But a nurse came to the door. "Dr. Randolph, I need you in room two."

"Is blood involved?" he asked.

"No, just an impatient gentleman."

"Then I need five minutes. Stall him. Give him a bottle of water or something."

Five minutes. How he must hate going from patient to patient like this, not giving them the time he felt they needed. Was this what all of medicine was becoming? Maybe so.

Seth took a tablet from a drawer and found a pen on the counter.

He explained, "Fortunately, from what the X-rays show, I think Timmy just has a greenstick fracture. That means the bone isn't broken the whole way through. But I'm not an orthopedic doc." He drew a picture on the tablet of the kind of fracture Timmy had. After he asked Bella if she understood and she said she did, he addressed Caprice. "Are you going to stay with her, maybe drive her home?"

"I can drive," Bella protested.

But Caprice understood what Seth was saying. Bella was worried about Timmy. Since she was concerned about him and everything else that was going on, she might not have her mind on what she was doing.

"I'll drive her home," she assured him. "Nikki can bring me back for my car later."

From the counter, Seth took a sheaf of papers that were stapled together. On the top, Caprice could see a business card. He handed the papers to Bella.

"I need you to sign down at the bottom that you understand everything I told you. Do you have any more questions?"

"No. I just want to get him home."

"I know that. But his arm has to be properly taken care of. You don't want it healing the wrong way. The card on top belongs to the doctor I called. His practice is in York, and he'll fit you in tomorrow. This appointment isn't with a P.A., but with him. It's clinic day there, and everybody will be lined up on gurneys in a long room, but he's good, Bella. He'll study those X-rays, and he might ask for more. He'll make sure Timmy gets the best care."

"Oh, Seth, thank you."

"No thanks necessary. It's my job." He tapped Timmy on the head. "I just want to see you back out on that field, reaching for those fly balls, swinging at the good ones."

"But I won't be able to play," Timmy complained.

"Probably not this season. But next season should be great." He helped Timmy down from the table and said to Bella, "I've given you a prescription there for pain medication. Follow the directions exactly. If he says he doesn't want it, watch him, because if the pain gets too out of hand, and then you give it to him, his discomfort will take a lot longer to settle down. For tonight, use it as directed, and tomorrow talk to the orthopedic doctor about it. Got it?"

Just then, Caprice heard a voice she recognized in the hall. Joe Santini had arrived, and he wasn't as quiet as he'd been at their last Sunday dinner. He was full of spurting energy, and growling stress.

"Where are they?" she heard him ask.

"Come right this way," one of the staff informed him. Soon there he was, in the cubicle with them all, face-to-face with Bella. Caprice had never seen him look exactly like that before—over-the-top anxious, ready to break down.

"Is he all right? What are we going to do? Does he have to go to the hospital?"

Although Caprice knew Seth felt pressured by waiting patients to move on, he didn't rush. He stood

there and told Joe everything he'd explained to
Bella.

"Take him home and try to make him forget
about it for tonight."

Joe and Bella exchanged a look, and Caprice
wasn't sure what it meant.

Then Joe went to Timmy. "I'm sorry I wasn't at
your game, Bud. I know I haven't been around much
lately. That's going to change."

Seth pointed to the paperwork. "Just take that
with you, and you can leave. But if you want to talk,
just stay right here."

Then Seth was gone, moving on, the way doctors did.

Joe looked at Bella, really looked at Bella, maybe
for the first time in weeks. The perfectly coifed,
manicured, and made-up Bella was nowhere in sight,
and hadn't been for a while.

"I can leave, too," Caprice said.

But Joe protested. "No need. You might as well
know where I've been too. You can tell your parents,
Nikki, Vince, and anybody else who wants to know.
I've been talking with Father Gregory at Saint Francis. I've always respected him. When I was in high
school, he kept me on the straight and narrow."

Joe turned to his wife. "I didn't just meet up with
him by chance. I had an appointment with him.
That's why I had my phone turned off. I wasn't trying
to avoid you. I just needed some privacy while he and
I talked."

Bella's voice was shaky when she asked, "What did
you talk about?"

"I talked about us. Not the murder. Not Bob. But

us. He wants to have a session with both of us. He thinks he can help."

When Caprice thought about Father Gregory, she thought about a short, rotund man with kind brown eyes and a practically bald head. Could he possibly put Joe and Bella's marriage back together again? No, but maybe they could. Maybe it wasn't too late. Maybe it wasn't too far gone. Just the fact that Joe was bringing this to Bella meant so much.

Joe took Bella's hand—the first sign of affection she'd seen between them since this whole thing had blown up. "Will you come with me on Wednesday? He's free at two."

"But you have to work."

"I have vacation time coming. This isn't the busiest time of the year. I might have to take off an afternoon once a week for a while. That's what Father's suggesting. Will you make the time, too?"

Now Caprice felt that she shouldn't be here. If Bella and Joe had issues to work out, they needed to do it with the priest. Or in privacy. Hovering family could hinder the whole process.

Still beside Timmy, Caprice dropped her arm around his shoulders. "How about you and I go out to the front and wait. It'll only be a couple of minutes."

"Can I go home in your car, Aunt Caprice? It's cool."

"I'll be glad to drop you off at home, if your parents want me to."

Joe came over to Timmy and gave him a hug. "I know that son-of-a-gun has to hurt, but you think it will hurt a little bit less if you ride in Aunt Caprice's rad car?"

Timmy smiled, the first smile Caprice had seen since she'd come in. "It might help," he agreed.

Joe chuckled. "All right. You go with Aunt Caprice, and I'll drive your mom. I'll walk back here later tonight and get her car. For now, I'll settle up at the desk and meet you outside."

It looked as if Joe was taking charge again, doing what he thought was best for his family, protecting all of them in his way. Maybe he and Bella could put things back together with a little guidance.

As Joe spoke to the receptionist who took care of checking out patients, Timmy wandered over to the window to stare outside at Caprice's yellow Camaro.

Bella touched Caprice's arm.

Her sister looked worn-out and a little shell-shocked, as if her world had suddenly taken a ninety-degree turn and she wasn't quite ready for it. It had been doing a lot of that lately. "I'm scared," she almost whispered.

"Of Joe?"

"No, of what's happened to us. What if we can't fix it?"

"If you can't fix it, you'll find the next best thing to do. Father Gregory can help."

"You really believe that?"

"I do. You know how he used to come over for dinner, and then stay long after we all went to bed?"

"Yes, I do."

"If you think about it, he was there the most when Mom and Dad were having skirmishes with Vince about school. I think he was unofficially counseling them on what to do." She hoped Joe and Bella could resolve whatever problems they were having so they could welcome Timmy's brother or sister with open arms . . . so they'd be a happy family again.

She caught a glimpse of Seth as he came to the front desk to speak with the receptionist.

And her and Seth? Only time would tell what was going to happen there. Seth was obviously too busy to spend even two minutes with her tonight. That was just as well because she had a presentation to prepare. It wasn't an official presentation, but an informal one. A builder of midrange model homes, a man who had introduced himself as Derrick Gastenaux, had expressed interest in her services. She was going to inspect those homes tomorrow and hope they could come to an agreement. So tonight she'd be thinking about bare drywall and hardwood floors, and houses families wanted turned into homes.

She just hoped the Santini home would be peaceful once more.

The following morning, Caprice didn't know when she was aware of the feeling that she was being watched. She just knew at some point that she was. She had errands to run before she was supposed to meet Derrick Gastenaux at the model home site. Her calendar reminded her she had a client meeting in York at nine, and she intended to stop at the rental company on the way back to Kismet. She had a few more items to choose for the Sumpter estate open house. Fortunately, she found them at the rental company's warehouse. A checkerboard alpaca rug along with an old-world chest would fit in with the Wild Kingdom theme beautifully.

Maybe it was when she exited the rental company

and climbed into her car that she noted the white
SUV with the tinted windows in the same parking lot.
On the road again, she thought she spied it in her
rearview mirror. But that was silly. There were a lot of
white SUVs on the roads. She really didn't think a
whole lot about it, not then anyway.

Still . . . she had chills running up her arms that
couldn't be explained. Her Nana had always told her
to pay attention to anything her body was trying to
communicate to her. Caprice did most of the time,
but this watched-over feeling was new.

Maybe she was just getting paranoid. Maybe investigating Bob's murder was something she should
leave to the police. After all, Grant, Seth, and her
family all thought so. She'd had an experience with
someone in an SUV when she was investigating the
murder several weeks back.

Maybe it was just SUVs that spooked her . . . or
tinted windows.

Brushing it all off as anxiety over Bella and
Joe—or nervousness about the awards dinner or
distraction because of the possibility she and Seth
could be through before they'd hardly begun—she
drove through the countryside outside of Kismet for
about a half mile. She couldn't help glancing in her
rearview mirror.

Now she saw no one.

Yep, she'd watched too many suspense programs
on TV.

However, when she arrived at the model home
site, the property had a deserted feeling. She was
supposed to meet the builder at 1 Drury Lane. Numbers 3 and 5 were in the construction process, but

number 1 was under roof and almost complete. He'd said he'd be there at noon.

It was noon. She pulled her car into the gravel driveway and cut the engine. Taking her tablet computer with her—it had her presentation notes—she climbed out of her car and looked around.

Kismet was located in an area of Pennsylvania where rolling hills were the norm. From all angles of the development, green fields led into the distance. It really was a bucolic setting. These homes weren't mansions, but they looked to be anywhere from three to five thousand square feet and were designed for families with upper middle incomes. She knew staging them would be her best advertisement for future work.

Walking around the side of the house, she did see a pickup truck parked out back. Maybe that belonged to Derrick Gastenaux. Possibly he was doing something inside and waiting for her.

She walked to the front door of the house. It was one of those overly expansive doors with a row of windows across the top. She turned the knob and found it unlocked.

Stepping inside, she was met by newly framed rooms and the smells of lumber and fresh drywall.

She called, "Mr. Gastenaux?"

There was a hollow echo, and she didn't hear any response. Stairs in the foyer led up to the second floor. It never really entered her head to hesitate or to first go outside and call to see if the builder was out there. After all, he could be doing something upstairs.

After she climbed the stairs, she peered into one of the four huge bedrooms. The master suite was going to have a gigantic bath with a whirlpool tub and step-in shower. Wandering back through the bedroom, thinking about what she wanted to do next, she heard a noise downstairs. Maybe Gastenaux had seen her car and was ready to start their meeting.

She called out again, "Mr. Gastenaux, I'm up here."

But no one answered.

Now she was getting those chills up and down her arms again. A sixth sense? Or just fear.

She supposed the best thing to do was to return downstairs, right?

But what if—

No what-ifs.

Taking her pepper-spray gun from her heavily macraméd purse—a girl never knew when she might need such a thing—she slipped her tablet under her arm with her purse and held the spray gun. Descending the steps slowly, she listened but didn't hear a sound. Not right away. But then she heard the purr of an engine and the crunch of tires on gravel, and she hurried down the rest of the stairs.

The door was closed. Hadn't she left it open? She hadn't heard it bang shut.

Rushing to it, she opened it, and there was a white SUV surging down Drury Lane away from the model home development. Had someone followed her here?

If so, who? More important . . . why?

Chapter Eleven

"You could have painted stripes on the piano," Denise said as she nudged Caprice's elbow on Sunday.

Guests had arrived at the Sumpter estate even before the official four o'clock open house began. Quite a property, the estate boasted a high security gate, a long driveway, and a sprawling floor plan. It had sunken rooms, modernized bathrooms featuring neutral-bowl sinks, a pool, and a pool house that was bigger than any studio apartment. Caprice and the estate's owner, Colin Sumpter, had decided a Wild Kingdom theme would be perfect. Colin had told Denise, as well as Caprice, that he didn't care what they did to the house as long as they sold it. The estate had once been his home base, but now that he was making more frequent trips abroad, he'd decided he'd rather own a villa in Tuscany.

"Stripes would have been over the top," Caprice remarked, as one of the guests commented on the metalwork wall hanging that depicted a savannah with lions, as well as the low-slung, off-white sofa decorated with leopard-print pillows.

"You do over-the-top quite well. I really doubted you could pull this one off—the color scheme is almost theatrical."

Caprice understood what Denise was saying. She'd used a palette of rich rusts, golds, black and white, and deep chocolate against an off-white background. There were black and white striped lampshades as well as caramel and chocolate colored, rich faux-fur throws. In the bedrooms, she'd mixed gold and brown brocade comforters with lighter tan fabrics that almost resembled burlap. After searching high and low online, she'd found unique pieces—for instance, the three-foot-long sleek panther statue that stood in the archway to the dining room like a sentinel. In alcoves and on shelves she'd employed pottery in various sizes in red and orange and black. Against a cream backdrop, they were well placed and uncluttered. The overall scheme made a statement that this house was indeed special.

Denise gestured to the wall near the stone fireplace.

"Just where did you get that sisal hanging? It looks as if you brought it in straight from Kenya." The hanging portrayed a trio of elephants heading toward a water hole.

"You won't believe it, but I found that in one of those little shops in Peddler's Village."

"In Lahaska?"

"Yep. I've had it in my storage shed for about a year."

"Those lounge chairs you located for around the pool—patterned with vines entwined all over the cushions—are perfect. How do you get your ideas?"

"I don't know. And that's the fun of it. I see a wall

and know what I want to put on it. I see a sofa and love seat and can envision the exact coffee table that should be there. Nana tells me not to think about it too much because that will upset the mystery of it. I believe she's right." She was having tea with Nana tomorrow afternoon and was looking forward to it. Maybe Nana would have insight into what had happened at the model home before Mr. Gastenaux arrived. Maybe she'd just agree that Caprice was paranoid.

"Speaking of mysteries . . ." The real estate agent's expression became very serious. "I heard there wasn't going to be a funeral for Bob Preston. Is that true?"

"He left instructions with his lawyer that he didn't want anything at all. He was cremated, and I don't have any idea what happened to his ashes. I guess they'll be buried without a service."

"How odd," Denise said.

"Maybe not so odd. He didn't have any family."

Nikki suddenly waved to Caprice from the kitchen, and she looked a bit frantic. Nikki never looked frantic, not when she was catering anyway. With her brown, highlighted hair and her wide, golden-brown eyes, she was the pretty girl next door. For this bash she wore a black, short-sleeved Oxford shirt and black slacks that sort of matched the background. All the servers were dressed the same way.

Caprice excused herself from her conversation with Denise and went to Nikki, who grabbed her arm and led her to the quiet corner of a room that wasn't occupied—yet. Soon they'd all be occupied with the crowd that seemed to be pouring in.

She said, "I have Jocelyn watching the boar paninis and the bison meatballs. Mom just called."

Caprice reached into her flowing, calf-length skirt—leopard-print, of course—for her phone, but Nikki stayed her hand.

"No, she called me. She thought I wouldn't be quite as busy as you." She rolled her eyes. "Bella stopped in and she was pretty upset."

"Bella told me she didn't want to involve Mom and Dad."

"I know, but I guess we weren't available, so Mom's the next best thing."

"When I asked Bella about her and Joe's first counseling session, she gave the impression it went okay."

"Okay's a relative term. Father Gregory listened to them both, had them listen to each other, and then made a suggestion."

"Which was?"

"Every day they're supposed to spend a half hour talking to each other and looking at each other straight in the eyes, while someone else watches the kids. He doesn't want them to do it late at night when they're both tired."

"Okay," Caprice said warily. "So what's the problem?"

"Apparently Bella, Joe, and the kids, Mom and Dad all went to noon Mass. Then Mom and Dad took the kids home with them. Well . . . when Joe and Bella came to pick them up, there was a whole lot of static in the air. Bella was close to tears. Apparently Joe asked her if this baby is his!"

Caprice gasped and then realized if *she* was that shocked, she could only imagine how her sister felt.

"He thinks it's Bob's?"

"Your guess is as good as mine. But I don't know how they're ever going to get over this one. Father Gregory might have to call down a few saints. Don't give me that look," Nikki added. "I still pray to Saint Jude for anything impossible I want to do."

Caprice almost smiled, but then she shook her head. "I don't know how to help them."

"I don't think we can. But if the real story behind Bob's murder came out, I think it might help. Maybe then Joe can see Bella was just looking for a little innocent attention. Who are the suspects?" Nikki asked.

"Jackie Fitz was Bob's girlfriend. The way Bob flirted and dated, she could have a motive, even if it isn't his coffee date with Bella."

"You met with Jackie?"

"Briefly."

"Does she seem the type?"

"I don't know. We've got calculated murder on the one hand, or . . . a crime of passion on the other. Who knows what a woman's capable of when she's riled up enough, or a man for that matter? On the male side of the equation, we have Bob's partner, Kent Osgood. I'd like to find out what happens to Bob's side of the business now that he's dead. From what I understand they haven't been partners very long. And then there's Danny Flannery. He had an argument with Bob before Bob was murdered. He's sullen and defiant enough to get into a fistfight, but I can't imagine him swinging a ball-peen hammer. My guess is the murder weapon was one of the tools lying around for the construction and remodeling at the center. The police confiscated some of Joe's tools, but if they found blood on them and analyzed it, he would have been arrested by now."

"Unless the labs are backed up."

"I just don't think it was Joe. I can't believe that."

Nikki shook her head, "I can't either. You mentioned Danny Flannery. I know his mom, Sharla. She works at the Cupcake House. She's blunt and honest, and I think if you talk to her, she'd probably tell you the truth."

"About her own son?"

"She's spoken to me now and then about his problems in school. He doesn't get along with the other kids. She thinks it's because he's artistic, and that could be. Different doesn't sell well."

Caprice knew that firsthand. She'd gone to Catholic school, and she'd tried to be the good little girl who didn't ask too many questions and took everything on faith. But she just wasn't that type. The years she hadn't had teachers who understood her curiosity were rough. Classmates who didn't want to rock the boat didn't like her. It wasn't until she'd graduated from high school and gone to college that she realized her questions kept her excited about life. Her desire to search—for something better, something new, or something old—enlivened all of her experiences. She hung around with kids who liked her quirks, and she found being unique was not a bad thing. As an older sister, Nikki had seen that transformation in her and had applauded it. Nikki herself didn't much like rules and regulations, so they could be a real pair. Maybe that's why Bella had taken an overly traditional route for her life.

But now Caprice wasn't so sure she was happy with

it. "I'll make sure I stop in at the Cupcake House tomorrow. Roz often buys their specials."

All of a sudden, something in the house seemed different to Caprice. When she'd joined Nikki, there had been groups of house hunters conversing. Noise of one sort or another was generated from every room. But now there seemed to be a stark silence.

"Do you hear it?" she asked Nikki.

"Hear what? I don't hear anything."

"That's exactly my point. Something must have happened or the house wouldn't be so quiet. I can't believe everybody would have left."

"What if there's another murder?"

"Don't even think it."

Caprice and Nikki rushed from the room toward the hall. They could see into the living room and to the foyer beyond. Everyone was standing still, the crowd all turned toward the door.

"I wonder if this is Denise's famous client."

As Caprice and Nikki approached the living room, chatter began again. But it was all chatter aimed at the individual who'd walked in with two men at his side. One, big and burly, looked like a bodyguard. He had a full beard and appeared tough enough to wrestle anybody to the ground. On the center figure's other side stood a shorter man in a yellow linen jacket, white slacks, and a royal blue tie. *A manager maybe?* Caprice wondered, because she now recognized the man who had caused the fuss.

Ace Richland was a rock star from the eighties. He'd appeared on a reality show last year, and social media as well as an excellent publicist had given his career a huge upswing. Caprice had heard he'd planned a comeback tour. She recognized him because she liked his music and played his old stuff. Everything from "Gotta Keep Her Yours," to "Zingy Chick" to "Swinging for a Future" and "Wrestling the World." She could even sing some of the lyrics.

Denise must have been watching for him because she rushed over and shook his hand. She shook the hand of the man in the yellow jacket too, but not the big, burly guy's. Then, scanning the crowd, she spotted Caprice. She asked the burly guy to make way for her, which he did.

Seconds later, Caprice stood before Ace Richland, staring at his spiked-brown hair, which was stiffer than some of the plants in her garden. His earring was at least two carats of sparkling diamond. He was dressed in designer jeans matched with a navy silk shirt that clung to a body that had seen a lot of workouts. Ace might be hitting fifty, but he'd kept himself in shape. Or else he'd gotten back in shape to go on that reality show, and it had paid off.

When Denise introduced Ace to Caprice, she felt herself blush a little. She couldn't be star-struck, could she?

Ace was a tall, lean man, and there was a lot of power in his handshake. "It's nice to meet you, Miss De Luca. Denise told me you came up with the theme for this staging."

"I did. I just thought it seemed to fit. Many of the leopard spots and stripes can be removed, leaving a cream background for black leather furniture that would go well in anyone's home. Accents are usually the start."

When he released her hand, she looked up into his green eyes and said, "I read the reality show article. You related your experience in the jungle as you searched for a route out. You turned introspective about the experience."

"Yes, I did. During that god-awful isolation, when I was crawling up trees to find food to survive, I decided if I ever got out of there, I'd plan a comeback tour."

"I'd love a front-row seat," she said, before she could filter her thoughts.

"You're young to be familiar with my music."

"I like all music. I'm familiar with the Beatles, Chad and Jeremy, Paul Revere and the Raiders. Your group kind of reminded me of them. Your harmonies. Your guitar skill."

"Wow, you are a fan! I bet you might even know my real name."

"I do. It's Al Rizzo, and the reason I took an interest in it is because I'm Italian, too."

"And cooking is everything?" he asked with a twinkle in his eye.

"I don't know about everything, but it's a lot. It brings our whole family together."

"Mom makes me lasagna whenever I get home."

Denise said, "Why don't I show you around the property."

"If you don't mind, can Miss De Luca do it? If she arranged all this furniture in here, I'm sure she's familiar with it too. I just have to decide if I like it. When we're done and if I do, I'll talk to you about price."

Denise looked a little flustered, and Caprice wasn't sure how to handle this. The real estate agent always took over at the showing, and this was the first time a client had asked her for a tour.

"I'm Ace's manager," the man in the yellow suit

said, shaking Caprice's hand. "Trent Jarvick here.
I've spoken with Denise on the phone. Why don't I
get all the paperwork and statistics from her while
Ace takes a look around."

Ace looked over his shoulder. "Charlie can stay
with you."

"Ace . . ." Trent warned.

"No one's going to assault me here. Look at this
crowd. They're in their Sunday best. They know I'm
here, but the novelty will wear off. Come on, Miss De
Luca, let's take that tour."

What choice did she have?

As they passed through the dining room, with its
giant pedestal table, swivel rattan chairs, and six-foot
hutch layered with colorful pottery and collector's
items, Ace asked, "Did you know I was coming?"

"Denise told me someone important was coming,
but she didn't tell me who."

He thought about that as they walked. "You can
call me Al or Ace. I answer to both."

She laughed. "You can call me Caprice."

"That's an unusual name. It suits you."

He studied her maxi-dress, a throwback to his era,
though the colorful beads were as popular now as
they were then. "You're as interesting as your surroundings."

When she looked up at him, he shook his head.
"That wasn't a come-on. That was just a statement. I
had my midlife crisis a few years ago when I got my
divorce. Now I don't date anyone who's more than
two years younger than me."

"This is a big house for one person."

"Maybe. But I just want a place away from the
glitz, where I can have a quieter life. With my divorce,

I received partial custody of my daughter. I need a house she can enjoy too. I've toured other properties the past few months, but none were just right. This one possibly could be. I especially like the idea of the pool. I've seen the pictures of it."

"How old is your daughter?"

"She's eleven, and I don't know Trista as well as I should. I can't even blame touring for that because I'd almost stopped touring until the reality show. In lots of ways, that's what shook up my world."

"It sounds as if the past few years haven't been very settled."

He gave a grim laugh. "Settled they were not. I got a divorce the year before the reality show. Trista was nine then. Between nine and eleven I missed a lot. That's going to change now. She might even respect her old man again."

There seemed to be a lot of story he wasn't telling, and Caprice wondered if alcohol or drugs might have been involved too.

She imagined it was difficult to be in the spotlight, and then suddenly that spotlight was gone. How did a man keep his pride, keep his ego shored up, keep his head on straight? Ace seemed like he was thinking clearly once more.

In the media room, Ace stopped before a wall decorated with panels that were two feet wide by four feet high, one in a tiger-skin motif, one in leopard, one in zebra, and one in giraffe. The animal-print rug on the floor coordinated with those, and the black leather seating blended right in. There was a chest at one inset wall, painted in a gold and leopard motif. A floral print in a gold frame hung above it, and leather-bound book volumes stood on it next to a brass compote holding coconut shells.

He smiled. "How long does it take you to do something like this?"

"The media room?" she asked.

Though the huge flat-screen TV was the main component, it didn't overtake the room because of the prints.

"Not just this room. The whole place."

"The actual staging can be done in a couple of days."

"I mean finding everything to stage the house."

"This took about a month. Of course, I was handling other stagings, and living life in between."

"Living life," he said with a sigh. "This new tour my manager set up cuts into that. I'm not as young as I used to be."

"But only as old as you feel."

He narrowed his eyes. "Are you one of those optimists I hear about?"

Now she laughed. "I try to be. Don't you want to do the tour?"

"Oh, yeah, I want to. For the past year since the reality show, my manager's been booking me on late-night TV, morning talk shows, that kind of thing. At the end of the interview I perform, and it feels great. But a solid year of it . . ."

He glanced around the house again. "That's why I need a place away from the lights. This isn't about money for me. Yeah, I have a lifestyle I want to keep up. But I've done pretty well with my investments, and I'm involved in a couple of businesses that have taken off. I can keep busy without music if I want to. Still, a chance to be back in the thick of it again is just too good to pass up."

"What does your daughter think of it?"

"She wasn't around the first time I made good. She's seen the posters, the crazy outfits, the green hair. It's all one big circle. The truth is, I might use her as a consultant for some of the techno-glitter of the show."

"LED lights and fireworks?"

"Something like that."

As they wandered through more rooms, Ace asked her, "So you grew up in Kismet?"

"Sure did."

"You don't find it confining?"

"Not really. My family has always expanded my world. I have a brother and two sisters, parents, and a nana who keeps up with everyone else. There was always lots of activity and stimulation, so I really didn't need to look elsewhere."

"I know what you mean. I've got three brothers back in Scranton. They have no desire to leave, and every time I have a chance to get home, we sit around a pan of lasagna and talk. Though I've got to admit, it wasn't always that way. They weren't into music and often thought I was weird."

They stayed away from the kitchen to avoid the congregation of guests enjoying Nikki's food. Caprice led Ace through a den that had a door to the pool area. He stopped to study an art print of a tropical cheetah family. Absentmindedly, he toyed with a leopard-patterned votive candle holder with swinging panels that caught the air currents and swayed. The drape set at the window with zebra-patterned sheers caught his eye too.

Caprice liked the interest he was showing. It

seemed genuine. But she didn't know if that meant he'd buy the house.

Ace peered out the sliding-glass doors to the pool area, where some guests had gathered.

"Nice pool," he said. "Lights and heat?"

"Yes. Would you like to see it?"

"I think I'll pass. Too many people might want an autograph. I'm just not in the swing of that today."

She suddenly realized that Ace Richland was a persona. Underneath lurked Al Rizzo, a fifty-year-old man who wasn't sure what direction his life was headed in. He thought he wanted to go back, but he wasn't sure about that at all.

"How much time will you spend here?"

"Weeks between gigs. I'm selling my place in L.A. Marsha lives in Virginia with Trista now, close to her family. Kismet would be closer for Trista's visits. We wouldn't have to fly and worry about security hassles. I can have a car service drive her here."

"Or you could pick her up," Caprice suggested.

He was about to protest when he studied her more closely. "You're not in awe of me, are you?"

She laughed. "I'm in awe of the sunrise, or of a litter of kittens, or of a rainbow."

"So you already think I'm a rock legend has-been with no substance?"

"Of course not! I admire what you did, and what you're going to do. I like your music. I have it on my iPod."

"But?"

"No buts. I like to talk to people when I decorate or stage their houses. I try to get to the bottom of who they are. That helps. So I guess I do that in most of my conversations now. I don't mean to invade your privacy."

"Yes, you do. But that's okay. You're better than paparazzi with a long lens." He gave a last look to the expansive patio outside. "I've seen enough. My manager and I are flying back to L.A. in a couple of hours. Walk me out?"

"Of course."

Before they'd reached the foyer, Ace's burly bodyguard and his manager reappeared with Denise. Apparently they'd been monitoring his tour.

Denise unabashedly handed Ace her card.

"I have your number on my phone," he told her. "On the other hand . . ." He stared at Caprice. "Do you have a card?"

Caprice slipped the turquoise card with white print from her pocket. "You can always reach me through Denise. But I don't sell houses. I just stage them."

"I get that," he said, but he pocketed the card and winked. "I'll be in touch."

As Ace, his manager, and his bodyguard left, Denise turned to Caprice. "What's he going to be in touch with you about?"

"I have no idea."

"Did he seem interested?"

"He did. A lot is uncertain in his life right now, and I'm not sure he knows where he wants to settle in between gigs."

"But you convinced him Kismet was best, right?"

"No, I didn't try to convince him of anything. I don't think he's a man who is easily convinced. He needs to make up his own mind."

"I hope you didn't lose me a sale," Denise grumbled.

"You should have treated him like the celebrity he is, gotten him a boar panini and a drink."

"We could have a buyer here other than Ace Richland."

"We'd better," Denise muttered as she walked away.

Caprice wasn't sure what had just happened . . . or maybe she was. Her mind was on Bella and Joe more than it was on selling the Sumpter property. She couldn't do anything about Bella and Joe today. Work had to come first, or she'd lose the reputation she'd built up. She couldn't let that happen.

But she couldn't let Joe or Bella go to prison, either.

Chapter Twelve

The Cupcake House almost looked like a gingerbread house as Caprice approached it Monday morning. Cupcakes of all shapes, sizes, and colors decorated pillars that supported a portico. The awning sported pink and white stripes. Inside, cupcake pedestals displayed the latest trend in frosted cupcakes, plain cupcakes, and over-the-top huge cupcakes. The whole shop was a mix of frosting colors—pink, yellow, white, lilac, deeper blue, and purple. It was Caprice's kind of place.

But . . .

She baked a lot herself, as did everyone in her family, so she didn't need the additional calories from coming in here and buying a half dozen or a dozen cupcakes. Yet she knew from sampling them here and there that they were delicious. She thought about her and Seth sharing a few . . .

Her and Seth. Fade out to the discussion at hand.

Nikki had described Sharla Flannery to her, and Caprice had caught glimpses of her now and then.

After all, Kismet was small, and everyone knew everyone else.

Sharla was a flamboyant redhead, and Caprice wondered if that red had a little help. Nikki told her the woman's personality matched her hair color. So Caprice wasn't sure what to expect when she walked up to the counter to find her filling the display case.

"Be with you in a minute," Sharla said.

She wore a smock decorated with every kind of cupcake imaginable. When she straightened to address Caprice, she smiled. "How can I help you?"

Caprice really didn't want to believe Danny Flannery had anything to do with Bob's murder. However, after talking with him, she believed he was hiding something. If she could find out what that was, maybe she could eliminate him from the mix.

"My name's Caprice De Luca. I'd like to talk to you about your son."

Sharla planted her hands on her hips and looked resigned. "What did he do now?"

"I'm not sure he did anything, but . . . The truth is, I knew Bob Preston, the man who was murdered. He and Danny got into a tiff and scuffed around a little. Do you know anything about that?"

"Are you with the police?" Sharla asked warily.

"No. My sister found Bob. Because she did, the police are looking at her hard, so I'm nosing around. I don't want to invade your privacy, but I'm trying to protect her."

"I certainly understand trying to protect family. I've been doing that for Danny all his life." Sharla took two chocolate cupcakes from inside the case and slid one over to Caprice. "Let's have coffee and talk."

Chocolate, no matter what time of the day it was, wasn't a temptation she resisted well. She was going to go to Shape Up later to swim—and nose around there a bit too. Certainly she could work off one chocolate cupcake.

"It's a slow time, so we're good for a few minutes," Sharla said, as she took two mugs of coffee to one of the small tables, where she and Caprice sat across from each other.

They both unwrapped their cupcakes, and Caprice asked, "Do you make these?"

"I help bake them. The batter's already made up. Dana comes in around four every morning and mixes them all. She keeps the recipes secret. I don't blame her. They're good."

Caprice had learned from Nikki that Dana Hodgkins was the owner of the Cupcake House. "Dana's not here now?" she asked.

"Nope. After her stint from about four a.m. to nine, she takes a few hours before she comes back in."

Caprice took a bite of the decadent chocolate cupcake, closed her eyes, and appreciated it, seeing exactly why Dana kept the recipe secret. After a swig of coffee, she looked at Sharla. "So tell me about Danny."

"He's a good kid, but he's quiet. He's never had a dad around to play catch or throw a football, and the truth is, I haven't been around as much as I should be. I not only work here during the day, but I clean houses at night."

Sharla ate a bite of cupcake, licked icing from her lips, and then said, "I knew Danny was in a fight. His

hand was bruised, and I asked him about it. I might
not be around much, but I do notice things."

Good moms did. And although Sharla had to
work a lot, Caprice already suspected she was a
good mom.

"I always make sure he has plenty of food to eat
and that the neighbor keeps an eye on him. At least
when he was younger she did. But now he doesn't
want anyone watching over him, not even me."

"He thinks he can do everything on his own."

"Exactly. And he can't. Most of all, he doesn't have
close friends. Kids don't like other kids who are
different, and Danny is. He likes to draw pictures
instead of study, so teachers aren't too keen on him,
either. But he's got talent. I just wish I could pay for
art lessons. The budget's being cut in the schools.
There's not much room for artistic creativity in the
curriculum."

Caprice's mom talked about that all the time.
Teachers wanted to expand kids' horizons, but that
was tough with state regulations becoming tighter on
what to teach and not to teach. Education was getting boiled down to how well a student scored on a
standardized test.

"So Danny spends some time at the community
center," Caprice prompted.

"Yes, he does. I knew he'd been helping Bob with
the murals . . ." A look crossed Sharla's face, and it
was a look Caprice knew she had to explore.

"So you knew Bob?"

"Not well, but I did know him. One night, after I
cleaned one of those mansions in Reservoir Heights,
the owner left me a particularly generous tip. I was

so tired, maybe more tired of feeling defeated than physically tired. Do you know what I mean?"

"I do."

"So I just wanted a treat. The Blue Moon Grille has those big, soft pretzels, and they cover them with a mixture of crab and cheese sauce. I was so tired, I just decided to sit at the bar and have a beer with a pretzel, and then take one of them home for Danny. Well, this handsome guy with a great smile and a great body sat down beside me. Honest to goodness, I don't know how long it had been since I thought of myself as a pretty woman. But he started talking right away. He made me laugh. He made me feel . . . special."

Bob was good at that, Caprice knew.

"So I ate my crab pretzel, I had a beer, and so did he. Then we had a pitcher of beer. One thing led to another, and I went home with him. Believe me I know how stupid that was. But he wasn't a complete stranger. I'd seen him around. I've got to admit, I was hoping for more than one night. But one night it was. He never called again. When Danny mentioned he was working with Bob Preston at the community center, I figured that was probably just as well."

"Why?"

"I don't know how well Danny would take to having a man in his life, not at this late stage."

"You don't normally date?"

"Who has time?"

Caprice thought about her and Seth, and how they wanted to date, but how work and other responsibilities often kept them from seeing each other. A single mom with a teenage son and two jobs? When did she have time to date?

"Do you think Danny knew you and Bob had hooked up?"

Sharla shook her head. "I don't see how."

But it was possible Danny had found out. It was possible he didn't like the idea of a man in his mother's life. It was possible he had a motive for murder.

Shape Up, Kismet's workout center, was located on Oak Street near the Country Fields Shopping Center. It had been constructed about ten years ago. About three years ago a pool, a hot tub, and a warm-water arthritis center had been added. Memberships had increased.

Caprice had joined about a month ago, determined to add exercise to her weekly, if not daily, routine. Swimming was about the only exercise she really enjoyed. One evening last week she'd made a good attempt at fifteen laps. She knew she was probably out of shape and had to work up to it if she wanted to do more, but it had been a good start. She liked coming in in the evenings, when the pool area was quieter. If she timed it just right, sometimes it was just her and the lifeguard. She was self-conscious in her bathing suit, and the fewer people who saw her the better, as far as she was concerned. She didn't know how swimsuit models did it. Did they really not mind people watching them?

However, this morning she was going to swim and ask questions about Bob's habits and acquaintances. She already had a nodding acquaintance with the secretary at the registration desk. But as far as other members went, she didn't know many. When she

came to work out, she arrived ready to do just that.
So she didn't dawdle at the vending machines or in
the lounge area where there were a couple of
backgammon tables and magazines. The gym had
public Wi-Fi now too, but who needed that during a
workout?

So she didn't know exactly the best way to learn
more about Bob's habits and friends here, but she
was sure he had them. There was no way Bob could
have worked out without talking to everybody in
sight. That's just the way he was.

Should she ask questions before she swam or afterward? Better before. Afterward she was liable to be
worn out. She was having tea with Nana this afternoon, but her grandmother would understand if she
wasn't a sparkling conversationalist.

The first thing she did was go to the locker room
and stow her gear.

She supposed the only way to do this was to march
into the workout room, head over to one of the
bikes, and see if she could fit in.

She was surprised at the number of people who
were coming and going. Maybe they worked out on
their mid-morning breaks, or took an early lunch. It
was almost eleven.

After pocketing her key in her shorts, she left the
locker room and headed toward the computerized
exercise bicycles. She tried to remember everything
one of the fitness instructors had told her when
she'd taken a tour of the facility before she'd joined.
The buttons were fairly self-explanatory. However,
she really didn't want to climb on that bike, and then
pedal and sweat.

Looking around, she noticed three guys over by

the weights. They looked to be around Bob's age. As Giselle had mentioned the last time she was at Grant and Vince's office, nothing ventured, nothing gained.

With a smile on her face, and acting more confident than she felt, she approached the weight station. The truth was, she didn't know how to flirt, and she wasn't going to even attempt it. Bantering with Seth was one thing. Trying to get information by flirting was another. She didn't feel capable of it.

Instead she approached the three guys. "Hi. I wonder if any of you knew Bob Preston."

All three of them had worn relaxed expressions before, but now they didn't look so relaxed. Their lips thinned, and Caprice wondered if this had been a huge mistake.

Thrown a little off balance, she offered, "I knew Bob. I have a home-staging business and he did painting for me. My sister found his body just after he was killed and I . . . I sort of did, too. We're trying to find some answers about what happened."

One of the guys, a tall blond with a buzz cut, narrowed his eyes. "Isn't that the police's job?"

"Yes, it is," she answered quickly. "But knowing Bob, finding him like that, makes this personal."

The best-looking one of the three, with brown hair tousled over his forehead, his green eyes serious, studied her for a few moments. Then he asked, "Aren't you Nikki De Luca's sister?"

Ever since she was little, Caprice had been called that. Nikki was the older one, the smart one, the pretty one. Caprice had been the middle girl, and maybe that's why she tried so hard to be unique. Being in the middle wasn't always fun.

"Yes, I am." She extended her hand. "Caprice De Luca."

"Chad Hollister. Nikki and I have gone out on a few dates."

The third guy standing there, with russet hair, dressed in a muscle tank and board shorts, repeated, "De Luca. Like in Mrs. De Luca, the English teacher?"

Caprice had to smile. Yep, her mom was well known in Kismet. "She's my mom."

He shook his head. "I hated English, but your mom made it not seem so bad, except when she tried to teach me poetry." He extended his hand. "The name's Patrick."

Caprice laughed as she shook his hand. "Mom loves poetry, especially the nineteen-century English poets."

When Patrick looked blank, Caprice gave up that topic of conversation. Now that the ice was broken, so to speak, she asked, "So did any of you know Bob?"

They all exchanged a look that said guys didn't rat on each other. Guys stuck together. Guys had a man-code. Terrific.

Chad said, "I knew him by sight. Everybody who comes and goes here has a nodding acquaintance."

The blond shrugged. "We talked about the Phillies and the Orioles, how their seasons were going. We spotted each other now and then. But that's about it."

"Bob dated a lot," she said, and just left the statement out there like a helium balloon ready to float.

But there were those guy-looks again. Finally Chad seemed to speak for all of them. "You might want to check out the women's locker room if you want information about that."

"Are you saying guys don't gossip?"

"Guys don't admit they gossip, and they sure don't talk about what they gossiped about," he maintained.

"I understand that. But do any of you know specific women or maybe jealous guys who didn't consider Bob one of their favorite people?"

"He dated and dropped a lot of women," the blond said.

Chad exchanged a look with him and then revealed, "And there were guys whose girlfriends strayed because of Bob too. But that's all I'm saying."

"You don't know anyone who had a specific grudge?"

All three shook their heads. Nikki said Caprice's truth meter was pretty good. They all looked her straight in the eye, and none of them were shifting around. She believed them.

"Was there anybody in particular Bob hung around with? A best guy friend, that kind of thing?"

"He was a loner," Chad supplied. "As much as he liked to talk, he didn't talk to one person any too long, and never about anything personal."

That had been her experience with Bob too.

The blond averted his gaze from Caprice's. "We've got to get back to it. I'm here on a lunch break."

Caprice knew their conversation was over. There was nothing more she could learn from them, at least not now. But she'd made contact. Maybe they'd spread the word she was looking for answers. Who knew?

In the locker room, she opened her locker door and slid off her shorts and tank, revealing her one-piece, peacock-blue swimsuit underneath. She pulled goggles and swim shoes from a duffel bag inside her locker, then closed it and locked it. She expanded the stretchy cord that held her key around her ankle, slipped into the swim shoes, and out to the pool area she went.

She spotted an open lane and quickly claimed it. After a few warm-up exercises, she started her swim, hoping fifteen laps wouldn't seem like forty today.

An hour later, after a shower that didn't begin to wash the chlorine out of her pores, she dressed and left her hair wet. It would dry soon enough in the beginning-of-August heat. Nana wouldn't mind, Caprice was sure.

After she put her shoes and swimsuit in a ziplock bag so they wouldn't get everything else wet and made certain everything from the locker room bench was tucked in her duffel bag, she closed the locker door. She dropped her key off at the registration desk and headed for the parking lot. She had just walked outside and shielded her eyes from the midday sun when a tall shadow fell across her path.

"Miss De Luca."

Darn, she didn't have her pepper spray at the ready. But then a mugger wouldn't call her by her name like that, would he?

She turned to find Patrick, her mother's former student. Yews dotted the landscape along the building, and he motioned to the walkway behind them. "Can we talk back there? I don't want to do this out in the open."

How remiss of her not to have given these three guys her business card. Then they could have called her. Maybe she needed a course on how to investigate something.

He must have seen her hesitation. "This will only take a couple of minutes, and if you yell, somebody's going to hear you."

There were cars coming and going in the parking lot, and two women strolling up the walk approaching the fitness center. He was right. She had a good set of lungs on her, and if he made one wrong move, she'd scream bloody murder.

She gestured to the walk behind the trees, and he went back there first. She stepped in beside him. Unzipping a side compartment of her duffel, she took out her card and handed it to him. "If we're interrupted or anything like that, here are my numbers."

He looked at the card and pocketed it. "I owe your mom," he said.

That wasn't what she'd expected from him.

He went on, "She spent extra time with me. She let me do extra assignments, and she let me retake tests so that I didn't flunk English so I could play football. So I owe her."

"I see. So the information you're going to give me is payback?"

"Exactly."

"Go ahead."

"You wanted to know if anybody held a grudge. Someone did. Jeff Garza."

That name had come up more than once lately, but not in reference to Bob. "What do you know?"

"Bob didn't share much, but one day, when he was working out, smoke was practically coming out of his ears."

"He was angry."

"More than angry. He knew he could trust me, so I told him he was going to drop one of the weights if he didn't calm down. He could blow off steam by venting. He swore me to secrecy first."

Secrets never really die, Caprice thought, even if the person who wanted to keep them did.

Patrick continued. "Bob found out that Jeff Garza had skimmed off donations from the community center's building fund. Bob had just come from a meeting with him. Apparently he'd warned him to pay back the money or he'd go to the authorities. Since that didn't happen, I'd say Bob's death was timely, or maybe Garza had something to do with it."

"Does anyone else know you know about this?"

"No one. And I want to keep it that way."

"What if the police find out? Surely they're going to want to question you."

"They haven't yet. I'll deal with that problem when the time comes. You said you're looking for answers, and I think what you're looking for is Bob's murderer. I hope you find him. Just keep me out of it if you can."

He turned to go the opposite direction from the fitness club's entrance, but then he stopped and turned back to her. "Do me a favor. Tell your mom thank you."

Then he was striding away, and soon he disappeared around the corner.

Caprice stepped out from behind the yews, glad she was having tea with Nana. Maybe tea with Nana would help put everything in perspective.

* * *

Caprice was fortunate to have a lot of favorite people in her life. But one of her most favorite was her Nana Celia. She was seventy-five and five-three with silky, long gray hair that she wore in a knot to one side of her nape. She had a favorite tortoiseshell comb with seed pearls she often used to hold that knot in place for special occasions . . . like dinners with her family. Her husband had given it to her, and she treasured it. Nana's dark brown eyes saw much more than her surroundings.

Now her surroundings consisted of a little apartment built onto Caprice's parents' house. Her parlor was one of the prettiest places in Caprice's world. There were antiques and lace, and small flowered patterns in lilac, yellow, and pink.

For tea, the two of them always sat in the wing chairs near the window, where they sipped from teacups her grandmother had kept safe for years. Small pink roses edged the rims. The Victorian marble-topped table held a tray with a teapot and the biscotti her Nana often made when she knew she was having guests. Caprice had the recipe and made them too, but they never turned out quite like Nana Celia's. These biscotti, unlike their commercial counterparts, were small biscuit cookies with lemon icing. She intended to make two batches for the community center fund-raising fair on Saturday.

Now she stared at the sweet treats knowing she should bypass them. However, what could be wrong with a biscotti to top off the chocolate cupcake? It was a good thing Nana was serving yogurt with them.

"Did you skip lunch?" she asked Caprice now.

"This is lunch," she said, taking a spoonful of yogurt.

Nana shook her head. "What am I going to do with you?"

"Just continue giving me your decorating advice. Mom told me recently it's really life advice in disguise, and I take it better from you than anyone else. But you know I like listening to you."

"You're not as stubborn as your sister."

"Which sister is that?" Caprice asked with a smile.

"Bella. The ones who are the most traditional are the ones who are the most rigid. That's true in decorating and in life."

Thinking that over, Caprice suspected her Nana was right. Her Nana was usually right.

"I heard you're trying to help Joe and Bella."

Her mom usually kept Nana in the loop. "I'm trying, but I don't know how far I'm getting."

Nana studied her. "Are you stirring up a hornet's nest again?"

That was Nana's way of asking her if she was putting herself in danger. She remembered the feeling that someone was following her and seeing that SUV zooming away at the model home. So she was honest.

"I might be."

"Carry your pepper-spray gun."

If nothing else, Nana was practical. "I do." She remembered that she hadn't had it on her when she was at the gym. "I was just talking to someone who knew Bob and gave me a lead."

"A lead to someone who murdered him?"

"Someone who might have had a motive to murder him. I just have to figure out how to follow up."

"While you're doing that, you are seeing your new young man, aren't you?"

Nana had liked Seth. Everybody had liked Seth. She didn't even realize she was frowning until Nana asked, "What's wrong? Did you two have a fight? Tony and I had lots of fights when we were first dating."

It was hard to think about her Nana dating. She'd married at age seventeen. She and her young man, Anthony De Luca, had come to the United States from Calabria, Italy. Caprice admired them immigrating to a new country and making a life for themselves. Her grandfather had been a barber with his own shop. They'd lived in New York for a while but then had made their way to Pennsylvania. Nana had run a fruit stand at a farmers market in York for years after her children were in school and finding their own way in life. She was a homebody at heart but knew about the world and wasn't afraid to let it in.

"Do you remember the barbershop?" Nana asked Caprice.

"Of course, I do. I sat in that big chair in front of that huge round mirror. Gramps would spin me around and I'd giggle."

"Nikki got seasick," her Nana remembered. "Bella, she wanted no part of it. It scared her. But you were the adventurous one."

"Because I sat in the barber chair and spun around?"

"Because you wanted to know everything about the shop, from what was in every bottle your gramps kept on the shelf, to the towels I put through the ironer, to the spittoon on the floor. I have never seen a more curious child."

Her Nana had lived in a two-story row house in York when Caprice's grandfather had run the barbershop. Their living room had been upstairs. When he'd retired, they'd turned the shop space into a living room downstairs. But he'd been retired for only two years before he'd passed on.

"I miss the old place sometimes," Nana admitted. Then she looked around. "But I like it here, and I know your mom and dad worry about me less since I'm with them."

"They don't just worry less. They like having you close."

"I think you're evading the subject. We were talking about your young man."

"He's thinking about taking a fellowship at Johns Hopkins, Nana. I don't know how that's going to work out."

"It's not for sure yet?"

"Not yet."

"Then don't borrow trouble. When are you seeing him again?"

They were supposed to have another Cherry on the Top date. "Wednesday night. And officially he's going to escort me to the awards dinner."

"You're going to win."

"It doesn't matter if I do or not. It will be a fun night."

Nana narrowed her eyes. "It always matters if you win. But even more important than winning is finding the answers. You will find answers, Caprice. It's your nature. Just don't take too many chances while you're doing it."

Caprice couldn't see that she was taking any chances, at least not yet. After all, she was just asking questions.

But the last time she asked questions when someone was murdered, she'd almost gotten killed herself.

Chapter Thirteen

The August Saturday was going to heat up fast, and humidity would intensify the heat index. Most of the stands in the park across the street from the community center relied on the protection of a canopy. Caprice strolled along a row, breathing in the early-morning air and enjoying the sun on her face. She was having trouble shooing her ice-cream date with Seth away from her other thoughts and the reason she'd come to the community center's fund-raising event. Whenever she didn't stay focused on her investigative objective, Seth's smile and good-night kiss were uppermost in her thoughts. They'd enjoyed ice cream and each other's company. They hadn't talked about the future.

Gearing her mind to her mission, she was glad the fund-raising day for the community center had been set to go on in spite of what had happened there. The park had been tended to by volunteers and enthusiastic residents who lived nearby and wanted a safe place for their kids to play. The swings were the old-fashioned sort with long chains and wooden seats. The monkey bars were big enough for only a few kids. In the open areas, volunteers coached soccer games and dodgeball.

Today, however, Caprice scouted the stands that were everywhere—housing everything from games to food to bingo to vendors selling crafts. She knew these vendors donated a percentage of their profits to the center. From the baked goods booth, the center received one-hundred percent profit.

Nikki had agreed to coordinate the stand and, of course, had reached out to her mom, Nana, and Caprice. Caprice's mom baked three cakes, all chocolate—one with a fluffy white icing, one with peanut butter icing, and one with dark chocolate icing. Nana had baked a few peach pies. Contributing too, Caprice had decided her biscotti would sell well. She'd baked a double batch because everyone who tasted them loved them, even though they hadn't turned out exactly like Nana's this time either. She'd rolled, cut, and baked them early this morning. The lemon icing had had to firm up before she'd packed them for the bake sale.

When she arrived at the baked goods stand, Nikki was busy arranging the offerings on the table under a red canopy, along with two other women who Caprice didn't know.

After Nikki introduced her to them, Caprice said, "It looks as if Mom and Nana were here already." Their cakes and pies were on display.

"They're looking around, but I have the cash box ready. I got change and small bills at the bank yesterday."

Without hesitating, Nikki opened the box that held Caprice's biscotti. "I think I'm going to leave

these right in here to display. Last year, the baked
goods sold out in two hours, so we shouldn't have to
worry about the heat affecting them."

"Are you open for business?" The deep voice came
from behind Caprice's shoulder.

She recognized it immediately. "I didn't know
you were interested in the community center's fund-
raising."

Grant's expression was passive when she turned to
look at him. "Right now I'm interested in everything
about the community center. Isn't that why you're
here?"

"Nope. I donated baked goods."

"So you did," he said, studying the biscotti. "I'll
take a dozen of those."

"Seriously?" Nikki asked.

"Seriously. I've tasted them. I know they're good.
I'm working in my office today, and they'll see me
through to lunch."

"No breakfast?" Caprice joked.

"The cookies will be breakfast and a snack too. I'll
pick up coffee at the convenience store on the way
back."

While Nikki quickly boxed up the biscotti, Caprice
studied Grant in his more relaxed clothes. She usually saw him in a suit. Today, he wore black shorts and
a tan polo shirt. Although it was more casual than his
suit, he still looked . . . staid.

"Are you going to go inside and ask questions?"
she prodded.

"I thought I would. You're not the only one who
can investigate, you know."

She knew.

"That's not usually part of your job."

"One of the De Lucas in danger of going to jail, let alone two, isn't an ordinary occurrence. I like to have my bases covered, too, so I know what to expect next."

"I don't suppose you want me to come with you."

"No, I don't."

Stalemate. She'd push if she thought she could ferret something out that Grant couldn't, but at this point she was going to let him try. She'd look in other directions. Grant might be going inside the community center for his questioning, but she was going to buzz around here for a while to talk to the other vendors, as well as the parents and kids who ran in and out of the center.

Happy with his box of biscotti, Grant paid Nikki—giving her extra as a donation—and turned back to Caprice. "How's Shasta?"

"Holding up. Sophia seems a little less indignant when she's around. Thinking about one of those pups?"

Whereas before he'd dismissed the idea completely, now he shrugged. "I doubt it."

That wasn't an out-and-out no.

"I'd better get going. You be careful," he said in that authoritarian way of his that rubbed Caprice the wrong way.

"You know I will," she responded.

Before he had the chance to comment, Sharla Flannery walked up to the stand with a ziplock bag filled with chocolate-chip cookies in one hand and a huge box in the other.

As Grant strode away, Caprice took the box from her and opened the lid. "Cupcakes."

"The Cupcake House donated them. The cookies

are my donation, and I'm here to help if you need it." As she handed off the baked goods to Nikki, she said, "I don't know what Danny would have done without the community center. I just wish . . ."

"What do you wish?" Caprice asked.

"I wish Danny could find a real job. I know he's only seventeen and that's a problem some places, but he needs a sense of purpose."

"Maybe he'll be able to help finish the murals in the center."

"I hope he can."

"You know, those T-shirts he wears that he hand-paints are pretty nifty. Did he ever think about trying to sell them online? You know, taking orders for what someone wants painted, charging good money for it?"

Sharla looked surprised at the thought. "I wonder if he could."

"He'd just need a stake to buy plain T-shirts. Someone could take pictures of them and post them on a Web site. It's just a thought." She remembered the detail work on the mural. "He's a talented kid. There are places online where you can set up free sites."

"I'll talk to him about it," Sharla said. "Thanks."

Already customers were approaching the stand. Someone bought one of her mother's cakes, while another bought a peach pie and brownies. Business was starting to boom.

Caprice told Nikki, "I'm going to nose around a bit. If you need me, beep my cell."

"What are you doing when you're finished here?" Nikki asked.

"I have a couple of jobs to work on back home,

virtual redecorating. I haven't placed orders yet for the clients."

Two more customers came up to the stand, selecting a bag of this, a box of that.

Nikki nodded to the line forming. "We might be sold out in an hour and a half this time. I thought maybe you and I could go shopping for a dress for you. You know, for that awards banquet? You need to buy something that will knock Seth's socks off."

Knock Seth's socks off. If he was still free to take her that night. If they decided they were still dating. If the fellowship he'd applied for didn't change everything.

"I do need something dressier than I have," Caprice admitted, "but I'd still like something with a vintage look."

"We'll start at Secrets of the Past. But if Suzanne doesn't have anything, we can drive in to York. The work can wait till later, can't it?"

"I have to check on my furry duo first."

"Of course, you do. We'll make a pit stop."

That's what Caprice liked about Nikki. She was flexible as well as practical.

Maybe Caprice should think about being a little more practical.

Nah. That would be boring.

"I love it," Nikki said as Caprice studied her image in the dressing-room mirror at Secrets of the Past.

She studied the price tag. "I've never paid this much for a dress."

Nikki bumped shoulders with her, as she'd often

done since they were kids. "Just look at you. Seth will fall at your feet."

That was an overestimation if Caprice ever heard one, but she had to admit, the dusky pink reproduction of a 1920s flapper dress was exquisite. It was hand-beaded in glass beads with gorgeous embroidery and layers of beaded fringe.

"You've never been up for an award before, either. You're a successful entrepreneur. You have to dress like one."

"It's not too much?"

"Turn off that Catholic guilt, Caprice. It's not too much. It's perfect. I'm sure Mom has some vintage jewelry that will look perfect with it."

"Nana might," Caprice mused, thinking of the aurora borealis crystal beads her grandmother some-times wore.

Her thoughts turned to what Nikki had said about being a successful entrepreneur. With hard work and perseverance Nikki had become successful in her catering business—Nikki's Catered Capers—just as Caprice had become successful with home-staging.

So Caprice asked her, "Don't you ever feel like maybe you're just a little too fortunate. Don't you ask why our businesses are thriving when so many others aren't?"

"That maybe we deserve a little hard luck?" Nikki asked with a scowl. "No. It's not like any of what we have was given to us. Sure, we got some help along the way, and we have supportive family behind us. But we've worked hard. You know that. I think you're doubly afraid because you saw your home-decorating business almost go down the tubes before you switched to home-staging. But that's the whole point, Caprice. We have to be adaptable."

"And not only in business."

"You're thinking about Seth and the fellowship?"

"I can't stop thinking about it."

At least when she was analyzing murder suspects, she was distracted from the idea of Seth leaving. However, she hadn't learned one little new tidbit at the park today. She wondered if Grant had been more successful.

Caprice's purse sat on a shelf by the dressing-room door. Now her cell phone played, and she wrinkled her nose at it. But she hardly ever let it go to voice mail when she could reach it. So she grabbed the purse and fished in it for her phone. When she plucked it out, she put it to her ear. It was Denise Langford.

"Hi, Denise. What's up?"

"Ace bought the house! Not only that, he wants you to redecorate a few of the rooms, as well as the pool area. He's having a party soon. Can you meet him there at three-thirty?"

"That was quick."

"Apparently this man moves fast when he knows what he wants. Fortunately, there's no reason why he can't. So can you be there at three-thirty?"

Ace wanted her to redecorate for him. She could get a hefty commission from that. She smiled. "I'll be there."

Ending the call, she dumped the phone in her purse and grinned at her sister. "I'm taking the dress. How would you like to meet a real rock star face-to-face?" Ace and Nikki hadn't been introduced when he'd stopped in at the open house.

With some excitement, Nikki accepted Caprice's invitation to accompany her, although she asked, "Do you think Ace will mind?"

"I don't think so. Besides, it will be great to have another pair of eyes looking around with mine. I have the floor plan for the house, and I know practically every square inch because of staging it. But you might spot something I don't."

"Just like you send recipes my way?"

"Sure, if I think they fit the staging. We've always been a team, haven't we?"

"Always," Nikki agreed.

At three-thirty on the dot, Caprice stopped at the gate to the estate, then climbed out of her car and punched in the security code. The black wrought-iron bars spread apart slowly.

"Do you think Ace will hire a security team?" Nikki asked her once she was back inside her Camaro.

"It's possible. This place is going to need a staff."

To Caprice's surprise, Ace himself answered the door. She introduced Nikki, and he shook hands with them both. "It's good to see you again." He studied Caprice. "Do you think I need to change the code on that gate?"

"That would probably be a good idea. Will you be hiring a security team?"

"Do you think I need it? Won't the cameras themselves keep intruders away if they see they're being taped."

"Kismet usually isn't a high crime center, and you're out of the way here. But there was a murder recently at the community center, and word will spread one way or another that you're in Kismet, even if you tried to hide the transaction of buying a house and your address."

"Yeah, but I'm not thirty and hip anymore. I don't think anybody's going to break in and ravish me."

Caprice's lips twitched. "Maybe not. But because you live on an estate this size, because of who you are, someone might think you have valuables in here."

"Did you know Sumpter had a temperature-controlled room with a steel door for his art collection? I don't have anything like that."

She did know. But of course she hadn't told anyone about it.

Ace pointed his finger at her. "You're like a priest, aren't you? Clients tell you things and you don't leak a word. I like that."

"She's one of the few members of our family who can keep a secret," Nikki offered. "At least she usually can . . . when it's not about a member of the family."

Caprice elbowed her, knowing Nikki was referring to Bella's pregnancy, and turned back to Ace. "Are you keeping any of the Wild Kingdom theme or do you want to redo the whole place?"

"Actually, I think Wild Kingdom suits me." He grinned, and his grin still carried a powerful punch. "It's probably why I bought the estate. I want this party to happen fast. I've hired an event planner. I've used her before and she's good."

He studied Nikki. "Denise told me Caprice's sister did the catering at the open house. Are you that sister? Trent said the bison meatballs were the best."

"Yes, I am."

"Good. I'll give your name to Alyssa, my event

planner. Maybe you can fit my party into your schedule."

He started walking, and it was easy to see he was a person with high energy who liked to make use of it. "The first thing I want you to redo is the pool area. I want bigger tables with colorful large umbrellas around the pool instead of those little ones. Give me color in the chaises, and of course I'll need a lot of chairs. Bright color there too. There are enough animal prints inside."

She didn't want the pool area to be garish or decorated in something that would clash with the inside. Her mind started clicking with ideas. "How about if we give the pool area a Sea World theme? Inside is kind of wild creatures on land. Outside could be wild creatures of the sea. I can go with bright blues and greens, and incorporate some black and white to coordinate with inside."

They were standing on the patio now, and Ace stared at the pool and the surrounding area as if he were trying to imagine it. "Not bad for off the top of your head. You are good."

"I try to be," Caprice gibed.

Ace laughed. "I'll leave the details up to you, and Alyssa, of course. Maybe you can consult with her. She'll handle laser and holographic lighting over the pool, that kind of thing. How about the pool house?" He quickly headed that way. "What do you suggest there?"

A few minutes later, he threw open the door and they peeked inside. Caprice stepped over the threshold. There was a daybed with a tawny gold coverlet, club chairs in tan leather, a powder room, and two dressing cubicles. A wet bar seemed out of place, but there it was. On one wall, a grouping of framed prints told a story about the African veldt.

"Do you want this space to match the pool area?"

Ace nodded. He also waved to the wall above the daybed. "Can we do something different in here? I get tired of pictures and metal sculptures." He was observant and obviously cared about his surroundings.

Caprice studied the space once more, particularly the wall he'd pointed to. She remembered her conversation with Sharla Flannery at the community center fund-raiser. "What would you think about a mural on that wall? Maybe of dolphins? I can possibly find someone to paint it for you."

Ace narrowed his eyes and squinted at the wall. Then he nodded. "I like that. Yeah, go for it."

"We have to talk about a budget," Caprice said.

"We will. But I have to show you everything I want you to do first. There's one room upstairs that's going to be special."

He didn't say any more until they'd made their way inside and up the staircase. He stopped at the room next to the master suite.

Caprice wondered if he was going to put up a paramour there. After all, he did have a reputation in that area. Right now, the room was staged with a brass bed covered with a green patterned comforter.

"This will be my daughter Trista's room," Ace explained. "Here's what I want. I want a canopy bed and white furniture. Do lots of pink and frills on the bed and at the windows too."

Caprice thought that sounded more like a bedroom for a four-year-old than an eleven-year-old, but she didn't know Ace's daughter.

"I don't want you to spare any expense. It has to

be ready in time for the party. Trista will be here with me then, and so will my parents. It's going to be one big open house, not a wild party, so keep that in mind."

"Do you have any idea when you're going to have this party?"

"I'm thinking August nineteenth."

Caprice went still, and Nikki gave her a look. "You want me to do all this in ten days?"

"Is that a problem?" he asked, with an amused, quirked brow. Apparently he snapped his fingers and what he wanted immediately happened.

She'd have to put other projects on hold, contact Danny, check into suppliers, and expedite delivery on everything. But she could do it. She would do it.

"No problem." She turned to Nikki. "Are you free on the nineteenth?"

Nikki laughed. "You're lucky, Ace, I'm free. What kind of menu are you thinking of?"

"I want it good. I want it tasteful. I want plenty of help here. Hire who you have to. Just be sure you can trust them not to sell photos to the paparazzi."

"Got it," Nikki assured him.

"Got it," Caprice repeated, wondering how she was going to arrange everything in ten days.

One of the things Caprice had learned was that when she was busiest, that was when she needed to take deep breaths. She dropped Nikki at her house so she could pick up her car, then she spent some time with Shasta and Sophia, giving her feline an extra rub of catnip on her scratching post. While she did that, she let her mind pull ideas from wherever she could find them. The Cupcake House was closed on Saturday evening. Fortunately, she found Sharla's home phone listing and reached her there. Caprice ran her idea by her, and when Sharla approved, she spoke with Danny.

"Are you interested in a job where you'll get paid for your art?"

Silence met the question until finally he asked, "Seriously?"

She might be taking a risk with Danny, but not just anyone could paint designs on sneakers . . . or a mural. Her instincts told her this was a risk worth taking, for both her and Danny. "Did you ever hear of Ace Richland?"

"The music guy?" Danny asked.

"That's one way to put it. Yeah. He bought a place outside of Kismet, and he needs a mural on his pool house wall. I was thinking the ocean, dolphins, something like that."

Again there was silence. "This would be a wall like at the community center?"

Could she count on a seventeen-year-old to pull this off? Thinking again about Danny's talent, she realized, yes, she could. "Yep. Are you interested?"

"What's the money like?"

She named a sum.

Danny whistled. However, he asked warily, "What's the glitch?"

"It has to be complete before the nineteenth."

Finally he said, "It's a good thing I don't have school. I'd have to cut class."

Caprice smiled.

"Do you want to see a sketch first?"

"That would probably be best so Ace knows exactly what you're going to do. Is that the way you work?"

"I can. I'll work on it tonight and have it for you by tomorrow."

"That sounds good. Call me when it's done, okay? I'll pick it up."

"I will, but . . . Miss De Luca, why are you doing this for me?"

She didn't hesitate. "A couple of reasons. One of them is that I like your art. The other is, I think you'll like Ace. From what I hear, he didn't feel like he fit in anywhere when he was a teenager because of his music. He had brothers, but they weren't into it. His music kept him out of trouble."

"Okay," Danny said, understanding her broad hint. "I'll call you."

After Caprice ended the call, she fed Shasta and Sophia, then told them both, "I need some exercise to wind down. I'll feel better about myself, and it will get my energy up for next week. So you girls have to entertain yourselves for a couple of hours. But I'll be back soon and we'll snuggle, okay?"

Shasta barked. Sophia licked her lips and started eating.

Caprice swung her duffel by her side as she entered Shape Up, remembering her conversation with Patrick. Was Jeff Garza involved in Bob's murder? She'd called Vince about him, and her brother was supposedly looking into the businessman—his background and financial dealings. Would he uncover anything?

In the locker room, as she slipped off her shorts

and top, revealing her swimsuit, she realized she liked coming in here on Saturday night the best. The gym was busy, though not as busy as during the week, and the pool was practically deserted. She was grateful for that. She really didn't like an audience. The pool closed at eight, so she had forty-five minutes to swim laps.

She tied her hair back in a ponytail so it was out of her way, slipped on her swim shoes, grabbed her water goggles, and headed into the pool area. The humidity was high. Out of the water, the atmosphere was almost stifling. She'd just gone down the steps and decided to use the end lane when the lifeguard waved at her and came around the pool. She knew Brenda. The teenager had graduated from high school in the spring and had been one of her mom's students. She'd been thrilled about her job here.

She said, "I have to go to the laundry room and take the towels from the dryer. It hasn't been working right, and I'm afraid it's going to burn them. Will you be okay?"

Caprice had been swimming since she was a kid and was comfortable in the water. "I'll be fine. I'm just going to swim laps."

"I won't be long," Brenda assured her.

Caprice slipped her goggles on and adjusted them. Then she pushed off from the edge of the pool and began her lap session.

Swimming laps could almost be hypnotic. Although physical exertion was involved, after a few laps gliding through the water almost became a Zen experience. She reached, she breathed, she kicked. Momentum pushed her forward.

On her third lap, she suddenly felt pressure on

her back . . . something pushing her deeper under the water.

That pressure again. Harder now . . . and it hurt!

It took a few moments for her to realize something out of the ordinary was happening. She was in the deep end, and she couldn't simply let her feet drop to the pool floor. In the deep end . . .

She panicked. She tried to do anything to get away from the debilitating push on her torso. She couldn't raise her head out of the water. Her breath was running out. Instinctively, she twirled and ducked deeper, slipping out from under whatever was pressing her down.

Gasping, she rose to the surface. When she did, she heard the clang of the door.

Had someone just tried to kill her?

Chapter Fourteen

Someone had tried to kill her. Someone had tried to kill her. Someone had tried to kill her.

Holding onto the rail along the side of the pool, Caprice caught her breath and attempted to calm down. Her back not only hurt from the pressure, but it burned, too. Had she been cut? Adrenaline still raced through her body, and she suspected if she hadn't been holding onto the rail, she'd be shaking.

Hand over hand, she pulled herself along the side of the pool until she stood in the shallow end.

She heard the door leading to the gym area open and close.

Brenda appeared, carrying a stack of towels. When she spotted Caprice leaning against the side of the pool with her head down on her arms, she ran over and asked, "Are you all right?"

Caprice shook off the remainder of her panic and fear. She had to find out who'd tried to drown her!

"Do you know who was in here with me, Brenda?

Someone came in while I was swimming . . ." She stopped.

Brenda gave her an odd look. "Someone came in to swim?"

Caprice wasn't sure what she should say. Maybe it was better not to say exactly what had happened. "Someone came in. Do you know who it was?"

"I didn't see anyone. I was in the laundry room the whole time. Paul was helping one of the clients. So was Netta."

Thinking more clearly now, Caprice checked at the side of the pool, looking for something in particular. The skimmer was usually propped near the corner, but now it was lying next to the edge of the pool. Shape Up personnel used it to fish out small floaty hand weights or toys from a kids' class that floated out of the shallow end. They sometimes used it to guide someone who was suddenly afraid of being out in the middle of the pool over to the side. The basket that hung at the end of it was made of some type of net material. The pole attached to the basket was about six feet long. The end of that pole near the basket could have been used on her back to push her down and hold her. Something on the skimmer must have scraped or scratched her.

Goose pimples prickled all over her arms, and if she let herself, she'd go into full panic all over again. But she wouldn't let herself. First she asked Brenda to check the workout area and ask if anyone had been seen coming into the pool.

Ten minutes later, Brenda reported to Caprice that no one had been seen entering the pool area. Caprice had quickly changed, but her skin still gave off a strong aroma of chlorine because she hadn't showered. Taking her cell phone in hand, she realized she was shivering. That was probably just shock setting in. Her legs wobbled a bit, and she sat down on the bench and speed-dialed Seth's cell. If he was at the clinic, he wouldn't answer. But if he wasn't . . .

"Hey, Caprice. I got off fifteen minutes ago. I was going to call you to see if you wanted to drive out to that new place that opened up. It's supposed to be like the fifties, with waitresses on roller skates."

"Seth, someone tried to kill me." To her dismay, her voice shook a little.

"Where are you?" His tone was worried and sharp.

"I'm at Shape Up, in the locker room. I'm safe here now. I was doing laps. Brenda left to get towels. I felt this pressure on my back. I think someone used the skimmer on me and tried to hold me underwater. I don't know if they actually wanted to drown me, or just scare me."

"Did you call the police?"

"No."

He hesitated for only one beat. "I'll be right there. Don't move."

"I'm in the women's locker room."

"Don't move. Just stay there until you hear me outside the door. Got it?"

"Okay."

Not even ten minutes later, there was a loud knock on the door, and she heard Seth's voice. "Caprice? Are you in there?"

She pulled open the door and stepped out into the gym.

He put his arm around her. "Are you okay?"

"I'll get you all wet." Her hair was still sopping, but she really didn't care. She was so glad to see him, she could kiss him right then and there. He looked as if he wanted to kiss her too, but other Shape Up customers were still working out, and neither of them wanted to cause a spectacle. Though if she had drowned in the pool, there would have been a real spectacle.

Seth kept his arm around her as she dropped her key at the registration desk and he guided her outside. "If I take you home in my truck, can you pick up your car tomorrow?"

"Sure. Mom or Nikki can bring me over. But you really don't have to . . ."

He took her by the shoulders and held her firmly. "You've got to stop."

She blinked. Stop? Stop liking him so much? Stop wishing he wouldn't get the fellowship?

"Stop asking questions. That's what got you into this mess."

He was sounding just like everybody else in her life—Grant, her brother, her dad too, if she gave him the chance.

"I'm obviously onto something or this never would have happened."

"Do you know exactly what you're onto?"

"No, but . . ."

"There are no buts. You want to save Bella and Joe, but you can't put your own life in danger while you do it."

Her mind had been spinning while she was in the locker room, thinking about where she'd asked questions, who she'd talked to, who might feel threatened.

"I must have rattled somebody's cage. At the community center fund-raiser, I was asking questions about Bob, who he palled around with, who his friends were. I also found out that Jeff Garza was skimming money from the building fund and that Bob confronted him. But I don't think anyone knows I know that."

"You're not going to stop, are you?"

She looked into Seth's very blue eyes and told him the truth. "I can't. Not until I know that Bella and Joe aren't Detective Jones's number-one suspects."

She'd never seen Seth angry before, but he looked angry now. However, unlike the De Lucas, who usually vented vocally, his lips compressed, and he simply said, "Let me get you home."

At her house, Seth insisted on seeing her to her door and coming inside. Shasta ran around his legs and sat on his foot, and he patted her, noticing Sophia high on her cat tree.

After Seth stood, he concluded, "I don't think Shasta's such a great watchdog. She's too friendly. And Sophia's not the type to claw anybody's eyes out. Maybe you need a bodyguard."

"Are you applying for the job?" Wouldn't that be a hoot? Seth staying here watching over her.

"I'm not sure that would be the best thing for either of our reputations. If Kismet was bigger, nobody would notice. But it's not. I know you won't let me hire a bodyguard, but how about if Nikki stays with you for a few days, or you stay with her?"

"The animals," Caprice said, as if that said it all.

"All right. So ask her to stay with you. I really don't think you should be alone."

"Let me think about it."

"How long are you going to think about it?"

"This house has sturdy locks. I have a baseball bat

upstairs that Vince lent me earlier this summer for a game in the park. You might not think Shasta's a good watchdog, but she hears everything. If anybody would try to get in, she'd know before they even thought about it. Really, Seth."

"Maybe you should buy a gun."

"I have pepper spray."

"Maybe you should buy a gun," he repeated somberly.

"I'm not going to overreact. The more I think about it, the more I think it was just a scare tactic—a warning."

He gently touched her face and pushed her wet hair behind her ear. "I don't want anything to happen to you."

"I don't want anything to happen to me, either," she assured him with a weak smile. Then because she didn't want to think about what had happened or buying a gun, she asked, "Why don't I make us something to eat?" She started rubbing her arms, "Though I think I better take a shower first. I'm starting to itch from the chlorine."

"Then why don't *I* make us something to eat. I make great BLTs. You do have bacon, don't you? Every good cook does."

She laughed. "Of course I have bacon. He'd told her he made great BLTs during one of their first meetings at Grocery Fresh. She hadn't had a BLT in a while.

"Could you let Shasta out while I get that shower? Then we can give Sophia her nightly dollop of cream and make the BLTs together."

"We're going to make more than BLTs, Caprice, because I'm not leaving here until very late. I want to make sure no one's going to surprise you tonight."

"I just happen to have a couple of old movies we can watch."

"Such as?"

"*Roman Holiday* with Audrey Hepburn and Gregory Peck. What do you think?"

"I think you're trying to distract me from the real reason I'm here, but I'll let you. Watching *Roman Holiday* will be a lot better than me imagining what could have happened to you tonight."

"Oh, Seth." He almost made her want to cry.

He pointed to the stairs. "Go get your shower. I'll give Sophia her cream and let Shasta out. Then we'll replace eau de chlorine with eau de bacon."

Turning toward the stairs, she said over her shoulder, "Thank you."

"For what?"

"For being here." Then before she thought about the fact that he might not be here the next time, she hurried up the stairs.

Seth left after midnight and only then because Caprice promised she'd keep her cell phone beside her on her pillow, and she'd call him if she heard any unexpected noise. In spite of what he'd said about their reputations, he'd offered to sleep on her sofa. But she wasn't a damsel in distress who needed to be rescued. Yes, she'd be practical and cautious, but she was not going to cower and expect someone else to save her.

She did call Nikki Sunday morning, though, and Nikki said she'd be right over to take her to get her car. While she waited for her sister, she gave Sophia a dollop of cream—she was one of the fortunate

felines who could digest it—and then sat at her desk
to read e-mails. After finishing her cream and dain-
tily washing, Sophia climbed on her lap. Handling a
keyboard with a cat on her lap wasn't always the eas-
iest thing to do, but sometimes Sophia liked to be
close, and Caprice liked that closeness too. So she managed. After a morning run in the yard, Shasta was
contenting herself by gnawing on a chew toy close by.

While Caprice was reading her e-mail, her program dinged and an incoming correspondence
flashed on the screen. It was from Derrick Gastenaux. She opened it. After she read it, she wanted
to give a cheer, but she knew that would scare
Sophia, so she grinned instead.

Mr. Gastenaux wanted her to sign an agreement.
He was hiring her to decorate three model homes, or
stage them, however you wanted to look at it. That
would bring in a nice chunk of change. Although she
put back a reserve every time she did a job, not only
to pay taxes but also for savings, she knew she was set
for the rest of the year. But she still worried. Hers
wasn't a stable income. She'd been fortunate so far,
but she knew that, like anyone else, she could have
a dry spell eventually, and she wanted to be prepared
for that.

When Nikki rang the doorbell, Sophia gave
Caprice a look that said, *I know you're going to disturb
me, aren't you?* Normally Caprice didn't have her door
locked and Nikki could just walk in. But this morning was different.

"Sorry," she said to Sophia as she picked her up
and set her on the office chair she'd just vacated.
Shasta, of course, followed her to the door. The

dog was getting rounder, and her pregnancy was supremely evident now.

When Caprice opened the door, Nikki rushed in and hugged her. "Are you sure you're okay?"

"Except for a little water up my nose and some scrapes, scratches, and a little bruising on my back, I'm fine."

"Why didn't Seth stay until I got here?"

"Because I told him to go home last night. He has to get some sleep, too."

Nikki gave her one of those sisterly, knowing looks. "You're afraid to depend on him."

Caprice sighed. "It's too early in the morning for sisterly therapy. Let's just go get my car and go to ten o'clock Mass. I told Vince I was going to stop by his place around noon."

"To talk about what happened?"

"No, to talk about Jeff Garza."

"Do you think he tried to drown you?"

"I don't know. Either the person who did it belonged to the gym and no one noticed them, or they followed me and snuck in."

"Is that possible?"

"Oh, sure. The receptionist at the desk is busy. She's often away from her desk in the evening too, because it's slow, and she wanders around, talking to the clients and to the trainers who aren't busy."

"No answers there," Nikki determined. "So let's go."

After Mass, Caprice headed for Vince's condo, while Nikki went home to get ready for a catering gig. She'd be back at Caprice's tonight with her travel bag.

Sitting in Vince's first-floor condo in the refurbished school building, Caprice glanced up at the tall windows with white grids, then at the living room decorated in masculine comfortable style with leather and nubby-fabric furniture. Vince had asked her to go over again what happened at the pool and she had.

He looked worried. "Nikki's going to stay with you tonight?"

"She's going to stay with me for a few nights."

"Do you have that 'being followed' feeling today?"

"Not really. And tomorrow I have two appointments in the morning, another in the early afternoon, and one in the evening. Nikki can't be with me when she has catering jobs. I figure as long as I'm with other people and driving on a main street, I'll be fine."

"You aren't going anyplace out of the way?"

"My last appointment tomorrow is at Ace Richland's."

"Not many cars on that road."

"No, but once I get through his gates, I'm safe. Vince, I have my cell phone."

"I don't like this, Caprice. I don't like it at all."

"There are a lot of things in life we don't like, but we get through them. Now what did you find out about Jeff Garza?"

"I looked into him. He looks clean."

"Then I'm going to talk to him."

"You're not going to talk to him alone. Why don't I set up the appointment with him, tell him it's about community center business. Then it will seem a little more . . . official. He won't be expecting the questions you want to ask."

"Like if he embezzled money from the community center?"

"Especially if you ask him that. Let me call him and see what we can work out. When will you be free tomorrow?"

"From four to seven."

Caprice had Googled Garza and found his address online. He lived in a very nice neighborhood—the kind of neighborhood where you wouldn't think people would have to embezzle money. But just like with a marriage, no one knew what happened behind closed financial doors. Tomorrow's meeting, if they had one, would be interesting at the least, illuminating at best.

Jeff Garza's house was probably about five thousand square feet. It was an L-shape, with garages to the left and the main house directly ahead. There was lots of stone, a few gables, and clerestory windows over the garage. It definitely wasn't a cookie-cutter home. He'd probably had an architect draw up the plans.

Jeff Garza himself came to the door with a smile that definitely wasn't genuine. He invited Vince and Caprice inside.

As he studied Caprice, it became obvious he had not expected Vince to bring anyone with him. "Is this a colleague?"

Vince shook his head and said honestly, "No, she's my sister. She has an interest in what we're going to discuss."

"An interest?" Jeff asked with an arched brow.

He was probably in his late forties, with thick, dark

brown hair that was starting to gray, a crooked nose, and a pointed jaw. Still in a dress shirt and suit slacks, he looked fit, and Caprice wondered if he worked out at Shape Up. That's one of the questions she'd like to ask him. She decided to shake up this businessman a little.

"The police are looking at my sister and her husband for the murder of Bob Preston."

Vince gave her a startled look, but she just shrugged.

Jeff glanced over his shoulder as if he were checking for . . . his wife? His family?

"Let's go to my office," he said. Then looking over his shoulder again, he quickly shepherded them to the right, down a short hall, and into his home office.

Caprice had seen lots of home offices, and this was as ordinary as they got. Built-in bookshelves lined one wall, stained in a deep walnut. The L-shaped desk was actually scattered with papers and folders, and it looked as if this was an actual workspace. The artwork on the wall looked like it had been chosen by a decorator, but she could be wrong. Maybe Garza was into the English countryside and foxhunting, but somehow she doubted it.

Once in his office, he shut the door, and he didn't invite them to sit on the upholstered love seat or the chairs in front of his desk.

"I don't know what Bob Preston's murder has to do with me." His voice was haughty, and he gave the impression he was above the idea of murder.

"Then why did you bring us to your office and shut the door if you know nothing about it?" Caprice asked.

"I . . . I knew Preston."

"How did you know him?" Vince asked.

"How do you think I knew him?" Garza returned.

Vince shook his head. "I'm not playing that game. We're here for a reason. We have information about you and Preston. I'm just trying to ferret out the truth."

After a few beats of silence, Garza answered, "He and I were on the board of the community center."

"Is that all?" Caprice asked.

"Yes, that's all."

"Bob didn't have anything to do with the building fund?" Vince asked. He knew how to tag team with the best.

"No, why?" Garza asked suspiciously . . . or maybe guiltily.

"We heard you're having financial problems," Caprice offered.

Garza's cheeks flushed and he looked away.

Caprice wanted to say that she knew he'd pulled his financing from Eliza's business prospects, but she didn't gossip about what her clients told her. Mostly she kept the information confidential unless she was permitted to divulge it by the client.

What she did say was, "A lot of people's investments have dived. Yours too?"

Glancing from Vince to Caprice made Garza realize they weren't going to leave without a few answers. Maybe he realized they had more information than he thought they did.

"Yeah, I took a hit, but things will come back. Historically they always do."

"But historically it could take a while, right?" Vince asked, though he already knew the answer.

"I suppose," Garza said, crossing his arms over his chest, a totally defensive body-language gesture.

Finally, as if tired of the whole cat-and-mouse, question-and-answer game, Vince said, "Look. I have information that you skimmed money from the building fund. I also have information that you and Bob Preston got into it about that building fund and about that skimmed money. He confronted you, and maybe you got so angry that you picked up a tool and . . ."

"Wait a minute! I don't know where you got your information, but that's slander."

"I'm going to give this information to the police. I'm going to tell them what I know. Do you think slander will enter into it then?"

The right detective digging in the right place could discover information that Garza wanted to keep private. The right detective could see him as a viable suspect.

The haughtiness left his expression, and he sank against the corner of the desk, sitting on it heavily. "Preston was supposed to keep this quiet. He promised he would."

"Promises don't mean a lot to some people," Vince offered.

Garza snorted. "Ain't that the truth. Look, I don't know where you got your information, but I didn't kill Preston. After he and I talked, I swore I'd pay the money back, and I am doing that. I can't do it all at once. I sold one of my cars, a restored roadster. It was more like a toy than a vehicle to drive. Instead of funding my retirement, I'm siphoning that money back into the building fund when I can. I didn't kill Preston. You know, he wasn't a saint. He cheated on every woman he's ever dated. What about them? What about the husbands of the married ones?"

Caprice and Vince just stared at him. Silence sometimes shook out more information than the longest question.

"Something happened with Preston," Garza tossed out there.

"What do you mean, something happened?" Caprice asked, this time because she couldn't help it.

"A few weeks before he was killed, he seemed to have a changed outlook on life. I heard that he and Father Gregory had a very long talk. I don't know. It seemed like he got a conscience or something. He was spending more time on the murals at the community center. He seemed distracted, like his mind was on something else."

"A new woman?" Caprice asked, thinking about Bella.

"No. I don't think so. It was more like what happened with me. When I got in this financial mess, it was all I could think about. I'd be at a meeting but wouldn't really be there. I'd be having dinner with my family but wouldn't really hear what they were saying. It was more like that."

"You said that was a few weeks before he died?" Vince asked.

"Yes."

Caprice knew Father Gregory would be a dead end. He certainly wouldn't talk about anyone he'd counseled. "How do you know Bob saw Father Gregory?" she asked.

"One of the women on the board helps out in the church office now and then. She happened to be there when Bob showed up for an appointment with Father Gregory. She told me she'd seen him there."

Garza could be telling the truth, but that truth also didn't mean he didn't kill Bob. He was fit enough and strong enough to have used that skimmer too, so she asked, "Do you have a membership at Shape Up?"

His narrowed eyes turned wary again. "I do. Why?"

"Caprice ran into a little trouble there Saturday night," Vince revealed. "There's someone who doesn't seem to like her asking questions."

Garza remained silent.

"Let's put it this way," Vince said. "If any harm comes to Caprice, I'll know who to come after first."

"You're not serious." Garza straightened, squared his shoulders, and appeared outraged.

Caprice knew it could all be an act. He could have murdered Bob whether he was putting the money back or not. He could have murdered Bob *and* tried to harm her.

"We're finished here," Garza said, going to the office door and opening it.

Vince responded, "For now."

Straight-lipped and sullen, Garza saw them out.

Once outside, Vince took Caprice's elbow and guided her to his car. Once they were inside the vehicle, he turned to her. "What do you think?"

"I don't know. He certainly had motive. He has a membership at Shape Up. He could have been there and slipped into the pool area without anybody seeing him. He's fit and strong enough to have used that skimmer."

Vince started up his car, made a K-turn in the immense driveway, and drove away from the house.

"I've been thinking about buying a gun. Maybe you should think about it too."

She knew Grant had one. Before coming to Kismet, he'd worked in a big city. "I don't want to go that route."

"With your penchant for trouble, you might need backup."

"That's not the kind of backup I want. It's not me, Vince. I'll carry the pepper-spray gun. I'll even get another one if it makes you feel better. But I do not want to buy a weapon that could kill someone."

Vince gave her a long look. "I hope you're not making a mistake."

Chapter Fifteen

Caprice was nervous. Not because she felt followed. That feeling had gone away, and yesterday she'd insisted Nikki go back to her condo. No, today she was nervous because tonight she might become an award winner. She chided herself for being silly about her anxiety. But tonight was the awards dinner for Women for a Better Kismet at the Country Squire Golf and Recreation Club. She couldn't help but think about winning . . . or about Seth taking her.

So that she wouldn't become caught up in reverie about either, she concentrated on Ace Richland as he opened his door to her.

Ace was really just an ordinary guy. Okay. An ordinary guy who was used to being waited on sometimes. An ordinary guy who was accustomed to chauffeurs and limousines. But a guy who also remembered where he came from and, when he was alone, did let his hair down, so to speak.

After her appointment with him on Monday, knowing she'd have to put all her design skills on speed-dial and fast forward, she'd promised she'd have Trista's room and the pool area ready by the end of the week. Thanks to her business contacts and additional "rush delivery" extra payments, she'd accomplished what she'd set out to do.

Today, when Ace let Caprice in, his hair wasn't gelled up, but rather flat against his head. She wondered if he wore makeup when he was out in public. Today the lines on his face cut deep. The temperature outside was in the nineties, but inside Ace's mansion, it was around seventy-four in most of the rooms. Those more exposed to afternoon sun might be a little warmer, so that's why instead of being dressed for outside, he was dressed for inside, wearing a gray T-shirt and blue, very washed jeans.

"It's coming along." He led her to his den. His platinum records decorated the walls, while a Grammy sat high on a shelf. Guitars that he no longer used but kept as memorabilia hung on another wall. The glass-and-black-enamel desk had a modern look. That's what he'd wanted. The flat-screen computer monitor and keyboard formed another station over in the corner so it wasn't the main focus. There was a dock for his electronic devices and a Bose system that surrounded him with music. Or he could wear earphones to listen to demo tapes and recordings.

"I'm comfortable here," he said now, motioning to the guitars. "What would you say if I said I'm thinking about becoming a record executive and finding new talent to put on my own label?"

"I think that would be a great way to branch out, if you have the investment money to put into it. You certainly have the wherewithal and the right contacts for publicity and public relations. You're in the perfect position to do it. But when are you going to have time if you're touring?"

He pointed at her. "Now that's the sixty-million-dollar question. I don't know. But I do know that I have downtime on a tour. I need something to keep me busy so I don't get into trouble. I haven't done drugs for years, and I don't intend to do them again, but women were a problem in the past. Granted, I might not have as many coming after me now, but I don't want them to be the reason I'm on the road. So I need work other than the singing and the sound checks. This will keep me busy."

He led her out of his den and headed for the back stairs to go up to Trista's room. As he let her precede him up the stairs, he said, "Danny's working in the pool house now. He says he's almost finished. What's his story?"

"He hasn't told you?" she asked with a small smile.

Ace snorted. "That kid's quieter than a church mouse, but certainly not as meek. He has an attitude that I certainly recognize. I had the same one. But he's got talent, too, so he might be able to live with the attitude. It just depends. As soon as you e-mailed me his sketch, I knew it was what I wanted. How did you know he'd be capable of doing this?"

"I saw his artistry at the community center, and his T-shirts and hand-painted sneakers. How do you like his T-shirts?"

"Come to think of it, I like them a lot. I asked him if he'd custom-make a few for me for the tour."

"That's wonderful. He could get his name out there."

"I like the sneakers too, for that matter. We'll see what he has time to do. I can tell he's something of a perfectionist." He paused, then added, "I found out today Trista's coming on Sunday. That will give her a couple of days to get settled before the party."

Up in Trista's room, Caprice had done exactly what Ace had wanted. The room was painted pale pink. She'd bought pink-and-white striped curtains and a matching frilly spread for the canopy bed, though it made her cringe to think she was decorating for an eleven-year-old. Ace had ordered a few American Girl dolls that sat in a hutch in the corner. He had his assistant choose the doll clothes to go with them. There was also some doll furniture—a canopy bed, a wardrobe, and accessories that Megan would love dearly to have but never would. They were simply too expensive. Ace had insisted on a bookshelf but had no idea what Trista read. Caprice wondered if the shelves would even be necessary. Maybe she had an e-reader. When she asked him if he wanted her to set up a computer station, he said no. Trista was too young for that.

Just how much attention had Ace paid to his daughter, to her likes and dislikes, to her hobbies and pastimes?

"I know it's a bit unusual," he said, "but I'm not having Alyssa send out invitations to this party. It's for family, friends, and a few associates. I'm not going to go formal. You will come, won't you? Bring a plus-one. I don't care, but I want to see friendly faces, not people who want something from me."

"I'd be glad to come, and I'll think about the plus-one. The doctor I'm dating might be on call."

The rest of the house was basically as Caprice had staged it. She'd made a few adjustments here and there that Ace had wanted, switching out furniture, changing a painting, using a bedspread in a different color in one of the spare rooms. He'd added photographs of his family and of him and Trista, along with memorabilia gathered during his travels. The place was rapidly becoming his.

They returned downstairs. When they walked out to the pool area, he said, "This makes me smile. I like it."

Although the umbrellas weren't open, the colors were easy to see. Caprice had styled the furniture in groupings, and all the pieces were nautical colors, from sea green to the deepest blue, including the umbrella fabrics.

"I feel peaceful out here. I wrote a song here today, even in the heat."

"I'm glad your muse is visiting you."

"Just so she stays. I need new material for this tour, and I don't have a lot of time to add it."

They were approaching the pool house when Caprice heard rap music coming from inside.

"He brought along one of those old-time boom boxes. What can you do? Everybody's inner artist is fed by something different. I told him I don't care. He switched it off when I was out here writing and didn't seem to mind doing it. I think we've got a little mutual respect going on."

Caprice was glad of that. Even if Danny wouldn't talk, just being around someone he respected was a benefit.

When they opened the screen door to the pool house, Danny said over his shoulder, "I'm almost out of iced tea."

"It's not Mrs. Wannamaker," Ace said with a smile as he stepped over the threshold. "She's my housekeeper," he explained to Caprice. "She's been keeping him fortified while he's here."

Danny looked a bit embarrassed when he saw Caprice and Ace. "Sorry," he mumbled as he switched off the music. "I didn't know it was you."

Immediately, Caprice's attention went to the long wall. The mural was almost finished.

"Danny, this is gorgeous. Oh my gosh, you are so talented."

Now he really looked embarrassed. "I've never done anything all by myself before. It's kind of weird. I can do whatever I want, use whatever colors I want, put as much in it as I want."

There were three dolphins cavorting in waves.

"I was going to do the sun glinting off their backs, like in the morning, but then I thought I could really do something fantastic with the sky if I did evening and a sunset."

"It's perfect for in here. You could get more business after Ace's party. Are you ready for that?"

"I don't know."

"Well, you're doing a good job."

"Yeah, and I'm getting paid, too," he said with the first real smile she'd seen on him.

"We'll let you get back to it," Ace said. "I'll tell Mrs. Wannamaker you need more iced tea."

After he and Caprice left the pool house, he shrugged. "That's more than he's said in the few days he's been here."

"He's excited about the work. This is good for him. Thanks, Ace, for giving him a chance."

"No problem. I remember too well how I needed an outlet for my music when I was his age."

As her Nana often told her, *memories were life's*

jewels. She herself might be making a few memories tonight that she could keep locked in her heart for a lifetime.

"The winner of the Women for a Better Kismet Woman of the Year Award is . . ."

No drumroll accompanied those words, but Caprice held her breath anyway. She was seated at a huge round table in the dining room of the Country Squire Golf and Recreation Club, and her palms were clammy as she waited for the announcement. Seated on her left, Seth held her hand under the table. She *had* wowed him tonight in her flapper-style cocktail dress. Roz, Monty, Juan, and some other friends also stared at the podium with her and her family.

Under the twinkling lights of crystal chandeliers, Caprice held Seth's hand a little tighter.

Ginny Malcolm, president of Women for a Better Kismet, announced, "Congratulations go to . . . Wendy Newcomb."

There was a happy squeal from the table behind Caprice's and much applause in the whole room. Caprice kept a smile on her face. Wendy was certainly a deserving recipient. She'd been a major force in getting a women's shelter set up in Kismet, and Caprice would happily congratulate her.

Seth leaned close. "I'm sorry."

"Don't be. Wendy deserves it."

"So do you," he said loyally, and she could have kissed him right then and there. But she didn't because Nikki was leaning toward her on her other side.

"You'll win next year."

"How do you know I'll do something to even be nominated?" she teased.

"You will."

Wendy was at the podium then, thanking everyone. After another round of applause, she returned to her seat. Ginny said a few more words, closing the formal part of the evening, and then many of the guests stood.

After Caprice's mom and dad had given her consoling hugs, Roz had given her a thumbs-up sign, and Vince had patted her on her back, she told them all, "We had a fun night of it, didn't we? What more could we want?"

"An award for your wall," Nana grumbled.

"All of you know as well as I do that Wendy gives her life to that shelter."

"There's a story there," Bella said with conviction.

There might be. But if there was, Wendy never talked about it. It was hard to maintain privacy in Kismet, and the fact that she'd done so up to now meant she hadn't told anyone if there *was* a story there.

Monty came over to her now and said almost shyly, "It's a shame you didn't win."

"Something for me to aspire to another year."

"I'd better get going," he said, looking around. "This isn't a crowd I usually run with."

This was the first time Caprice had ever seen Monty dressed up. He wore a navy suit, a striped tie, and a white shirt. He'd done that for her, and she appreciated it.

"Thanks for coming." She'd received free tickets for the dinner, and she'd given one to him.

"It was a great meal, but not as good as what Nikki serves at your open houses."

Caprice laughed. "She'll be glad to hear you say that."

"I'd better be going, but I did want to remind you, I still have Bob's stuff in my garage."

"I forgot all about that. It's just tarps, right?"

"Some other stuff, too."

"Painting equipment?"

"Mostly. And a backpack."

"Is it in the way?"

"Nah. There's an old detached garage behind my apartment, and I store equipment in it. I usually park my truck on the street."

"I'll either pick it up myself, or give Kent Osgood a call. Thanks for reminding me."

After a good-bye to Roz and Juan, Monty left.

When Bella approached Caprice, she looked a little less troubled than she had for the past few weeks. She and Joe had sat next to each other at the table, leaned close, and spoken in low tones now and then.

"I'm sorry you didn't win," Bella said. "If you had won, I'd be jealous, but that didn't mean I wasn't rooting for you."

Bella's honesty amused Caprice. Diplomatically, she responded, "I know you're in my corner."

"Always. And speaking of corners, thanks for being in mine."

"How are you doing?"

"A little better." She glanced over at Joe, who was talking to their dad. "Joe doesn't go out at night anymore, and he's trying to help me more around the house. I guess he's getting in practice for when I'm more pregnant."

Caprice didn't think Joe had ever helped Bella around the house, not even during her other pregnancies. "Maybe he feels guilty about hiding his gambling."

"He does, just as I feel guilty about things. Father Gregory's helping. Discussing it with him can be really painful, but we're trying."

"Do you think you can be happy again?"

"Maybe happier than before. I don't know. A new baby could be another strain, or it could be a real bond. It all depends on how the two of us handle it." Bella's voice dropped a little lower. "I think Joe finally believes me that I didn't have an affair with Bob. I told him, if he wants a DNA test after the baby's born, we'll do that."

"How would you feel if he wants it?"

"Probably hurt. But he's been hurt, too, by the idea that I even wanted to have a coffee date with Bob."

They both looked toward Joe. Some of the dinner guests were starting to leave.

Bella said, "Oh, my gosh. There's Lauren Jacobs. I haven't seen her in years."

Caprice knew exactly who Lauren Jacobs was. She was the woman Bob had slept with while he was dating Bella.

"You don't see her when you go to the mall?" Lauren was the manager of a shoe store there—The Shoe Tree.

"I never go into that store," Bella explained. "Not that I hold a grudge. Not after all these years. But it's still awkward seeing her. She and I never really knew each other. She was ahead of me in high school."

Caprice nodded as she watched Lauren pass from the ballroom to the reception area. "Do you think she and Bob were still friends?"

Bella shrugged. "I have no idea."

Since Caprice was having trouble finding any true friends of Bob's, she put Lauren Jacobs at the top of her list. She just might have to make a visit to the mall tomorrow.

The Shoe Tree had an expansive display in the front windows, purses hanging to one side, colorful socks on the other. But basically, it was a do-it-yourself warehouse. Shelves with stacks of boxes lined the aisles, and customers pulled out the style and tried on the shoe that might suit them. Clerks checked the aisles to help, but they mostly went to the back to find an odd size rather than really helping fit a shoe to a foot.

Nana often told Caprice she shouldn't buy shoes in a place like this. She should go to the little store in the oldest part of Kismet where the smell of real leather wasn't just a memory. But Caprice liked fashionable shoes as much as the next woman. She also didn't want to pay an exorbitant amount for an odd color to go with a specific outfit. So she was a customer of The Shoe Tree at least once a season.

She'd arrived here early on purpose this morning, knowing the store wouldn't be well populated yet. Business always picked up toward afternoon.

When Caprice walked into The Shoe Tree, she didn't see anyone around. But then she heard a clatter along one of the side shelves, and she walked that way. She was pleased to see Lauren herself, unboxing several shoe designs and arranging the shoes on the top shelf.

Caprice said, "Excuse me."

Lauren swung around as if she hadn't heard Caprice approach. She put her hand over her heart and looked totally startled. "I didn't know anyone had come in. I didn't hear the bell," the auburn-haired woman said.

Another redhead. Bob seemed to like red hair on his women. But then she thought about Bella. Maybe he didn't have a preference at all. Maybe he just liked women in general.

"I'm sorry if I surprised you."

Lauren tilted her head and studied her. "Don't I know you?"

"Caprice De Luca."

Lauren nodded slowly. "Oh, yes, Bella's sister. Can I help you with something? My clerk is supposed to be handling the cash register, but she had car trouble this morning, so she's late. Is there a particular style of shoe you're interested in?"

"I'm not interested in shoes, at least not today."

Lauren looked puzzled. "I don't understand."

"I wondered if you were still friends with Bob Preston when he died."

Lauren's chin quivered. "I can't get Bob off my mind," she said. "But why do you need to know if we were friends?"

"Bob didn't seem to have many real friends. My sister, Bella, found him after he was murdered. I'm just trying to figure out what might have happened, who might have had a grudge against him. Were you friends?"

"I liked to think we were."

"Did you see him often?"

"We ran into each other now and then at the Koffee Klatch. We had lunch together every couple of months. All those years ago, we weren't involved very long romantically, but we gravitated back to each other now and then, if you know what I mean."

Oh, yes, Caprice knew what she meant. Two people who'd been intimate had a familiarity that could be comfortable. When they were lonely, they sought each other out, or they sought comfort any way they could.

"When was the last time you spoke to him?"

"A few days before he died. We had coffee. He'd called me because . . ." She stopped, as if maybe she didn't know if she should go on.

Obviously, Lauren was looking for a good reason to spill what she knew. "The truth is, the police are looking at my sister for the murder. I'd like to give them other viable suspects. Anything you can tell me will help."

After a pensive pause, Lauren said, "Originally Bob called me because he was excited about a new business venture. He'd developed an app for smartphones that had something to do with a contract with a painting company and a home-improvement chain. He was all excited about it. He told me about that, but then he told me something else, too. He'd been out of town recently."

Maybe Lauren knew where Bob had been when Caprice had had to call Monty to come in and take over for him. "I knew he was out of town, but I didn't know where he went. He reneged on a painting job for me, and that was unlike him."

"I'm not sure where he went. He didn't say. But he did say he'd found family that he never knew he had."

"Close family?"

"I'm not sure. I got the feeling that it was still all new, and he wasn't sure how to handle it. He got a call that cut our conversation short. I don't know who called him, but it was something about signing papers. He left and . . . I never saw him again."

Those papers could have had to do with a painting contract, or something to do with his company. Signing papers was a nebulous clue. Finding family he didn't know he had wasn't so nebulous.

Just who had unexpectedly dropped into Bob's life?

Chapter Sixteen

"You have to come over right away," Ace had said when he phoned Caprice Sunday afternoon. "There's a problem and only you can fix it."

So Caprice had zoomed over to Ace's. Mrs. Wannamaker let her in and told her to go right upstairs.

From the landing, Caprice could hear a shrill young voice. "I hate it! Dad, I can't believe you did this."

Ace's daughter ran from the pink-ruffled room, passed Caprice, and clomped down the stairs, platform sandals clacking on beautiful hardwood.

Ace called after her, looking woebegone. "Trista. It's pretty."

His eleven-year-old yelled back, "It's not *me*. It's for a little girl. I'm almost a teenager!"

So much for being on the mark with this decorating venture!

When Ace spotted Caprice, he looked defeated. "I know this isn't your fault. It's mine. I'll be right back." He went down the stairs after his daughter.

This *was* her fault. She hadn't pushed Ace away from a concept that had bothered her from its inception. Pink ruffles suited a four-year-old, not an eleven-year-old.

Caprice went into the room she'd decorated for the daughter that Ace thought he knew. Apparently, he didn't. Caprice should have insisted on a call to Trista, or an e-mail, or something. Yes, there were home-improvement shows that surprised house owners with brand-new living rooms, or made-over family rooms, or a functional office. But Caprice understood the truth. Most people, children included, knew exactly what they wanted, and they didn't like their ideas tampered with. If you brought in colors that weren't favorites or made them cringe, they could pretend to be happy, but they wouldn't spend any time in the room. She was experienced enough to know that.

So why had she let Ace convince her that he knew what was best for his daughter?

Because he was a celebrity, and she didn't want to push back? Because he'd been complimentary and she'd wanted him to think well of her? Back to her parochial school training. Not asking the important questions. Not looking behind pat answers. Trying to be the good girl.

Caprice wandered around the room. The cream carpet could go with anything. Thank goodness, they'd decided not to go with the wallpaper with lines of pink roses that Ace had thought Trista would like. But Caprice guessed the pale pink walls would have to go too—overnight. This was going to be a rapid redo.

She took her phone from her pocket and speed-dialed Juan. He answered on the second ring.

"You called?" he joked.

"I need to redo a room quickly."

"How quickly?"

"Yesterday. Are you free this evening?"

"You do like to mess up a guy's plans, don't you?"

"Hot date?"

"A date. I don't know how hot. Not hot at all now if I'm not going to be there. Do you want me to call Monty?"

She heard Ace and Trista climbing the stairs again. "You call him and see if he's available. In the meantime, I'm going to talk to my actual client and find out what she wants. Hopefully we can pull this off fast."

"Charge him extra."

"It's my fault, too. I should have known better."

Juan hummed a few bars of that Beatles song.

Caprice shook her head and ended the call.

Ace's daughter looked sullen and defiant as she stepped into the bedroom. She was a pretty girl and would be a striking teenager. Tall and lanky, she didn't seem quite comfortable with those long legs and nice shoulders. She took after her dad, not only in his lean lankiness, but also in his long face, her chestnut hair, her very green eyes.

"Trista, this is Miss De Luca. She decorated your room, but I told her what to do."

Caprice contradicted him. "This is my fault, Trista, as much as his. He might be paying the bill, but *you* are my client."

Her honesty seemed to surprise the pre-teen. Caprice went on, "I think you and I need a little one-on-

one time." She was pretty sure Ace and his daughter needed one-on-one time too, but that would have to come later.

"What are we going to do?" Trista asked. "The room's finished."

"A room is never finished, and I might be able to work some quick magic. But we need to have a serious discussion first. Come on, let's sit."

They sat in two puffy, pink bedroom chairs that were positioned catty-corner to each other at the window. Caprice had her electronic tablet with her, and she took it out and put it on her lap.

"Should I stay or go?" Ace grumbled from the doorway.

Immediately Trista said, "Go, Dad. Let us get this right."

But Caprice wasn't so dismissive. "I might need your help, and I might need your okay on what I want to do. So can you stay close? As soon as Trista and I finish, you and I have to talk."

Ace cast his gaze one last time at his daughter and left the room, looking as if he'd failed.

"Let's talk. How's your room at home decorated?"

"Mom did a lot of that, so it's not all what I want, either."

"What did you do to your room to make it yours?"

"I put horse posters all over the walls. I love riding. I like the outdoors. You know, swimming in the lake, fishing, that kind of thing."

"Does your dad know?"

"He knows I swim in the lake, but fishing . . . probably not. He's not the fishing type. He can't sit still for two seconds."

Caprice smiled. "He might, if he knows you'd like

to do it. He can always write songs while you're waiting for fish to bite."

Trista thought about that. "Maybe."

"So what's your favorite color?"

"Green."

"Green, like lime green? Or green like grass green or pine green?"

"I guess there are a lot of colors of green. Grass green."

"In other words, you like natural colors."

"Yeah, I guess so."

"My guess is your dad would like to do something more special for you than horse posters on the wall."

"Yeah, but that's what I like."

"You like horses, but they don't have to be on posters, do they?"

"I guess not."

"Did you see the pool house?"

"Yeah. Those dolphins are cool."

Ah ha. Progress. "I commissioned the artist who painted them. Now I don't know if it's possible, or if he's available, or if he can do it in one day, but what would you think about him painting a horse on your wall?"

"Really?"

"Really." Caprice woke up her tablet, put a few words in the search engine, searched, tapped a few times, then placed the tablet in front of Trista. "Let's talk furniture."

"No canopy bed," the preteen said, wrinkling her nose. "I don't like all that frou-frou around me. I don't like something on top of my head. I just want a plain bed."

Caprice really did smile this time. "Does it have

to be wood, or would you like brass?" She tapped a picture. "Or . . ." Caprice typed in the name of a specialty company she used sometimes, found what she was looking for, and showed the page to Trista. "How about an old barn door for your headboard? If they have one available, I can probably get it here in a day or two." The right amount of money could buy almost anything . . . or any service.

"Oh my gosh! That would be so cool."

Thank goodness the windows in the room were standard size. Caprice thought about what kind of curtains or drapes she could find on short notice. There was a specialty shop in York that stocked something Trista might like.

"Instead of standard curtains at your windows, I think I can find something lighter, like scarves we can swirl around a rod, or swaggy valances that come just three-quarters of the way down. And how about a quilt for your bed? Maybe patchwork with lots of colors."

"I think I'm going to like my room."

At that, Caprice laughed out loud. "That's the whole idea."

Trista glanced at the ruffled bedspread. "What are you going to do with that?"

"Lots of little girls would love it. I'll see what your dad wants to do. I can try to return it, or if he's willing, he can donate it to a second-hand furniture store and somebody who really needs it can buy it for a good price."

"Do you think I should have told him I liked it?" Trista screwed up her face as if that were a terrible idea.

"You have to be honest with your dad."

"We don't have much time together, and when we do, I don't like to make waves. But this . . ." She waved around the room. "It was awful for me."

"You're going to have a week with your dad now, right?"

"Yes."

"Tell him what you like. Tell him how much you like horses. And definitely tell him about the fishing."

"He'll think I'm a bumpkin. He's into rock and glitz and parties."

"Is he really? Or is that what's in the tabloids all the time?" She knew there was a difference between publicity, public relations, and real life.

"You don't think he parties all the time?"

"I don't know your dad well, Trista, but if you have questions, ask them."

"Can you ask *your* dad anything?"

"Mostly I can, but it takes practice. Once you start asking a few questions, the next ones won't be so hard."

At least they wouldn't be for Trista. She didn't know how Ace would like answering them, but he might as well get into the rhythm of it if he wanted a real relationship with his daughter, especially as she grew into her teenage years.

"Now I have to talk to your dad about all this."

"You mean how much it's going to cost."

"The cost, but also about deliveries, and when he's going to be here, and how much I can get done right away."

"You're going to start now?"

"I sure am. My assistant's on call."

"You like what you do, don't you?"

"I do. Especially when I get it right."

For the next couple of hours, Caprice called Danny, phoned other contacts, prepared a list for Juan, and gathered up bedding. Juan's list consisted of items he could pick up in the storage unit and bring right over. She'd stored a stained-glass lamp she suspected would fit the new decor, a swan-armed rocker she'd had reupholstered in a pretty plaid fabric in yellow and taupe, a wooden coatrack that would be practical for a girl Trista's age. She could hang her backpack on there, a pair of jeans she didn't feel like hanging up, her purse, her belt, or something decorative. They'd figure that out when more of the room was finished. If she remembered correctly, she had a two-tiered hobnail milk-glass light that would be perfect for a nightstand. Nightstands. She'd do some searching online for those. This room would come together and come together before Ace's pool party. In the morning, Juan and Monty would disassemble the bed and move furniture in and out. She was just about to find Ace and tell him she'd done as much as she could for tonight when her phone played.

She thought it might be Nikki, checking in on her. However, instead of Nikki's number, she saw Seth's and smiled. "Hi," she said brightly, even though she was tired after the long day.

"Hi. I just got finished my shift. Are you home?"

"No, but I will be in about an hour. Why?"

"I'd like to stop over."

Cherry on the Top closed at ten, and it was after ten. "All right. I'll see you at my place in an hour."

"Caprice?"

"What?"

"Never mind. I'll see you at your place."

Caprice didn't like that somber note in Seth's voice. She didn't like it at all.

Caprice was ready when Seth arrived. Ready, in that she'd brewed a pot of choco-mocha coffee and placed a few biscotti from a new batch she'd baked yesterday on a yellow plate. She thought about icing the coffee, but she could do that if that's what Seth wanted.

Shasta had made herself comfortable by the sofa. Although she barked when she was alerted by Seth on the steps outside, she didn't get up. Caprice wondered how near labor she was. A few days? A week? It was hard to know. But she'd be taking her to Marcus for a checkup tomorrow.

Sophia lounged on the top perch of the cat tree, her tail and front paw hanging over the side. She might get up for a stroll around the house before bed, but this was as active as she got on a hot summer night, air-conditioning or not.

Caprice opened her door to Seth, as always eager to see him. He smiled, but she thought that smile looked forced.

"I have coffee," she said. "I can ice it, if you're too hot."

"Iced sounds good. You can tell me about your day."

She didn't really want to tell him about her day. She wanted to know why he was here. She didn't need a sixth sense to know this wasn't entirely a routine social visit. But she could be in denial as well as anyone else, and she wasn't going to ruin any time she could have with Seth.

He stooped to pat Shasta and rub his hand down

over her back and along her tummy. "Is she slowing down?"

"She is. Are dogs like humans? Do they suddenly get a spurt of energy before they deliver?"

"I imagine that, just as with women, each case is individual."

"Spoken like a true doctor."

When they went through the dining room into the kitchen, Seth spied the plate of biscotti. "Were you working when I called?"

"I was at Ace Richland's. He and I made a real mess of decorating his daughter's room. She hated it, so I'm redoing it. Danny's going to start a mural tomorrow. I have to look for bedding and drapes, among other things, and get it done quickly. A little cream in your iced coffee, or pure caffeine?"

"Tonight, a little cream might be nice. I know yours is the real stuff from the White Rose Dairy."

She laughed, but she didn't feel like laughing. Delaying the inevitable might make the moment bearable, but it also made it fraught with tension.

After she'd fixed two glasses of coffee, they sat around the corner from each other at the table rather than going into the living room. That was a sure indication this was going to be a discussion, not a makeout session.

They each took a biscotti. They each sipped their iced coffee. But then their eyes met and Caprice wanted the truth.

"What's happened, Seth?"

He gave a little shrug. "I got the fellowship."

The fact that her heart sank to her toes must have been obvious on her face. He reached across and took her hand. "I like you, Caprice, and more than that, I care about you."

"I care about you too."

"That's why saying what I have to say is so damn hard."

"Then just say it, and put us both out of our misery." She tried to keep her tone light, but that was highly impossible.

Looking troubled, he squeezed her hand, then released it. "My fellowship is for a year. I know better than to ask you to stand by and wait until I have free time to spend with you because I'm not going to have any free time. No, Baltimore isn't that far away, but it's a lifetime away in what I'll be doing, and what you do here. Trauma medicine is important to me, and at the end of the year, I don't know where my new training will lead."

"So you're dumping me." She couldn't help but be blunt about it.

"No, I am not dumping you, but . . . we both have decisions to make. Do you want to stay in touch and e-mail when we get the chance?"

"Christmas cards?" she joked. Humor usually helped heartbreak, didn't it?

"Certainly Christmas cards."

While she was being blunt and Seth was being honest, she decided to take both to their limits. "What do *you* want?"

If she'd asked Travis what he'd wanted, maybe he would have told her he still had dreams of getting back together with his ex-wife. At least she'd learned to ask.

"I know this is terrifically selfish of me, but this is what I'd like," Seth said. "I'd like to stay in touch now and then. At the end of the fellowship year, if both of us are still unattached, we can pick up where we left off."

"If you don't decide to take a job in Alaska or Timbuktu," she muttered, realizing sometimes honesty was harder to take than pretense.

"I know all of this is iffy, and no woman wants iffy, not about a relationship. But you asked what I wanted, and that's what I want."

Her iced-coffee glass was sweating on the table. She kept her gaze on one of the condensation dribbles. "You might meet a pretty young intern who wants to work with Doctors Without Borders. You might want to do that, too."

"That's true. But if I meet a pretty young intern, and if I'd get serious, I'd certainly let you know, just as I'd like you to let me know if you meet anyone you want to get serious with. Could that be our deal?"

As deals went, it wasn't much of one. On the other hand, she and Seth would still have a tenuous connection, at least for the next year.

He went on decisively, "What I don't want, Caprice, is for you to put your life on hold for a year. I'm not asking you to do that. I've put mine on hold since . . ." He abruptly stopped.

"Since?" she asked gently.

"Since I lost a patient during surgery and decided maybe I didn't want a general surgery practice. I came to Kismet to get my bearings and figure out where I wanted a practice to go. The chance for this fellowship was like a tap on the shoulder, guiding me. Being accepted into the program was another sign that this is the right direction. You believe in signs, don't you?"

Yes, she did. Nana had taught her how to recognize and even wait for them. "I do."

Reaching for her hand again, he held it in his. "Meeting you and getting to know you has been a sign too. Before I can have a real personal life, I have to figure out where my professional life is going."

She could see how that was true. Gazing into his eyes, she asked, "When are you leaving?"

"Two weeks."

"That soon."

"I'm taking over a slot someone vacated, so everything is rush-rush."

"What about the urgent care center? Will they be short-staffed?"

"I found someone for them, a friend I went to school with. He's been practicing in Philadelphia and isn't overly crazy about it. He thinks Kismet might be a nice fit."

With a reluctance she felt too, Seth unclasped their hands, pushed his coffee away, and stood. "I'd better be going. I know you have a full day tomorrow, and so do I."

Now being around Seth hurt because she knew she was going to miss him. She suspected the same was true for him. Her heart heavy, she walked him to the door.

"You will say good-bye before you leave, won't you?"

"Of course, I will. I'm not going to lie and tell you I won't miss you."

"You couldn't lie if your life depended on it," she said, meaning it.

DEADLY DECOR 269

He wrapped his arms around her, brought her close, and kissed her gently. Then he backed away.

He didn't say good-bye, and Caprice knew that was going to be hard for both of them to do.

She watched him walk to his truck and get in. She watched him start it up and then drive away. Her heart hurt, but she knew neither of them were to blame. She'd dated Seth with her eyes wide open. Tonight when she closed them, she'd see his face and wonder what they could have had.

For the next two days, Caprice worked to the exclusion of everything else, except taking care of Sophia and Shasta. She simply didn't want to think about Seth's leaving. Now as she drove to Ace's on Tuesday afternoon, she asked herself if Seth could have made the grand gesture and said he was giving up the fellowship for her . . . for them. But they hadn't dated long enough for that. They hadn't known each other long enough for that. He had to figure out what and where he wanted to practice. He had to figure out if she fit into his life and he fit into hers.

After Shasta's appointment with Marcus yesterday, Caprice had readied everything she'd need for the birth of Shasta's pups because Marcus had decreed it would be soon. She'd sanitized the garage as much as possible over the weekend, setting up the borrowed whelping bed inside a modular containment pen. Leaving the pen's gate open, she'd encouraged Shasta to explore the box often. On a previous visit to Marcus, Caprice had talked to him about supplies she'd need to deliver the pups and what she should do to help that happen safely. He'd given her a list of instructions. After she'd prepared the box with layers of newspaper, then laid an old quilt in one corner, she'd spread wood chips on a rubber mat around it within the pen. The whelping box, borrowed from a friend of Marcus's who raised Labrador retrievers, would be roomy enough for Shasta and her brood. The pups would be making a home in the garage for at least six weeks.

After the garage was ready, Caprice had led Shasta to the box several times and the cocker had lain in it, even taken a nap there while Caprice weeded flower beds in the front yard with the garage door up. Since the garage's thick, cement-block walls kept it cooler than the rest of the house, and since the windows were shaded by poplars all day, the area should be perfect for Shasta and the newborn pups. Everything was ready, down to the latex gloves and the heat lamp.

Now all she had to worry about was Trista liking her redone room. Danny had called earlier today and said he'd be finished with the mural this afternoon. So she was headed there now. Trista and Ace had been barred from the bedroom until she was finished with it. This would be the great reveal. Tomorrow the pool party would create a different type of excitement.

When she arrived at Ace's, she spotted new security cameras. However, her code still opened the gate. After she rang the bell, a pretty young woman in royal blue slacks and shirt opened the door.

"I'm Alyssa," she said, shaking Caprice's hand. "The event planner. I'm making sure we're all set up for tomorrow. Ace said you could go right up. He and Trista are in the pool."

She was glad they were getting father and daughter time. She was hoping they were getting to know each other better. After she ran up the stairs, she walked down the hall to Trista's room and opened the door. Danny was packing up his paints.

When he saw her, he smiled. "What do you think? If you don't like it, there's not much I can do at this late date."

She did like it. A mare and a foal were standing at a fence in the foreground, nibbling grass. The scene was vibrant and alive. The horses' coats caught the light of a late-day sun. Everything about the scene was captivating.

"Danny, this is fabulous. It's even better than the dolphins."

"The dolphins were a practice run."

He continued putting his things together, stuffing them into a backpack. He glanced up at her once and then twice, and she guessed he wanted to ask her something.

"What?"

"Ace saw this when it was almost finished even though he knew he wasn't supposed to. He made me an offer."

"What kind of offer?"

"He said if I push my grades up this year and earn my diploma, he'll invest in sending me to art school."

"Oh my gosh, Danny, that's huge . . . and crazy wonderful. What did you say?"

"I said I'd talk to my mom, but I was sure she'd approve. Painting is what I love to do, Miss De Luca, and if I could do this and earn money from it, maybe

I could help Mom, too. She's had it tough. I want her to find a guy she can really count on. I guess I got so mad at Bob because he only wanted that one-night stand. I heard Mom talking to a friend. She was crying. Bob didn't think past that night to the next day. I fought with him because of Mom. She deserves the best, not a schemer like him. And I don't think it's just his scheming with women that might have gotten him killed."

"Do you know something else?"

After a long pause, Danny seemed to make up his mind. "You know that Kent who works with Bob? Some people say he's just a partner. But he's really Bob's half brother. I overheard Bob on his cell with a lawyer. That lawyer was changing Bob's will."

If Kent would be the beneficiary, he had a lot to gain from Bob's death. However, if he didn't know it was changed, that left a lot of possible brother-to-brother controversy, didn't it? A different dad? The same mom? The same dad? A different mom? More questions to add to her list instead of fewer. But for right now, she was happy with the room they'd created for Trista.

"Thank you for telling me."

"Do you know who did it yet?"

"Not yet. But I'll keep working on it. Now, however, let's see if Trista likes her room."

She glanced around. The headboard was perfect, and so was the distressed dresser and matching desk. The plaid valances and the patchwork bedspread that looked like an old down quilt added the colors to the room that Trista liked most. Caprice had found throw rugs too. One said "Build Your Dream," and bright hearts danced all over another. A third was designed with horses running across it. Trista's bathroom transitioned into the same theme, with a shower curtain, rugs, and even towels decorated with a band of horses. Everything was colorful, and pieces of it could be changed as Trista grew older and her taste changed. But for now, Caprice thought it was nearly perfect. She called Ace on his cell.

"Ready for us?" he asked.

"As ready as we're going to be. You've got to watch Trista's face. When she first sees it, you'll know if it's what she envisioned."

"And if it's not?"

"Then I guess we start all over again, or we take it apart and fix what she wants to change."

"A woman has the right to change her mind."

"Something like that."

"Okay, we'll be up."

In less than five minutes, they were outside the door. Ace rapped and Caprice opened it. Trista stepped inside, her dad's hand on her shoulder.

Her face broke into a wide grin. "This is more like it. It's wicked good, Caprice. Oh, look at this mural."

She went over to the horses and said, "Can I touch?"

"You better not pet the little one yet," Danny advised. "He might still have some wet spots. But the rest is dry."

She touched the ears on the mare, then stretched her hand down toward the floor, where the painted grass grew. "It looks so real. Look at these tiny little wildflowers. Oh, Daddy, I love it."

Daddy. From the look on Ace's face, Caprice

had the feeling his daughter hadn't called him that in a while.

He regained his composure quickly and looked at Danny. "What's your next job?"

"Nothing as great as this. I'm going to start on those T-shirts."

Ace rubbed his chin. "I might know a guy who could set up a Web site for you. I'll check into it. I want to see you move forward, understand?"

"Yes, sir."

Caprice hadn't heard that deference in Danny's voice since she'd met him. She liked hearing it.

"So we're ready for tomorrow night, everybody. Danny, you're invited, you know. Bring your mom if you want. This is a family party. Oh, and Caprice, your brother and Grant Weatherford are invited too. They're doing some work for me. Didn't want you to be surprised when you got here."

She would have been.

Ace crooked his finger at Caprice to follow him into the hall. Once there, he studied her. "You're not yourself. You haven't been the past two days."

"Of course I'm myself."

"You know what I mean. You've been quiet— quieter than usual anyway."

"I have a lot on my mind. I'm just strategizing a bit and figuring out the best way to go forward in finding Bob Preston's murderer. I ran into a little trouble."

"Does someone not want you asking questions? Did someone threaten you?"

"Ace, this isn't your concern."

"I can put a bodyguard on you. I know plenty of them."

"I don't need a bodyguard. Really. Tomorrow night will take my mind off everything that's happened."

Not only the murder investigation, but Seth's leaving too.

Chapter Seventeen

On Wednesday evening Ace's party was in full swing when Caprice arrived, and she liked the vibe she was getting from everyone there. She was so used to overseeing open houses that it was hard to act like a guest, and she kept reminding herself this wasn't an open house. Ace had made it clear that he wanted her to be his guest, so she'd dressed like a guest, in a gauzy, strapless maxi-dress. It was easy to get in and out of if she wanted to change into the bathing suit she'd brought along and stowed in the pool house.

She really didn't want to change into it or go near the pool. For one thing, her nightmare experience of being pushed under until her breath practically ran out was still very fresh in her mind. The second thing? She just didn't like wearing her bathing suit and feeling "exposed" around . . . anyone.

So she migrated from room to room and had a more than pleasant conversation with Ace's parents. They were down-to-earth and reminded her very much of her own mom and dad. Whenever she passed Nikki bustling around the kitchen, her sister tossed her sympathetic looks that brought home the fact that Caprice wished Seth could be here too. But besides his shifts, he had a lot to tie up before he left. Nikki knew how down she was about him leaving.

Caprice was determined not to stay down. What if she'd been dating Seth a year and this had happened? Or two years? What if they'd been more than dating? She knew his practical attitude was the best one they could both adopt, but that didn't make her feel much better.

She speared another one of Nikki's crab balls and popped it into her mouth. Delicious, as always. She'd spotted Vince earlier, but he'd said he wasn't staying long, and she wondered if he'd left already.

A few minutes later, she was involved in a conversation with Ace's public relations consultant about the difficulty in getting the word out about any business when they heard strains of music coming from down the hall.

The consultant said, "You can't keep him away from his guitar very long."

Caprice smiled. "I'm going to take a look."

Following the sounds of the music, Caprice stood in the doorway of the sitting room beside the media room. Ace and two of his band members were strumming acoustic guitars, jamming as musicians do. Because of the music, Caprice didn't hear anyone coming down the hallway, but suddenly Trista was by her side.

"That's it," she moaned. "You won't see him the rest of the night."

Caprice laughed. "You know your dad well."

"I know he loves music more than anything else."

Caprice heard the "more than me" element in her voice, and she simply responded, "It's been his life."

"It's really why he and Mom broke up, not because of some other woman."

Kids knew a lot more than adults gave them credit for.

As if she needed to change the conversation quickly, Trista said, "I do really like my room. You nailed it."

"I'm glad. I can't earn my fee if I don't nail it."

Trista finally smiled. "I like you. You're different from the people Dad usually gets to work for him."

"Different how?"

"I don't know. They're impressed by his money. Sometimes I even think they're scared of him."

"Nope, I'm not scared of him," Caprice assured her. "Are *you* scared of him?"

"Gosh, no. I've seen him first thing in the morning when he can't even get his eyes open." Looking a little bored with the whole music scene, Trista asked, "Will you get in the pool with me? This night's going to get real boring if I have to sit here and listen to him play all night, or talk to Grandma and Gramps."

There weren't any other kids here, and Caprice could see how Trista would be bored. On the other hand, it wasn't her job to entertain her. Still, she liked Ace's daughter. Feeling out of place wasn't comfortable for any kid.

"Maybe I could just sit by the side of the pool while you get in."

"That's no fun. There are some people playing water volleyball. I didn't want to just jump in with strangers, but if I know somebody who's playing, somebody like you . . ." Trista's grin was as disarming as her dad's.

Caprice gave a resigned sigh. "My duffel's in the pool house."

"Okay, let's go get it. My suit's there too."

Once out back, Caprice and Trista wended their way through the tables and umbrellas. Caprice glanced into the pool, where people were laughing and shouting and . . . stopped cold. Grant was playing water volleyball. She hadn't seen him come in. She certainly hadn't expected to see him in board shorts, bare-chested and with his hair soaking wet.

His gaze caught hers, and they stared at each other for a moment. But then he smiled and waved. She waved back, now doubly sure she didn't want to change into her bathing suit and step into the pool.

"Come on," Trista said, "This is going to be fun."

"Fun," Caprice muttered. "This is going to be fun."

There were women wearing bikinis in the pool, and they looked like the women on a TV reality dating show. Earlier she'd heard one of them talking about Ace's tour. They were his backup singers.

Ten minutes later, stepping out of the pool house with Trista, Caprice tried not to think about their svelte figures in bikinis compared to hers. Her bathing suit was sporty rather than stylish, with modestly cut legs. However, it was peacock blue. Her penchant for her favorite colors reached into every aspect of her life, from flowers to furnishings to clothes.

Trista's eagerness combated Caprice's nervousness as they traversed the patio, working their way around groups of guests. The night was absolutely balmy. Caprice had thrown a towel around her shoulders, but now she dropped it on a lounge chair as she followed Trista down the steps into the pool. If she was under water, no one could see her. The problem was, she couldn't play volleyball under the water.

She was usually a confident woman . . . when she was dressed. But in a bathing suit, she felt like a geek at a popular kid's party.

Unfortunately, she and Trista waded into the pool at just the time two of the guests who had been playing volleyball decided to climb out. That meant she and Trista were on Grant's team. So be it. Most of the time, her life was in the hands of fate, and fate definitely had an odd sense of humor.

Just as in a real volleyball game, they rotated their positions in serving. At least Caprice did know how to hit the ball over the net. As she did when engaged in most athletic activities, she soon forgot her self-consciousness and entered into the spirit of the game. Grant was their powerhouse, but the rest of them helped, even Trista, who had a lot of oomph behind her hits. Caprice even spiked a ball, and their team surged ahead.

Somehow in the rotation, she ended up standing next to Grant in the back row. That didn't matter. She still intended to hold her own. Caprice watched a pretty brunette from their team serve to the other side. A guy on the other team whacked the ball hard. It sailed toward her and Grant, and looked like it would come down right between them.

Caprice knew she'd have to jump to hit it. She could just let Grant handle the shot, but in a split-second decision, she decided not to. She jumped. She didn't know if she lost her balance or Grant brushed against her trying to reach the ball . . . or what. She just knew that one minute she was above the water, and the next minute she was under it. However, she wasn't there long, not long enough to once again experience panic. A strong arm snagged her around the waist and hiked her up to the surface.

She coughed.

Grant asked, "Are you okay?"

She looked up into his very gray eyes, coughed again, then realized he was still studying her face.

"Caprice?"

She couldn't look away. She couldn't find her voice. She couldn't . . .

"Breathe," he suggested.

She did, and then felt so foolish she mumbled, "I'm fine," and turned away from him, eager to get back into the rhythm of the game, eager to escape his steady perusal.

Though she took a few steps away, he clasped her shoulder to stop her. "What are those scrapes on your back? Did Sophia use you for a scratching post?"

She swung around. "What?"

"You have scratches and faint black and blue marks on your back. Did you fall?"

It had been ten days since her scare at Shape Up's pool. But she supposed the scratches weren't completely gone. A few of the volleyball players were studying them inquisitively now. She certainly couldn't explain what had happened here.

Trista was watching them too. She gave Caprice a little smile as if she thought something more than volleyball was going on. It was, but not what the preteen thought. Caprice smiled back, though, and gave a little wink because she needed to talk to Grant. As bullheaded as he was, he wouldn't let this go, and she wasn't going to explain what had happened while she stood in the middle of a pool in her bathing suit.

"I'll get dressed and meet you in Ace's study."

"There are two dressing rooms in the pool house. We could change and just talk there."

"All right," Caprice agreed. "But I need a head start. It will take me longer than you to get dressed." She was not having this conversation with him in her suit.

He gave her one of those patient looks that said he didn't understand but he'd go along with it.

As she waded across the pool, she stopped next to Trista. "I'm going to get out now, okay?"

"Are you and Mr. Weatherford gonna have a drink or something together?"

She was surprised Trista knew who Grant was. Trista must have seen that surprise.

"He came over before tonight. He's helping Dad do some legal stuff."

That made sense.

"We're just going to have a little talk, but then I'm going to head out." She hadn't intended to stay long because of Shasta.

Before Caprice had left for the party tonight, Shasta had napped in the bed in the garage and tried to dig in it. That came from her nesting instinct. According to the radiograph Marcus had done, the cocker would be having five puppies. The idea of it made Caprice a little nervous since she'd never taken care of a dog during labor and delivery before.

But she was excited about it, too. There was a first time for everything.

"You can always come over when all these people aren't here. You and I could just hang around the pool," Trista suggested.

"Do you think you're going to be bored? Maybe your dad has plans for the rest of your time with him."

Trista just rolled her eyes. "If he does, I bet they're lame."

Caprice suppressed a smile. "Give him a chance." She had a thought. "Do you like dogs and cats?"

"Sure, who doesn't?"

"Lots of people, I'm afraid. But I have a cocker and a feline who both like lots of attention. Maybe your dad could bring you over to my place."

"That would be cool."

"All right. I'll try to set something up with him."

"You won't forget?"

"I promise, I won't forget."

As she made her way out of the pool, she had the distinct feeling that Grant's gaze was on her back, probably studying those marks and trying to figure out what had caused them. He'd soon know.

In one of the pool house dressing rooms, she'd just dressed and stuffed her swimsuit into a ziplock bag in her duffel when she heard the door open and close.

"Caprice, are you in there?"

"I am. Almost ready." She was almost ready if she didn't count her wet hair and a not-ready-to-face-Grant attitude.

If Grant was like most men, he'd be dressed in two minutes. Spotting the hair dryer on the dressing table, she switched it on and did the best she could in a couple of minutes. Then she added a touch of lipstick for self-confidence, slipped on her sandals, and opened the dressing-room door.

She'd been right about the difference between men and women dressing. When she stepped outside the dressing room, there was Grant in navy shorts and a white polo shirt, looking all crisp except for his damp hair. She wondered if he ever wore yellow or a Hawaiian shirt. Probably not.

She was trying to distract herself, that was for sure. She plopped her duffel bag on one of the sea-blue leather chairs.

He crossed his arms over his chest and stared at her. "Tell me what happened, and don't make up some story like you fell in the bathtub."

"I would never do that."

He tilted his head. "All right, you wouldn't. What happened?"

She had the feeling that if he had to ask it again, he wouldn't be so patient. She didn't know how to soften the impact of what she had to say, so she just said it. "Somebody tried to drown me."

Rarely had she seen Grant look surprised, but now he looked surprised and concerned and horrified, all at the same time.

She went on, "I was swimming at Shape Up. I was the only one in the pool. The lifeguard went to fetch clean towels. Anyway, I was swimming laps, and I felt this pressure on my back."

Reliving it a little as she told the story, she hurried on. "I couldn't get out from under it. I was in the deep end and couldn't drop my feet to the floor. I managed to twist away and swim over to the side. I heard the door clang. Whoever did it was gone. The pool skimmer was on the floor."

"Did you yell for help? Tell anybody?"

"I asked Brenda some questions afterward."

"You didn't call the police?"

"Grant, let's be serious. I was alone in there. The attendants had their attention on clients and helping them. Nobody saw anything. We asked. There's something else going on here, too."

"You mean besides somebody trying to murder you?"

She brushed that away. "Danny told me he overheard Bob on his cell phone with a lawyer making plans to change his will. Apparently Kent isn't just his partner, he's his half brother. But few people know that. Why do you think it's such a big secret?"

Grant stared her down. "Don't think I didn't notice you changed the subject."

"I didn't. We're talking about murder."

He gave a patient sigh. "You are the most exasperating woman I know."

"Then you must not know many women," she returned easily.

Again he shook his head. "Have you dismissed Danny as a suspect?"

"Danny fought with Bob because of his mom. He knew they'd had a one-night stand, and he thought she deserved better. Think about it, Grant. Kent has a huge motive. He had a lot to gain if Bob changed his will to make his new half brother his heir."

"Sometimes until a lawyer gets the paperwork together, it's a few weeks until the client signs. If Bob hadn't signed it, your motive's gone."

"Maybe. But there could be life insurance involved,

too. Maybe Bob changed his beneficiary for that. There are all sorts of possibilities."

After a few silent moments, Grant asked, "Are you telling me everything?"

She hesitated, then plunged in further. "Before the incident at Shape Up, I felt I was being followed." She explained about the model home and the SUV that had sped away. "But I'm being careful. I have pepper spray. Nikki even stayed with me a few nights. My cell phone is always at my fingertips."

"But you won't stop, will you? You're ruffling the feathers of a person who might get plucked."

Again they stared at each other until he threw up his hands in defeat. "I can see there's no point talking to you about this, so I'm going to do the only thing that I can do. I'm going to follow you home."

"Now?"

"Yes, now. The road between here and town is isolated. I wouldn't want someone trying to run you off of it."

She told herself Grant was a family friend. For that reason, he felt protective of her. She didn't like the idea of him trying to protect her, but she supposed there wasn't much she could do about it.

"I have to say good-bye to Ace and his parents, and I think Denise is here somewhere too. I don't want to just leave without thanking Ace. I told Trista I'd arrange with her dad for her to come see Shasta and Sophia."

"That's fine. I'll wander around out here a bit, then meet you in the foyer."

Grant had asked his questions and now she wanted information from him too. "You didn't tell me if you found out anything at the community center."

"That's because I didn't, except . . . Not many people like Jeff Garza, not the other board members, not even some of the volunteers."

"No surprise there. I guess Vince filled you in about our visit to him."

"Yes, he did. But this thing with the pool . . . Did that happen before or after you saw Garza?"

"Before."

"Vince didn't tell me you almost drowned."

"That's because I asked him not to tell anyone what happened."

"I'm not just anyone," Grant muttered, and she thought he looked hurt. But that flicker of emotion was gone so fast, she knew she'd imagined it.

Fifteen minutes later, after a quick conversation with Danny and his mom, who'd just arrived, and good-byes all around, Caprice and Grant gave their keys to the two young men who were acting as valets and had parked guests' cars in an area designated for that. As Caprice climbed into her Camaro and drove home, she saw the headlights of Grant's SUV shining in her rearview mirror. Those lights were steady, about fifty feet behind her, never getting too close, never drifting too far back.

What was the tension that always crept into her conversations with Grant? Why couldn't they have a simple conversation without one of them backing away?

Caprice thought Grant would just drive on by as she pulled into her driveway, where her van was parked since her garage would soon be housing Shasta and her pups.

After she switched off her ignition, she realized
Grant hadn't just driven by but had parked at the
curb. He met her as she climbed out of her car.

"We should talk," he said. "Especially because of
what happened to you at Shape Up. I need to know
every little tidbit you've learned. I don't want you to
hold anything back. A contact at the police department admitted there are rumblings in the D.A.'s
office. We need to be prepared with whatever ammunition we've got."

"Prepared for what?"

"Charges being filed."

Caprice felt her heart skip a beat. "Against Bella or
Joe?"

"I'm not going to speculate. Let's just make a list
and go over everything. If I have enough on any one
suspect, I'll go to Jones and talk to him about it."

"Do you actually think that will do some good?"

"I know you believe he has tunnel vision, but he
is a reasonable man."

Caprice didn't really know Detective Jones, but
she had been around him enough when he had suspected her best friend of murder to be wary of him.

After grabbing her duffel from her car's backseat,
she closed the door, took out her key, and went to
the house. When she let them both inside, she realized Sophia had come to greet her, but the cat wasn't
giving her a friendly hello. She was pacing, looking
up at Caprice, and meowing for all she was worth.

"What's wrong?" Caprice asked her.

Sophia meowed loud and long again.

Foreboding tapping her on the shoulder, she
asked, "Where's Shasta?"

Sophia quickly padded toward the kitchen.

Shasta had scratched the colorful rag rug Caprice kept at the door into a heap. She was pawing at it restlessly. She barked at Caprice and then lay on the floor on her side.

"Oh, my gosh," Caprice said. "She's in labor. She didn't eat much today and was restless. I should have stayed home tonight."

"What do you want to do?" Grant asked in a calm, even voice.

Caprice took a deep breath and then immediately went to Shasta. "I'm going to carry her to the garage."

"No, you aren't. I'll take care of it. You lead the way."

"Grant . . ."

She was going to say he didn't have to do that, but he said tersely, "Don't argue. Just open the door."

So she did. She opened the back door and held the screen door. She kept her garage door unlocked, so as soon as Grant stepped out onto the porch, she turned the knob and opened that, too. Hurrying inside, she switched on the light. Grant followed, with Shasta in his arms. When he got to the containment pen, he laid her on the bedding in the whelping box.

"I'm supposed to let nature take its course." She could see Shasta straining, so she knew delivery of the first pup was imminent, probably within fifteen minutes or so.

"So you do know what to do?" Grant asked, glancing around at the setup, including supplies Caprice had lined up on one of the shelving units against the wall.

"Can you boil water for me so I can sterilize the

scissors? I think I have everything ready. The puppy will be in a water bag. Shasta will probably chew the membrane from her, free the pup, and lick her dry to stimulate her to breathe and cry. But if she doesn't, I have to be ready with a towel to rub the puppy until she does breathe and cry."

"You're presuming the first pup will be a she?"

Caprice threw her hands up, frustrated with him picking her words apart. "I don't know. He or she. Can you toss me the box of latex gloves?"

Instead of tossing them, he handed them to her. She slipped her phone from her pocket.

"I'm going to call my vet and see if he's available if I need him."

"This late?"

"Marcus and I are friends. He won't mind."

Grant's eyes narrowed. "I'll go boil that water."

Caprice knew this could be a long night, and she didn't expect Grant to stay. After the first pup, it could be another hour or two until the second. Marcus had showed her an online video that explained how to cut the umbilical cord and tie it off. It was simple, he'd assured her. She told herself the same thing now as she dialed his number. She got his voice mail and told him what was happening, assuring him she'd call him after the pups were born.

She knew some dogs didn't want anyone around when they delivered their pups, but Shasta kept looking up at her as if she didn't understand what was happening.

Caprice stroked her head. "I know this is scary. But everything will be all right."

Caprice suddenly remembered she needed to fill the hot water bottle. As warm as the outside temperature was, the newborns might be okay without the heat lamp. But she had that ready too, in case she needed it. Marcus had told her that the first eighteen hours after the birth were the most critical. On his advice, she had a scale ready to weigh the pups. She knew she had to do that often, as well as taking their temperature the first few days. She'd bought a puppy supplement and bottles just in case Shasta couldn't feed her babies enough. But Caprice also knew she had to leave Shasta alone to take care of her brood. Marcus had explained more than once that the less she interfered, the better.

Not interfere. Right.

When Grant returned to the garage with a pan of boiling water, he dropped the scissors into it. "I washed up so I can help if you need it."

"You don't mind staying?"

"It's not every day I can see pups born."

"There are five. Delivery can take an hour or two between each one."

Grant crouched down beside her, his elbow brushing hers. "If you want me to stay, I'll stay. If you'd rather call someone else . . ."

Did he mean Seth? She couldn't call Seth for a lot of reasons. He was a doctor who needed his sleep. He was a doctor who was dedicated. He was a doctor who would be leaving.

She didn't answer Grant directly but rather said, "I can use the moral support."

She thought he looked glad that she wanted him to stay, but it was so hard to tell with Grant. She couldn't look deeper because Shasta whimpered and strained again.

"Can you fill the hot water bottle?" She pointed to it. "I'll wrap it in a towel. It won't be long now."

And it wasn't. Grant had no sooner returned with the hot water bottle and wrapped it in a towel than Caprice said, "The first baby's coming!"

Her heart in her throat as she knelt beside Grant, Caprice watched the miracle as the sac appeared and the first pup was born.

Shasta licked her baby into life.

Tears gathered in Caprice's eyes as she tucked in the hot water bottle. She felt all choked up, and she ducked her head so Grant wouldn't see.

But when he capped her shoulder with his large hand, she raised her gaze to his.

The silent communication that passed between them shook her a little. However, she didn't have time to think about it because Shasta and the pup needed her . . . and because at that moment Grant's cell phone buzzed.

He plucked it from his belt. His face went passive as he answered the call. "Hi, Jason. What's up?"

Caprice watched Shasta mother her pup as Grant asked tersely, "When?" He followed it with, "I'll bring him in myself at nine a.m."

A chill ran down Caprice's spine. When Grant ended the call, she asked, "What's happening?"

He looked as if he didn't want to tell her, but then he finally did. "Jones wants to bring Joe in again for questioning. But this time . . . I think he could charge him with Preston's murder."

Chapter Eighteen

Grant was blunt with Joe when he called him a few minutes later. "Prepare yourself to be charged. Do whatever you need to with Bella in case you don't come home again . . . right away."

After the phone call, Grant looked down at Shasta and her first baby.

Caprice couldn't leave Shasta and her pups, although she desperately wanted to go to Bella.

"I can't believe they have enough to charge him," Caprice complained.

"It's got to be circumstantial at this point, but my guess is the mayor's pushing the police department to do something, and Joe's their best suspect."

"Do they even know about the others?"

"They will when I take him in. Jones and I are going to have a little chat."

"As if that will do any good," Caprice muttered, watching Shasta, seeing she was about to deliver another puppy.

After studying her for a moment, Grant perceptively said, "I know you want to go to Bella, but she and Joe need tonight together. You'll have time to talk to her after I take him in tomorrow."

"I need to do more than talk to her. I need to figure out who did this."

"Another pup's coming!" Grant replaced his phone on his belt and appeared ready to do whatever he had to.

His hands were large and capable as he picked up a towel. It was easy to see he cared about Shasta and her pups . . . bringing her babies into the world . . . giving them a good chance at life.

The rest of the night was a mixture of excitement and worry. By the time the sun came up, Shasta's five pups were greedily nursing . . . and Grant had to leave.

He took a last look at Caprice and the pups and asked, "Are you going to be all right here with them?"

"Of course, I am. I'm going to document their weights, keep an eye on their temperature, and then give Marcus a call."

Caprice's cell phone rang. She checked the screen and said, "It's Bella."

Before she could even say "hello," Bella started. "I want to go to the police station with Joe, but he won't let me."

"Bee, it's probably better if you don't. It's better if you try to keep Megan and Timmy calm."

"They're going to want to know where he is. What am I going to tell them?"

Grant waved toward the door and murmured, "I have to get going. Tell Bella I'll be there in half an hour."

Caprice nodded and watched him leave the

garage. They'd shared some special moments last night. What had he thought about that?

She'd never know because Grant didn't tell her what he was thinking, not about anything but the case anyway.

She returned her attention to her sister, intending to give her every reassurance she could think of.

She'd just ended her call with Bella when her phone played its Beatles' tune. It was Marcus.

"How's it going?"

She told him about the five pups, how they looked, how they were nursing. Her veterinarian suggested, "Why don't I stop by on my way to the clinic? Shasta should have a posterior pituitary extract injection, and I can check out the pups."

"Are you sure you have time?"

"For you, I do. I know I can call you when I get a stray who needs a home. I'll be there in half an hour."

And he was. Marcus was big and burly but one of the gentlest men she knew. He examined Shasta and each of her pups, closely looking at how Caprice had tied off the umbilical cords.

"For your first time, you did a great job."

"I can thank instructions on the Internet for that."

He laughed. "That's where everyone goes for human and pet diagnoses. Sometimes it's an advantage and sometimes it's not."

"The Internet can't replace you."

He gave her a cautious look. "Flattery will get you everywhere."

"Will it?" She assessed him carefully. "Do you have a few minutes?"

"What will I be doing with those few minutes?"

"I'm trying to figure out who killed Bob Preston. I have all my notes on my tablet. I need to go over them with someone who has an analytical mind but isn't involved in the case."

His bushy brows arched. "Do you plan to set a trend solving murders?"

"Not intentionally. But my brother-in-law is being grilled as we speak, and I have to figure this out."

"I'll watch the pups. Why don't you make some coffee and get your tablet. We'll see what we can come up with."

"I just need a lead."

"We'll find you one," he said with assurance.

Twenty minutes later, sipping raspberry-chocolate-flavored coffee and with her tablet in her lap on the garage floor, she consulted with Marcus, who was seated in a lawn chair.

"So those are the suspects so far—Kent Osgood, Jeff Garza, Jackie Fitz, and Danny Flannery. But I've practically eliminated him. And, of course, Joe. I've eliminated him too."

"You've given me each one's motivation. That's fine. But maybe instead of looking into the suspects, you have to look into Bob's last days a little more. Do you have a timeline for the last ten days of his life?"

"That's a good idea."

"I sometimes have them," Marcus joked. "Tell me what you know."

She began tapping on her tablet. "Bob was working a job for me at Eliza Cornwall's, doing painting for staging."

"Did you notice anything unusual about his behavior?" Marcus asked.

She thought about it. "He asked my sister to go for

coffee. That was a little strange, considering they had dated years ago and she's married."

"Nothing strange in that if he really just wanted to catch up. Maybe he had some regrets about how they split."

"I suppose that's possible. Jeff Garza told us that Bob had gotten a new outlook on life, probably because he'd found out he had family—a half brother. Do you think he was looking back at his past because of that?"

"Could be."

"Changing his will would have been major."

"Let's get back to that timeline," Marcus said. "Bob had coffee with Bella, then . . ."

"Then . . . he went out of town without telling anybody. At least I don't think he told anybody. And he didn't finish the job at Eliza's. Bob was a charmer and devil-may-care, but he was always responsible. He never left a job unfinished and he left that one unfinished. I had to call in someone I'd been using temporarily. In fact, Bob even left his tarps and everything. Monty said he moved all that stuff to his garage." She abruptly stopped and suddenly snapped her fingers. "That's it."

"What's it?"

"My next lead. Monty said there was a backpack there too."

"Is he sure it was Bob's?"

"I don't know, but I'm going to find out. It's all still in Monty's garage. I'd forgotten about it. Actually, I didn't even know about the backpack until Monty told me at the awards dinner."

"Yeah, I'm sorry you didn't get the award."

"It really doesn't matter. I don't live my life to earn an award. You know that."

"Yeah, I do. Working hard and taking in strays is just part of your life." He glanced over at the pups. "Have you found homes for these yet?"

"No, but I'm working on it." She paused, then asked, "Do you think the pups will be okay for an hour or so if Nikki comes over to pup-sit? I have to check out the stuff in Monty's garage."

"Nikki's reliable and an animal lover. She's been around your strays often enough. I think they'll be fine with her. Show her how to take their temperature and stimulate them if Shasta doesn't. She keeps licking them and nosing them, so I think they'll be fine. But alert Nikki to all of it."

"I'll give her a checklist," Caprice assured him."

"You did a good job last night, Caprice. Not just anybody can deliver a litter of pups."

"I had help." She thought about Grant, and how he'd just stepped in . . . how he'd worried about the scrapes on her back . . . how he'd looked at her when the pups were born.

But she couldn't think about that now. She was still hurting over Seth's leaving, and a little confused about her feelings concerning both men. What was foremost on her mind was proving Joe didn't kill Bob. She was going to do that sooner, rather than later.

After Nikki had arrived and understood exactly what taking care of newborn pups was all about, and after a phone call to Monty, who told Caprice he'd leave the side door to his garage open because he had a job to work on this morning, Caprice drove toward the community center with Monty's address in her head. She hadn't realized he lived near there. In fact, he lived a street over from the renovation project where Roz's store was located. Even though Monty had been Roz's gardener and worked for Caprice now and then, she didn't know him very well. He was single and ran his own small business, tending to yards around Kismet. But that was about all she knew.

This morning, however, she'd learned more. Monty rented the downstairs apartment in a row house, and a detached garage in the back was his to use. He didn't park in it because he kept his equipment in it. However, there was a gravel lot next to the garage where she could park while she was searching through Bob's stuff.

After she found the address, she drove to the alley that wound behind the backyards. Monty had mentioned the clapboard garage had been painted yellow, so she easily found it. It was the old-fashioned kind with wooden doors that slid from one side to the other. She parked, glanced around a bit, then went to the side door. Since she'd promised everyone she'd stay safe, she patted the pepper-spray gun in her pocket and went inside, leaving the door ajar. After she switched on the overhead bulb, she looked around. There was one small window that was raised, so the garage wasn't stifling.

Monty had told her all of Bob's things had been dumped on the left side. She spotted the tarps right away as well as the two painter's trays and an assortment of brushes stuffed in a bucket. There was also the long-handled contraption for a ceiling roller, which reminded her of the pool skimmer.

She shivered. She couldn't let the creepies get hold of her now.

She thought she heard the hum of a car engine nearby. Was it coming down the alley?

It was. However, it didn't pause but zoomed right by the garage doors. She was letting her imagination run overtime.

She thought she spied blue nylon peeking out from under the tarp. Crossing to it, she pushed the tarp aside to reveal a backpack. It was worn and utilitarian. She picked it up, feeling strange as she handled something Bob had owned and used not long before he died.

Something in the backpack rolled to one side. A gun?

No, Bob wouldn't carry a gun.

She unbuckled the flap and lifted it, peeking inside. The rolling object was a bottle of water. That made sense. She pulled it out. It was still half full. In the bottom of the backpack she found two granola bars, a bag of barbecue chips, and another of pretzels. For snack attacks. This must have been Bob's food stash for when he was working. She dug deeper into the bag and found two pens, a pencil, and a ruler.

She'd explored the largest compartment first. Now she undid the Velcro flap on a smaller compartment, really not expecting to find anything. Bob wouldn't have left the backpack if there had been something valuable in it, would he?

A large yellow piece of paper, about eight-and-a-half by eleven, was folded over. She pulled it out and realized there were other papers inside it. Unfolding the larger sheet, she found a work order of some sort. It was for the rooms in Eliza's house. Bob had checked off those he'd finished. But inside that . . .

There was an old newspaper clipping. It too was folded in half, and now she opened it, smoothing it out. FIRE IN TROPICAL TAN, MEDIA PA. Media was a suburb of Philadelphia. Why was Bob carrying this around?

Caprice began reading the article carefully. Fire had broken out at Tropical Tan, a tanning salon located in a strip mall. The businesses on either side of it were spared. The owner, Elizabeth Crandall, was quoted as saying she was so grateful for that.

The name niggled in Caprice's brain. Elizabeth Crandall. Maybe it was because she was also holding the work order, but Eliza's name came to mind. Eliza Cornwall. Eliza Cornwall. Elizabeth Crandall. Awfully similar. Was that just a coincidence? Or wasn't it?

Why was Bob carrying this around, and why was it here in his backpack?

While Caprice thought about it, she made sure there wasn't anything else in the backpack. After that, she pawed through the tarps. Nothing else there, either. How could she find out more about this fire?

In her business, just as in any other, contacts were essential. She did have a contact at the newspaper, Marianne Brisbane. Marianne had interviewed her twice. Caprice and Roz had also done a favor for the reporter. Maybe Marianne would be willing to return that favor.

Caprice made the call, hoping Marianne would do some snooping for her. Fortunately, the reporter was at her desk at the *Kismet Crier.* "Are you going to spice up my day?" she asked Caprice.

"No big stories on your docket?" Caprice asked.

"Just Bob Preston's murder. You wouldn't have information for me, would you? The way you solved that last murder . . . Did you know him?"

"Yes, I did. Bob often painted the homes I staged."

Caprice suddenly heard a snapping noise. Apparently Marianne had snapped her fingers. "Bella is your sister. She found the body! So you are investigating this?"

Instead of answering, Caprice asked, "Will you do me a favor?"

Marianne's voice was wary. "If I can."

"I have a clipping from what I assume is a Philadelphia newspaper. The town of Media is mentioned in the article. The story details a fire in a business called Tropical Tan. The owner was Elizabeth Crandall. Can you see what you can find out for me?"

"And just what will you give me in return?"

"My undying gratitude," Caprice said quickly.

Marianne laughed. "Now, Caprice, you know that's not enough."

Caprice sighed. She could, of course, research Tropical Tan and Elizabeth Crandall on the Internet herself, and she would when she got home. But she didn't know exactly where to look, and she knew Marianne had databases at her disposal that she didn't.

"All I can say is that if this leads to anything, you'll be the first to know."

"And the first to get an interview with your brother-in-law? I heard they were bringing him in for questioning again."

"I don't know how Joe would feel about that."

"But you could try to convince him."

"I could. But Marianne, this might not be anything at all." Yet in Caprice's gut, she had the crawling knowledge that this article was very important in this case.

"It's a deal. I do have other work on my desk, but I'll get to it sometime today."

Caprice was just ending the call when her phone beeped because a text had come in. It was from Jackie.

Can you come to Connect Xpress? It's important.

Caprice texted back, **Be there in half an hour.**

She had to stop at home and check on Shasta and her brood, to see if Nikki was bored with pup-sitting or if she was as enamored with the pups as Caprice and would stay for supper. They could cook up something together.

She considered Jackie's text once more. Just what did the videographer have to tell her?

Forty minutes later—sure the pups were faring well under Nikki's watchful eye, yet eager to return to care for them herself—Caprice noticed that only one car was parked in Connect Xpress's side lot. She assumed it was Jackie's.

Caprice parked in the first slot, closest to the door, eager to find out what Jackie had to tell her. But after she opened the door and stepped inside, she found Connect Xpress eerily silent. Maybe she should turn around and go right back out.

No, that was silly. This was a public business, and Jackie had texted her. Certainly she would be close by. Caprice remembered the last time she was here and how Jackie had been working at the computer.

She proceeded down the hall as she had before, hoping to see Jackie at the opposite end of it. But she didn't see Jackie. Goose bumps broke out on her arms. One of those "signs." Now she really should turn around and leave. But her middle name wasn't "Curious" for nothing.

The taping rooms were just beyond the office. She went to the first glass window, and a gasp escaped her. There was Jackie on the floor! Blood dripped down her forehead. She looked as if she were unconscious or worse. Her hands were behind her back, secured with duct tape. Her ankles too were duct-taped together. Caprice rushed through the door and fell on her knees beside the young woman. Jackie was still breathing.

However, before Caprice could pluck her phone out of her pocket, she felt as if all the air had been knocked out of her, as if every muscle in her body was shooting pain to her brain. On top of all that, she couldn't move. Yet she collapsed to the floor, stunned . . . and incapacitated.

Caprice had never felt that kind of pain—like a thousand knives slicing through her all at once. When the sensations stopped, she felt like a rag doll and out of breath. Yet she was aware that someone had pulled her arms together behind her back and secured them with . . . duct tape? She moved because she now could.

"There's no point in fighting me," Eliza said. "I'll just tase you again."

Caprice finally got her breath, finally could make her mind work.

Eliza was ranting. "You couldn't stop snooping, could you? You and Jackie. You couldn't take the warning when I tried to drown you."

"That was you?" Caprice managed to say.

"I work out in my home gym, remember? And Shape Up has no security to speak of, except for an alarm when they're closed. It's easy to slip in and out of there. Jogging suit, baseball cap. No one knew who I was."

"Why hurt Jackie and me now? I might never have found out who killed Bob."

"Don't play stupid with me. I've been following you. I had to keep track of what you were doing. I could hear you on the phone in Monty's garage. I heard you call Marianne Brisbane. She's a pit bull. I knew if she researched the tanning salon, you two would find the road to me."

"What did Jackie find?" That was the only explanation for Eliza knocking her out.

"She found the video I took of the fire in Philadelphia at the tanning salon. I thought I'd buried it in the files."

"Did you know she texted me?"

"After I tased her and she hit her head when she fell, I checked her phone. I knew you'd be coming."

"Eliza, don't make this any worse for yourself. Whatever you're planning to do . . ."

"I'm planning to do the same thing I did to Bob, only in a different way."

Caprice knew she had to buy some time. Maybe

somebody would walk in. After all, Nikki knew where she was. Maybe she could get the drop on Eliza. Her feet weren't bound yet.

But just as she thought it, Eliza came toward her with duct tape and the Taser gun. "Try to kick at me or prevent me from securing you, and I'll zap you again."

If she struggled, she knew Eliza would do what she threatened. If Caprice got tasered again, it would be easy for Eliza to wrap her ankles. Either way, she was going to get bound.

As Eliza secured her ankles, Caprice said, "I don't know what you have planned, but I don't want to die without having answers. Tell me who you really are and why you killed Bob."

Eliza added another layer of tape and then smiled viciously. "Who I really am? You're going to find out exactly who I am when I set a fire to this place, and you go up in flames with it."

Chapter Nineteen

At first, all Caprice felt was panic, panic so horrifying she shook. But panic and fear were enemies now as much as Eliza was. She still felt exhausted from being tased, but her mind felt clearer, and she had to keep it that way.

Her thigh seemed to tingle, and she wondered if that was a leftover sensation from the Taser. But then her phone played "A Hard Day's Night." If only she could get to it!

After the music stopped, Eliza smiled with malice. "Your phone isn't at your fingertips now, is it? Always chatting with your sisters or your doctor boyfriend. You're as bad as Bob."

Didn't Eliza have family, either? Was she jealous of anyone who did? Caprice had to keep her talking.

"Why fire?" Caprice asked, trying to steady her voice.

That didn't seem to be a question Eliza had expected. "You mean the first time or this time?"

"Both."

Eliza had a huge ego, and if Caprice could just

feed it and nudge it and paw at it, Eliza would tell her the whole story. Time was her friend. She needed the story.

"The first time, it was all about the insurance money. I needed it to start over. Starting over isn't as hard as most people think it is. I knew someone who could find me an identity. All he had to do was use someone who was already dead. And it just so happened I could even keep my initials."

"But why did you have to change your identity? You could have just started over with the insurance money."

"If I'd stuck around Philly, my creditors would have moved in. I had a lifestyle to maintain, and I did it by borrowing to the max. But I owed everybody. I wasn't going to give them that insurance money. Are you kidding?"

"So you just disappeared."

"I did. I researched lots of towns, but Kismet seemed just right."

"So in about five years, you became a multimillionaire, right?"

"On paper."

"And you had a fling with Bob," she guessed.

"I did. I wanted it to be more than a fling. I thought he really cared about me." She stopped and seemed to think about that.

Caprice kept silent, waiting for Eliza to continue.

Finally, appearing to come back to the present, she looked down at Jackie, and her expression hardened. "Bob knew I was hurting for money and needed investors to expand. He promised me that once he sold his software app, he'd have money to throw away. But then Kent Osgood came to town and joined his crew. They got along well and decided to form a partnership. Lo and behold, suddenly last month, Kent confessed to Bob he was his half brother! You would have thought an old world ended and a new one began."

Prompting Eliza when she stopped there, Caprice said, "I guess Bob decided family was more important than anything else."

"I'll say. Bob felt protective of Kent. So instead of giving me the money, he told me he was going to invest in a fund for Kent to go to college. College. When we both could have become rich. If only he hadn't overheard my phone conversation after the June board meeting with my insurance agent—he's on the community center's board too—upping my fire insurance on Connect Xpress. If only Bob hadn't rifled through my desk and found that newspaper clipping."

"He went through your desk?"

"He was all over my house when he was painting, you know that. He seemed to think a lot of things about me didn't add up. Like if I was going to leave Kismet for California, why would I up my fire insurance on Connect Xpress? When he checked into my background, the only Eliza Cornwall he could find was a sixty-year-old woman who'd died."

"So he had questions, and I guess he came to you with them?"

Eliza's eyes narrowed as if she were remembering exactly what Bob had said. "He asked me point-blank if I was using an alias. At first, of course, I denied it. But he showed me that clipping, and he wanted to know what it had to do with me."

Caprice had read somewhere that criminals often

keep souvenirs of their crimes. That clipping had been Eliza's souvenir. So had her video of the fire.

"You told him the truth?"

"Not exactly. I just told him that, like Eliza Doolittle in *My Fair Lady*, I became a different person and started over. Was that so terrible? He even agreed that that wasn't terrible, that he felt like starting over too. But he wanted to know what I did that I had to leave my old life. Of course I didn't tell him, but I did invite him to go to California with me. I wanted him to so badly. I loved him. You understand, don't you?"

Before Caprice could answer whether she did or didn't, Jackie moaned and moved a bit. Caprice could see she was coming around.

Eliza could hear and see that too. She went over to Jackie and stood over her. "You know what Bob told me? He told me he loved Jackie. He told me he was thinking about asking her to marry him. He told me he was going to look out for his brother. Then he went out of town and left us both high and dry."

"Do you know where he went?"

"I didn't then. I do now. He went to Philadelphia. He asked questions. He even found an old picture I'd had taken for publicity for the tanning salon. After July's board meeting that night at the community center, we went out back. He told me all that. He told me if my place here suddenly burned down, he'd know for sure what I did in Philadelphia. So I told him the truth. I told him I loved him. I told him again that I wanted him to go with me, that we could have a great life in sunny L.A. And do you know what he said? He said he'd made a mistake in ever going out with me, and ever getting involved with me, and ever sleeping with me. Him, with so many notches on his belt it would never be long enough to hold them all! I was so hurt, and so angry. When he turned around to pick up a can of paint to take back into the center, I picked up that hammer and I smashed him. Then I ran around the building to my car and drove away. I drove all the way to the reservoir and dropped the hammer from the bridge."

Silence invaded the taping room, and Caprice could think of nothing to say. But her phone in her pocket played the Beatles' music again.

Eliza looked at Caprice's pocket. "I guess someone's trying to get hold of you. That means I better hurry up."

"Eliza. Don't do this," Caprice pleaded.

But Eliza had already left the room.

Caprice had missed the fact that Eliza was on the board of the center, along with Jeff Garza and Bob. Missing that important piece of evidence had put her in this danger.

She wiggled and wiggled and thought about screaming. But in the taping room, nobody would hear her. Her voice would never carry outside the walls of the building.

She called over to Jackie. "Jackie, are you awake?"

The videographer groaned and tried to lift her shoulders. But she flopped back down. "I'm seeing stars," Jackie murmured.

"Take some deep breaths," Caprice advised her, knowing they didn't have much time before Eliza murdered them too. She was really trying not to panic. She waited a few beats, then asked, "What happened to you?"

It was a few seconds before Jackie answered. "Not so long ago, I asked Eliza if she had any gum. She said there was some in her purse and I could get it if I wanted it. So I did. When I pulled it out of this little compartment, an old business card came with it. It was for Tropical Tan, and it had the name Elizabeth Crandall on it. I didn't think too much about it. But then this morning I was missing Bob and didn't have a lot of work, so I was just looking through old videos on the computer. I found the video file of Tropical Tan burning down. It seemed weird. It seemed to be too much of coincidence. You know what I mean? So I wanted another opinion and that's why I texted you."

The smell of gasoline or kerosene or some such product became evident. How far away was the accelerant?

Caprice heard Eliza moving around outside the door. Then she was back inside the taping room. She spotted Caprice's fringed macramé bag on the floor. Crossing to it, she delved inside and found what she was looking for.

"I'll be driving your car around the back so no one sees it. It's too noticeable. If the fire company doesn't get here in time, it will go up with the rest of the place. I'll be long gone on the private plane I chartered." She stared down at Caprice. "It's true what they say, you know. Nice girls finish last. You're going to finish dead."

Before Caprice could even register the fact that her car might go up in flames with them, Eliza disappeared out the door. Where had Eliza poured the gasoline?

She asked Jackie frantically, "Can you move?"

"I'm dizzy and I feel sick," Jackie responded weakly.

"But can you move?" Caprice prodded her, using her hands and her feet as best she could to scrunch toward the door. "We've got to get out of here. I don't know if she's going to detonate the fire from afar or light it before she leaves. Come on, Jackie. Move."

Jackie tried to push herself as Caprice had done. But she just couldn't. "You go," Jackie said. "Go as far as you can."

Straight into the fire, Caprice thought. Faces flashed on her mental screen—her mom, dad, Nana . . . Vince, Bella and her family . . . Nikki . . . Seth . . . Grant. She thought of Sophia and Shasta with her pups.

Caprice could move only an inch or two at a time, and she'd hardly made it outside the taping room when the smell of gasoline became stronger. Just what had Eliza doused? Wouldn't Connect Xpress's security system detect the smoke?

Not if she had turned the system off.

Caprice heard a noise, like a *whoosh*, then she smelled something burning.

She couldn't move fast enough. She'd never even get down the hall into the reception area. It was silly to think she could save herself, let alone Jackie too.

She saw the fire now. It had started at the back of the building. Of course Eliza wouldn't have splashed gasoline across the front. Someone might have seen her.

Caprice called to Jackie. "Try to get out here with me. Try."

But Jackie didn't respond, and Caprice didn't know if she'd passed out again or given up.

Smoke filled the entire area, and Caprice could hardly breathe, let alone see. Yet she saw red-orange flames eating up the walls . . . eating up the ceiling . . .

"Caprice!"

She must be imagining things. That sounded like Grant's voice. But imagination or not, she answered him. "Grant, I'm here. Down the hall."

The smoke was like a thick, icky fog, and she didn't even know if he'd heard her. She yelled again. "I'm on the floor in the hall. Outside the taping rooms."

The next moment he was there . . . on the floor beside her.

"I'm bound . . ."

"I'm getting it," he muttered.

Soon her hands were free. She saw he had a pocket knife and was slicing at the tape at her feet.

"Jackie's in the taping room. We have to get her out."

"I have to get you out."

"I'm fine." She wiggled her hands, shook her feet, got to her knees, and almost fell back down. But she didn't fall because Grant's arms were around her. He held her waist.

"You have to stay down so you can breathe. The fire started in the back. You can make it out. Go."

"But Jackie . . ."

"I'll get her. Go!"

It wasn't the authority in Grant's voice that made her find her feet, keep crouched down, and hurry out the hall. It was the fact that she trusted him. She trusted him to find Jackie and save her too.

And she soon realized she was right to trust him. She'd no sooner made it outside to the street than there he was, carrying Jackie in his arms, laying her down on the ground.

Caprice reached into her pocket and pulled out her phone.

"I already called nine-one-one," he told her.

"I'm going to call Chief Powalski."

Five minutes later, Grant had carried Jackie across the street and Caprice had followed him. The three of them sat at the curb while sirens screamed and fire overtook Connect Xpress.

Jackie was leaning against Caprice, and Caprice had her arm around her. "The paramedics will be here soon."

Looming above her, Grant hovered next to Caprice. "You need to be checked out too, and don't argue with me about it."

She glanced over her shoulder at him. "Just because you saved my life, don't think I owe you obedience."

He rolled his eyes. "Obedience is one thing I'm never going to get from you."

There was something in his voice, something in his eyes that made her ask, "What do you want from me?"

He looked as if he might say exactly what he wanted. But then the fire engine rolled down the street.

Grant answered her question with, "All I want for now is to know you're safe."

Without a doubt, Grant was the most frustrating man she knew. But without a doubt, she understood she'd always be grateful to him for saving her life.

Epilogue

Three Weeks Later

Caprice was standing on her front porch with Mr. and Mrs. Tavish and their daughter, Olivia—Livvie for short. Shasta was dancing around their legs, barking up at them, joyfully enjoying their presence. There was a reason for that. Shasta belonged to them, as much as a dog could belong to anyone. Her real name was Honey.

"We are so grateful," Mrs. Tavish said again as Grant's SUV rolled up to the curb.

Caprice's heart beat faster. She hadn't seen him in the past two weeks. That first week after the fire, she'd spent time with him at the police station, talking with Detective Jones, explaining everything they knew. But they'd come and gone on their own. Grant had acted as if saving her life was just another activity in his week . . . like going grocery shopping.

Now he climbed out of his vehicle and started up the walk. At her stoop, he smiled at all of them and bent down to pet Shasta/Honey, who rubbed against his hand eagerly.

"Another home for a pup?" he asked Caprice.

"More than that. Shasta—her real name is Honey—will be going home soon! Mr. and Mrs. Tavish are from Virginia. They were visiting relatives here when Honey slipped her collar, ran out of the yard, and apparently couldn't find her way back in again. They stayed for a while but had to return home without her. Mrs. Tavish's sister saw the flyer posted in one of the grocery stores."

Livvie, who was ten, explained, "We can't take Honey along now. Her pups need her for a while longer. But then we're going to have a pup *and* Honey." She clapped her hands. "I can't wait."

Mr. Tavish said, "You're going to have to. We're just grateful to Caprice for seeing her through a pregnancy and delivery. Honey doesn't have papers or anything, so we're thrilled if she can place the rest of the pups, the ones we're not taking. But we need to get going. We have a drive ahead of us and work tomorrow. We can't thank you enough, Caprice."

"No thanks are necessary. Honey's been a delight, and it was an experience delivering her pups." Her gaze met Grant's. "Wasn't it?"

After a few moments, he broke eye contact first. "Yes, it was. Is this a bad time, or do you have a few minutes to talk?"

"I have time," Caprice said.

As the Tavishes left, Caprice waved, watched them climb into their SUV and veer away.

Grant followed her and Honey inside.

"Do you want to see the pups?" she asked him, unsure why he was here.

"Of course."

"Biscotti and lemonade afterward?"

"Of course," he said again, matter-of-factly.

So matter-of-factly that Caprice's heart sped up a little faster.

As they went out the back door onto the porch and into the garage, Grant kept quiet. But once in the garage, he went right over to the pups' pen, followed by Honey, opened the gate, and went inside. Honey went straight to her pups.

"They sure have grown," Grant said.

"Yep, they have, and in just three weeks."

"Have you found the others homes?" he asked nonchalantly, as if it didn't matter much.

"Kent Osgood is taking one. The Tavishes are taking another. Ace's daughter is taking a third." Trista had fallen in love with the pups when she'd visited Caprice.

Grant crouched down in the middle of the pups, and they squiggled around him.

"I'm keeping the lightest one. I'm going to call her Lady—from *Lady and the Tramp*. It's my favorite Disney movie. That just leaves a boy who doesn't have a home.

"Is there a reason you picked the one you did?"

"She was the runt, though I don't like to call her that. She did need the most care and still does. I want to make sure she gets it."

"That's just like something you'd do."

So was that a compliment or what? she wondered.

"One left, huh?"

"Yep. And that one doesn't look like the others. See how his ears are shorter and his coat might have darker patches?"

When Grant was silent, she had a feeling there was a reason he was here today other than a friendly visit. After all, when did he stop by just for a friendly visit?

"I'd like to adopt him then," he suddenly said. "Unless you have someone else in mind."

She lowered herself on the little stool that she'd placed in the middle of the wood chips that made the pen comfortable and cleanable for the pups. Then she gazed at Grant. "I don't have anyone else in mind."

She thought he might sit with her, maybe talk about a name for his pup. But instead, he said in a gruff voice, "You almost died in that fire."

They hadn't talked about everything that had happened. But she'd been through it all over and over again, not only with the police, but with her family and friends.

"I know," she said simply.

"I don't want you to ever put yourself in that kind of danger again." The tone of his voice told her that he cared, but she didn't acknowledge that because she didn't know what it meant.

"You were in danger too."

"Yes, I was. And that's my point. What you do doesn't just affect you. Your investigation affected everyone around you."

"My investigation cleared Joe."

Grant impatiently concluded, "So you're saying the end justified the means."

"No. What I'm saying is that I can't just stand by when someone I care about needs my help. Let's face it, Grant. You can't, either. Nikki told me when you called my house after Jones questioned Joe again, you were worried because you couldn't get me on my cell. When she told you I went to Connect Xpress, you didn't think twice about running into the smoke and fire to save me . . . and Jackie. And here you are today, wanting to give a home to a needy pup."

He shook his head. "Only you could compare adopting a pup to tracking down a murderer who fortunately got nabbed before she could fly away."

They had learned Eliza had been apprehended en route to the airport and her chartered plane. Since then she had been arraigned and was awaiting trial. No bail had been offered at all in light of the charges. Caprice was glad about that.

"Detective Jones couldn't have been too pleased that Marianne Brisbane gave you all the credit in her article," Grant added.

"One of these days, Detective Jones is going to arrest me for something. Even if it's jaywalking."

"Probably," Grant agreed blandly.

She grinned at him. But he didn't smile back. In fact, he didn't seem able to look away.

He cleared his throat. "I heard Seth Randolph is leaving Kismet."

"He already left," she said softly, remembering their good-bye and how hard that had been. But Seth was doing what he had to do, and she couldn't fault him for that.

"You're not going to follow him?"

"He didn't ask me. Besides, I could never leave my family." And she couldn't. Almost dying in a fire had shaken her up. In those moments before Grant had arrived, she'd thought about everyone she loved and knew what she'd be losing. They were even more precious to her now than before.

As Grant seemed to absorb that, he leaned down,

picked up his pup, and cradled him. "I never imagined I'd want a dog."

He never imagined he'd care again? Caprice wondered. Maybe he was finally ready.

"I'll get the lemonade and biscotti." She rose to her feet.

Grant straightened too, still cuddling the pup. "I'm going to need help knowing what food to give him . . . how to train him."

"You can call me anytime. In fact, we could walk them together."

"That sounds like a plan."

Then Grant smiled at her, a really genuine smile that told her maybe . . . just maybe . . . they could do more than walk their dogs together . . . that maybe he could forgive her for putting their lives in danger . . . that maybe . . . just maybe . . . he accepted everything about her, including her penchant for solving murders!

Just maybe.

Original Recipes

Fran's Pasta Fagioli

Preheat oven to 350 degrees.
Prep time: One hour
Bake time: 40 minutes
Serves 6–8

1 pound ground beef. I use 85% lean.
⅛ pound sliced prosciutto torn into bite-size
   pieces
½ cup chopped fennel. I chop the upper portion
   of the stalks around the "heart." (The heart is
   a great crunchy snack!) You can substitute
   celery, but that will change the flavor of the
   casserole.
½ cup chopped onion
1 clove grated garlic
1 teaspoon salt
Dash of pepper
1 cup fire-roasted canned tomatoes
1 cup ketchup
¼ cup brown sugar
1 tablespoon mustard
1 tablespoon lemon juice
1 tablespoon apple cider vinegar

2 cans of cannellini beans (white kidney beans; 15.5 ounce cans). I rinse and drain these.

1 cup of shredded, apple-smoked mozzarella cheese. Using my hand grater, I grate the cheese and set it in the refrigerator until the casserole has baked for 35 minutes.

1½ cups fusillini or other mini pasta

5 quarts of water with 1 teaspoon of salt

Start water to boil. While waiting, chop the vegetables and measure out the other ingredients so they're ready when you need them. When the water boils, add the fusillini or other mini pasta and boil for 8 minutes.

The pasta should be finished about when the beef is browned. Drain your pasta after it cooks, and let it stand until you are ready for it.

In a large frying pan, brown the ground beef until there is no pink.

To the browned ground beef, add the prosciutto and stir well. Add fennel, onion, garlic, salt, and pepper.

Stir and let simmer for about 2 minutes to mix the flavors. Stir in tomatoes. Add ketchup, brown sugar, mustard, lemon juice, and vinegar. Add drained beans.

Cover the ground-beef mixture and let it simmer for 5 minutes. Then pour the drained pasta into the mixture and stir.

Transfer all of it into a 3-quart casserole; cover and bake for 35 minutes. Remove from oven, sprinkle with the grated apple-smoked mozzarella, and insert into oven again, uncovered, for 5 minutes.

Remove and serve with crusty bread.

Nikki's Baked Tomatoes

Preheat oven to 350 degrees.
Prep time: 15–20 minutes. This always depends on how much you enjoy the process of handling ingredients. Some cooks rush through prep, while others put on music and enjoy chopping and measuring.
Bake time: 60 minutes
Serves 6–8 as a side dish

2½ pounds tomatoes—washed, cored, and sliced about ¼" thick. I like to use large tomatoes.
1 medium onion, thinly sliced (⅛" thick)
2 teaspoons oregano. You will first use one half and then the other half later.
1 clove garlic, grated
1 tablespoon sugar, one half first, the other later
½ teaspoon pepper, one half first, the other later
½ cup shredded parmesan cheese, one half first, the other later
¼ teaspoon salt
1 tablespoon extra-virgin olive oil
2 cups shredded mozzarella cheese (8-ounce bag)
⅓ cup Italian-style bread crumbs. I use Progresso.

Layer half the sliced tomatoes in an 8" x 12" glass casserole. Spread half the onion over the first half, sprinkle with 1 teaspoon oregano, all of the grated garlic, 1 teaspoon sugar, and ¼ teaspoon pepper; then sprinkle with ¼ cup parmesan cheese.

Layer the remainder of the tomatoes and onion. Sprinkle with salt, pepper, 1 teaspoon sugar, and the remaining 1 teaspoon of oregano. Drizzle with olive oil. Cover with foil.

Bake at 350 degrees for 40 minutes.

Remove casserole from oven. Carefully spoon out excess liquid. Sprinkle with remaining parmesan, then mozzarella cheese and bread crumbs.

Put the casserole back in the oven at 350 degrees, uncovered, for 20 more minutes until the bread crumbs are toasty brown.

After removing, allow the dish to sit for 5 minutes before serving.

Caprice's Blueberry Vanilla Pecan Bread

Preheat oven to 350 degrees.
Prep time: 20–25 minutes
Bake time: 50–55 minutes
Makes 2 loaves

2½ cups flour
½ cup white sugar
½ cup packed brown sugar
3½ teaspoons baking powder
¾ teaspoon salt
4 tablespoons sour cream
4 teaspoons imitation vanilla extract
¾ cup milk (1½%)
2 large eggs
1 cup finely chopped pecans
1½ cups fresh blueberries, de-stemmed, washed,
    and well drained. I put a paper towel in a bowl
    and let them roll around on that before
    adding to batter.

Grease and flour two 8½" x 4" x 2½" loaf pans.

Beat all ingredients except nuts and fruit in a
mixer bowl, scraping bowl often, on mix or
blend setting until batter is smooth (about a
minute). Stir in nuts by hand, then fold in
blueberries.

Pour even amounts of batter into 2 pans. Bake
50–55 minutes at 350 degrees until a toothpick
comes out clean. Cool on wire rack.

After 10 minutes, remove from the baking
pans to continue cooling. Refrigerate uneaten
portions (if there are any). A slice of blueberry
bread with a dollop of vanilla ice cream on top
makes a great dessert.

Please turn the page for an exciting sneak peek of
Karen Rose Smith's next
Caprice De Luca Home Staging Mystery
coming in February 2015!

Chapter One

If her sister could run away, she probably would!

At least that's what Caprice De Luca thought after glancing at the expression on Bella's face, as well as the total disarray in Bella and Joe Santini's home.

This kind of chaos probably wasn't unusual for a mom with a three-week-old baby because *everything* changed when a baby entered a house. A baby or a pup.

Caprice patted her hip to bring her dog, Lady, to her side. But Lady's head swung back and forth between Caprice and the newborn infant in Bella's arms who began to wail again.

Caprice wished she had more time to stay and help her sister, but shortly she was due at an appointment with a client. During February in Kismet, Pennsylvania, houses sold slowly. On the other hand, if a house hunter was looking at this time of year, the prospective buyer was usually serious. When Louise Downing, her mom's best friend, hired Caprice to stage her house, Caprice was more than ready with a Valentine's Day idea. An open house in conjunction with the popular holiday would be different than anything she'd done before. Louise's home already was all about hearts and flowers so that would be the underlying home-staging theme.

All at once, Bella's son Timmy yelled at his sister Megan, "You don't know how to play hide and seek." At eight, he was an expert.

Although Megan was only six, she still knew the rules. "You didn't count. You cheated."

Their squabbling was born out of restlessness and change. The let-down after the holidays had segued into welcoming their new brother into their home. Caprice supposed that they'd expected a newborn baby to be more fun. Since their mom had to give most of her attention to little Ben, they were antsy and looking for trouble. That's where Aunt Caprice had come in. But she wasn't sure she'd done a very good job this Saturday afternoon. Bella was sleep-deprived and cranky, even though she loved her baby to bits. Trying to help out, Caprice had decided to keep them all company, do a little cooking and laundry.

Suddenly, the front door to the modest ranch-style house opened. Cold winter wind blew in with Bella's husband who'd been shoveling melting slush from the driveway so it wouldn't freeze. He looked as if he wanted to turn around and return to shoveling when Ben wailed again.

Suddenly Megan squeaked, "Oh, no," just as Lady squatted under the table and . . .

She'd obviously been trying to tell them she needed to go out and no one had listened.

Caprice sighed. No, babies and pups weren't that different sometimes.

She rushed over to Lady. "Come on, girl, let's go outside and see if you're finished."

Joe called from the middle of the living room as he unzipped his coat. "She's not going to want to go out there any more than you will. There's snow in the air again."

"She knows we have to make this quick. I'll clean up when we're done," she assured him, grabbing her sixties-style pea coat from a kitchen chair along with a paper towel and a plastic bag from the counter.

After pushing her straight, long, dark-brown hair over her shoulder, Caprice dropped the paper towel on the puddle, grabbed Lady's leash and headed onto the back porch, clucking to her dog to follow her. Caprice's bangs blew in the wind and she knew she should be wearing her hat, but it was in her van. She attached Lady's leash and had to laugh as the cocker romped in the snow patches and turned around to look at Caprice as if asking her if she wanted to play. After all, she *was* wearing boots. She ran to the edge of the yard with her and waited as she did her business.

After Caprice cleaned up, she followed the five-month-old pup back inside. Lady shook herself, leaving sparkles of water on the kitchen floor.

"I'll get it," she told anyone in the vicinity. She wasn't going to cause any extra work here today.

Taking care of a newborn wasn't easy in the best of households. Joe had seemed to form a new cooperation with Bella since Ben was born, but you never knew when that could end.

While Caprice cleaned up the kitchen floor, she saw Joe had taken the baby from his wife and was walking him.

Bella held a bottle. "He just won't take it from me. And he has to or I'll never get any sleep."

Her sister had been breastfeeding but was trying to transition her newborn to a bottle so Joe could handle some of the feedings . . . or a babysitter could.

Joe assured her, "Maybe he's just not hungry."

"He's a baby. He *has* to be hungry," Bella insisted.

Lady whined at the anxiousness in Bella's tone.

Focusing on the situation at hand, Caprice realized the best thing she could do for her sister was to take her kids out of the house, maybe ice skating, sometime soon.

"I thought Lady would entertain the kids," she said. "But we're adding to the commotion."

"And you didn't want to leave your dog home alone too much," Joe said, as if he'd heard it all before. "She's a pup. She can't be alone all the time, or she'll develop bad habits. I've got three kids, I know all about bad habits."

His expression was even, and Caprice couldn't really tell what he was thinking. Actually, she used to be able to tell better. Not that she could ever read his mind. But he'd turned over a new leaf last summer, and now it was hard to tell sometimes exactly what he was feeling . . . or thinking.

She crossed to Bella who looked close to tears. "Bee, you just fed Ben not so long ago."

Bella shook her head. "But he's crying again."

Caprice was at a loss. Pups and kittens she understood. Babies, not so much. "Maybe he just needs a little walk or something."

Bella glanced around her house. "It's not as if we have that far to walk, and I don't want to take him outside when it's this cold. I just wish the snow and sleet would stop and the sun would come out."

Bella had deep blue smudges under her eyes. Her hair didn't look as if it had been washed today. Her slacks and sweatshirt weren't anything a recent fashion magazine would advertise. Caprice wondered if Joe had been helping at night or if—

As if Bella could read her thoughts, she assured Caprice, "Joe's been getting up with me at night. He's been great," she said, smiling up at him.

Caprice had noticed that Joe had been kind and attentive soon after he and Bella had started counseling with Father Gregory last summer. He'd been by her side during every minute of her labor and delivery. He really *had* seemed to change from the arrogant man he'd once been. Caprice wondered, though, if he had changed for good, or if he'd changed for Father Gregory's approval . . . or the De Luca family's approval, for that matter. Seven months ago her sister's marriage had almost fallen apart when Bella had found out she was pregnant again . . . when both she and Joe had become suspects in a murder.

Now, Caprice and her family just weren't sure what to think about the couple. Hope for the best and prepare for the worst, she thought. Wasn't that the Italian Catholic motto?

Joe jiggled his youngest son and repositioned him on his shoulder. "It's really okay if you leave, Caprice."

She should. Leaving was better for them and better for her. As it was, she might be a few minutes late for her meeting with her sister Nikki—who was catering the open house—and Louise Downing.

"I made a mac and cheese casserole," she said. "With that creamy cheese sauce you like so much. Put it in the oven, ten minutes later shove in the chicken fingers, and everything should get done about half an hour after that. I even steamed broccoli and all you have to do is warm that up in the microwave. It's a semi-healthy meal. I brought along some new cookies I whipped up for Valentine's Day, too. Give them a taste and let me know if you like them."

"What's in them?" Joe asked suspiciously.

"White chocolate, cranraisins, and secret ingredients," Caprice answered jovially, learning that was the best way with Joe.

The infant had quieted now and Joe said to Caprice, "I'll walk you out. Can you get the dog okay?"

In no time at all, Caprice had buttoned her jacket, rounded up Lady and clipped on her leash once more. After giving the kids and Bella kisses and hugs, she walked to the door.

In a low voice, Joe said to her, "I appreciate everything you're doing. Don't think I'll forget it."

"We're family, Joe. We stick together, good times and bad. You and Bella have had enough of the bad," she added. "Just remember, she could still be going through post-partum baby blues—"

"You have to meddle, don't you?" he asked in a resigned, almost amused tone. "But I guess I can accept that now because I know it's for her own good . . . and mine. I'm making sure she does something for herself each day, even it it's just to take a bubble bath."

Perhaps Joe really had changed.

Lady was pulling on her leash and Caprice squeezed her brother-in-law's arm affectionately. "Thanks for taking care of my sister. I'll see you soon."

Once outside, Caprice opened her van. Because Lady was still a pup, she enclosed her in her crate in the back. When they traveled, that kept her safe. Fortunately, Louise and her husband Chet liked animals. They especially liked Lady, so she'd been a welcome guest at their house as they'd talked over strategies for staging to sell.

Snow was falling softly as Caprice climbed in the driver's side of her vehicle. She always smiled when she saw the swirling psychedelic colors and large flowers painted on the side. She loved the sixties and it showed in her fashions, in her house stagings, and especially in her home decorating. No matter who she was decorating or staging for, she chose colors because of the emotions they evoked. Sixties colors made *her* happy.

She switched on her windshield wipers but didn't really need them. The flurries were teeny dots that didn't even leave wet spots. She hoped the snow wouldn't fall heavier until much later. Then neither she nor Nikki would have to worry about driving in it.

With her own catering business, her older sister Nikki always helped with Caprice's house stagings, and together they made them events. This was a busy time of year for both of them. They'd be helping with Kismet's Give-From-The-Heart Day food and clothing drive, as well as the Valentine's Day dance. The next two weeks would be nonstop activity.

Dusk was wrapping itself around the town as Caprice drove her van down slush-filled streets. The temperature was hovering around thirty-two.

Crossing White Rose Way—the main street arrowing through the center of town—she headed for the outskirts of Kismet and the Downings' neighborhood. The streets hadn't been cleaned as well in this section where snowbanks lined the road. Expensive houses stretched along Middlebrook Drive where Louise lived. These homes weren't quite mansions, but they sprawled across acre lots. Many of them were older, unlike the new estates in the Reservoir Heights area. Country club patrons inhabited the homes on Middlebrook and had lived in them for more than one generation.

Louise and Chet Downing's property was elegant and pleasing to the eye. The house covered about forty-eight hundred square feet. Caprice knew almost every square foot since she was in the process of staging it. She drove around the front of the property, whose boundary was delineated by an intricate brick and stone wall. Sturdy brick pillars stood at ten-foot intervals. A broad lawn, now mostly snow-covered led up to the front entrances with the floor-to-ceiling unique window treatments, arches, and multipaned glass. A four-story sycamore, its branches still prettily snow-covered draped over the front lawn. Multilevel roofs and gables lent character to the house, and evergreen shrubs gave color to what could have been a drab winter landscape.

Louise was quite the gardener and had a hand in

the landscaping. Come spring, color would overflow from every planter, border, and manicured garden surrounding the house. Since she enjoyed dabbling in a greenhouse of her own out back, every January she started plants from seeds—impatiens, geraniums, and petunias.

Caprice drove toward the garage side of the house and the greenhouse, entering the driveway in the rear. She appreciated the architecture of the back of the house almost as much as the front. French doors on the first and second floors provided panoramic views of the gardens. Now, however, she parked her van, exited, and released Lady from her crate. After attaching the leash, she watched the pup jump from the back of the van onto the snow-cleared driveway. Lady walked beside her up the flagstone path to the kitchen entrance. This is where friends and family usually entered.

Louise's maid, Rachel Cosgrove, answered the melodic chime of the back door. She was about Caprice's age, thirty-two, with honey-blond hair she kept restrained in a low ponytail. "C'mon in. Nikki and Mrs. Downing have been chatting. It's surely cold out there, isn't it? I'll take your coat."

Caprice could hear voices coming from the breakfast nook. When Caprice removed Lady's leash, the cocker raced to the women, wiggling around their feet.

After Caprice shrugged out of her jacket, she handed it to Rachel as Louise smiled and made an attempt to pet Lady. But her smile seemed a little forced.

Nikki patted the seat next to her. She must have

had her hair highlighted recently because golden strands glowed under the lights along with the dark brown. She looked gorgeous.

Louise told Rachel, "Bring a cup of coffee for Caprice with cream and sugar." Her tone was a bit absent, even a little condescending.

Caprice took one of the seats, wondering if Louise was worried about this open house . . . or something else. The burgundy and green flowered chairs on wheels suited their staging theme, so she hadn't suggested Louise change them.

Louise's house was all about "pretty" mixed with "elegant." Lace curtains at the windows added a touch of old world. Heart-shaped pillows trimmed with ecru lace decorated the love seat by the small fireplace in the kitchen as well as the rose and green damask-covered sofa in the living room. Caprice had de-cluttered a bit for the house staging but, for the most part, had just rearranged furnishings Louise had chosen.

After greetings all around, Nikki nodded to the tablet computer in front of her. "We're brainstorming what to serve at the open house. I know your theme is hearts and flowers, but how over-the-top Valentine's Day do you want to make it?"

"There's no over-the-top for Valentine's Day," Louise maintained, possibly a little too firmly to be believable. "After all, Chet and I fell in love at first sight at the Pretzel Party's Valentine's Day shindig all those years ago."

Louise almost sounded as if she was trying to convince herself, as well as them. Caprice knew Louise's story well. Louise and her mom had become fast friends when they'd met at St. Francis of Assisi Church soon after Louise first arrived in Kismet. Back then, she'd been a secretary at the Pretzel Party, Chet Downing's snack company. She'd caught his eye, and they'd gotten married, practically thirty years ago. Theirs had been one of those Cinderella stories that had become a legend in Kismet.

But something about Louise's attitude tonight made Caprice wonder if Louise and Chet had argued about something. Obviously, Louise loved lace and chintz, flowers and hearts, velvet and ribbons. Her house reflected that. However, now she and Chet wanted to downsize to travel more. This house staging and open house was supposedly going to sell the Downing estate faster. Hearts and flowers had been the obvious theme, especially with Valentine's Day right around the corner.

"Do you really think Chet's going to be happy selling the Pretzel Party?" Caprice asked Louise now, guessing the man of the house was housed in his den away from their planning.

"He's always wanted to travel more," Louise answered. "With no restrictions on our time, we can choose places we *both* want to see." She hesitated, then added a bit thin-lipped, "By the way, he's staying overnight in Philadelphia tonight for a late meeting. At least he won't be on the road in this weather."

As Rachel set a porcelain cup and saucer before Caprice, Louise scolded Caprice. "You really should switch to herbal tea, or at least decaffeinated coffee. I had a latté at the Koffee Klatch just a few weeks ago. After I drank half of it, my heart skipped beats. The barista had used caffeinated coffee instead of decaffeinated. I could have gotten her fired but she was young and in a hurry."

Because her mom and Louise were friends, Caprice knew Louise had suffered a heart arrhythmia condition since she was a young girl. It didn't act up often, but caffeine would activate the problem.

"I drink tea with Nana. I'll try to switch from coffee to tea at home, too," she assured Louise, knowing if she didn't, the older woman would try more thoroughly to convince her. Louise's opinions were usually unshakeable.

Moving their meeting forward, Caprice asked Nikki, "So what did you have in mind for food for the open house?"

Lady had settled at Caprice's feet and her tail wagged against the floor in a *thump-thump-thump* rhythm. Some people found that thumping bothersome, but Caprice found it soothing.

Nikki glanced at Caprice, then read from her list on her e-tablet. "We talked about hor d'oeurves. They're easy—heart-shaped bruschetta, kiwi slices with tiny cream cheese hearts in the centers. I also have access to soup bowls shaped like hearts that would be great for tomato bisque. I can use red rose petals to decorate the plates, and carnations are edible too. They can taste spicy, peppery, even clovelike. Chrysanthemums have a more bitter taste so I could use some of their petals in the salads."

Nikki paused and thought about that. "Some people have allergies to flowers in food, though, so it might be better just to decorate the buffet with them rather than use them in the dishes. We wouldn't want anyone to have an allergic attack."

"Goodness no," Louise said, her hand covering her heart. "Chet would have a fit at the liability involved. No flowers in the food. Nevertheless, red rose petals on a white tablecloth would look fabulous."

"Not everything has to be heart-shaped," Caprice reminded them. "I just made a batch of white chocolate and cranraisin cookies. They'd be a great Valentine treat with chamomile tea, hot chocolate, or coffee."

"Not to mention strawberry cheesecake, and cherries with meringue," Nikki suggested with a lift of one brow. "The choices are endless with this kind of theme."

"I spoke with Jamie Bergman at Garden Glory," Louise informed them. "I placed an order for peace lilies, grafted hibiscus trees and, of course, palms. Jamie had the terrific idea of planting flowers in the base of the palms. She's going to look into exactly what varieties are available and get back to me."

Louise was one of those clients who liked control over the house staging. Since she knew plants and flowers well, Caprice had let her handle that, though she or her assistant would actually place them.

Caprice tapped Nikki's e-tablet. "What about our main dishes? When guests come to one of my stagings, they expect substantial food, too."

Nikki nodded. "I was thinking of prosciutto-wrapped stuffed chicken. Sliced correctly, the slices could look like heart shapes. Fettuccini would go well with it. Shrimp scampi is another possibility. I also thought about using those heart-shaped bowls for individual casseroles of shepherd's pie with lamb and pork. This time of year, with this weather, that kind of food can warm your heart."

"That sounds wonderful," Louise agreed. "But back to incidentals . . . Let's not forget chocolate-covered peanut butter creams. They're my favorite candy." Her eyes seemed to grow a little misty as she added, "Chet and I shared a few of those the first night we met."

Louise and Chet had been married for thirty years. Caprice's mom and dad had been married thirty-seven years, so the idea of a lifelong union wasn't foreign. Yet Caprice could hardly imagine being married to someone for that long. Still she wanted that kind of committed, all-in-for-life marriage. If it was happy. Was Louise still happy? Was Chet?

Rachel approached the table, her expression worried. "I don't mean to interrupt, Mrs. Downing, but the snow is falling rather heavily again."

The blinds in the nook were closed. Louise looked toward them and nodded. "Thank you for telling us."

"I think we're ready," Caprice announced. "The house is staged exactly the way we want it except for the plants, and Garden Glory will deliver them the day before the open house. The menu sounds perfect. By next weekend, we'll be ready."

A few minutes later after Rachel procured their coats and they hugged and said their goodbyes, Caprice led Lady to her van.

She happened a glance at the frosting of snow on the driveway. She caught the glare of headlights as a truck sped away from the driveway's entrance. A visitor who decided not to come in? A wrong turn on a snowy night?

Caprice gave herself a mental shake. She was just paranoid because she'd been followed before. She'd been followed and almost killed.

Nothing was going to happen tonight.

She followed Nikki's car out of the driveway onto Middlebrook Drive. Her sister's car had just turned off onto a side street when the snow swirled in almost blizzard proportions with a howl of wind. Recently snow squalls seemed to become more prevalent in the Pennsylvania winter weather patterns. She was glad she'd put Lady in her crate.

She was carefully slowing for a stop sign when her cell phone played the Beatles' "Good Day Sunshine" from her cup holder. She thought about not taking the call, but then her curiosity, as usual, got the best of her.

Checking the caller ID, she saw that it was Grant Weatherford, her brother's law partner. She listened to a few more notes of the music and took a deep breath. Lately Grant's voice made her feel both excited and nervous. They'd been getting along better since he'd adopted Patches, Lady's brother, but there was still so much tension between them.

She swiped her finger across the face of her phone and picked it up. "Hey, Grant, what's up?"

"I think we have a problem," he warned her.

She started off again across the intersection, wishing she had taillights in front of her to follow. "And what might that be?" she asked.

"I think your brother is in love with Roz Winslow. What are we going to do about it?"

The question so startled her and broke her concentration that she hit a patch of ice and slid sideways into a snowbank by the side of the road.